Her Line For A Wealthy Man Is Always Cast

OH SHIKSA!

Mayan Hadara

Outskirts Press, Inc.
Denver, Colorado

This is a work of fiction. The events and characters described herein are imaginary and are not intended to refer to specific places or living persons. The opinions expressed in this manuscript are solely the opinions of the author and do not represent the opinions or thoughts of the publisher. The author has represented and warranted full ownership and/ or legal right to publish all the materials in this book.

Oh Shiksa!
Her Line For A Wealthy Man Is Always Cast

v5.0

Outskirts Press, Inc.
http://www.outskirtspress.com

ISBN: 978-1-4327-5829-5

Library of Congress Control Number: 2010928438

PRINTED IN THE UNITED STATES OF AMERICA

Four Years Prior
Mexican Restaurant
Upper West Side Of Manhattan

The night is dragging like the line at the D.M.V. Maive can feel perspiration from her under arms beginning to trickle down her sleeves. Thank God she wore two layers! If they turn up the heat any higher in this place she'll be a puddle. It's probably not a good idea to order anything spicy. She'll order another margarita instead.

Having only been in the company of these girls for fifteen minutes it will hardly be appropriate to leave now, even though it is evident she will not be missed. The security wand they sweep you with at the airport is far more subtle then the once-over these girls are giving her.

They take in every piece of her jewelry, clothes, shoe brand, and purse type. When the four of them talk amongst themselves about a Bar Mitzvah she is not invited to, a nose job and how painful it is, and a sale at Bloomingdales which includes Tory Burch, she can tell they aren't impressed with her small pearl earrings, white blouse, Levis, imitation leather shoes, and Nine West handbag.

Maive excuses herself to the ladies room to make sure she doesn't have anything in her teeth and returns a few minutes later to find the girls have been seated at a table and are looking at menus.

"I know what I'm having to eat!" Janet looks up from her black framed Prada glasses after perusing the menu for ten seconds.

"I don't know what to have! It all looks so fattening." The skinny one grimaces.

Maive notices that Janet's friend is not just thin, but grotesquely so, with a sheen that covers her face like a freshly Zambonied ice rink. She also has a nervous habit of twisting her long, frizzy black hair around her pointer finger and chewing on it.

"Mmm...grilled salmon!" The frumpy one practically drools as she reads the menu.

"I think I'll get the Southwestern salad, minus everything, but the pepper and celery." Anorexic decides and shuts the menu.

"I'm having one of everything!" The one who had mentioned having a nose job says.

"What are you having, Marilyn?" Janet looks at Maive.

"It's Maive." She smiles apologetically. "I think I'm going to have a black bean burrito."

"I hope you're not planning on sleeping with David tonight!" Frumpy says and all four women burst into laughter.

Maive ignores the comment and turns towards Janet. "What are you going to order? The shrimp sounds yummy!"

Janet looks at Maive like she has four heads. "I'm kosher!"

"Sorry! I mean I'm not sorry that you're kosher. I didn't know."

Maive glances at her watch. Twenty-two minutes, fifty-six seconds and counting. An excuse! She needs an excuse. An excuse and a new napkin! If one more girl shows up that she has to shake hands with she's going to have to resort to the ole cough and hand clasp over the mouth bit. It always works for Grandma Henry when avoiding contact with "those people" at church. She wonders if "those people" are anything like these people here.

Forget the burrito! There's no way she's sitting through an entree! Maybe she'll have an appetizer, something that goes down quickly. Soup! Soup is good food. Great! Now she's reciting commercial jargon. She looks down at her watch for the tenth time in thirty minutes.

"Is that a Rolex?" The anorexic one asks.

"No, a Timex." Maive smiles.

"Really? I didn't think anyone wore THOSE anymore." She smirks and then chews on a piece of her long black hair.

Maive stops looking at her watch. She twists the chunky jade ring on her right hand instead until the frumpy one asks about the design.

"What is that?"

"It's a turtle." Maive nervously shrugs her shoulders.

"A what?" Her voice raises an octave.

"A turtle." She answers to the back of her head.

The polyester napkin she has is useless! She needs

a paper one. Starbucks has paper napkins. Why didn't they meet for coffee? She can kick herself for agreeing to meet David's ex-girlfriend and her entourage of yentas.

"Go on, Maive! It will be good for you to meet the ladies. After all, Janet has known me longer than anybody. The two of you can share stories." David had laughed, as he pushed Maive out the door of his apartment.

Her corner of the tablecloth is soaked now. The more Maive tries not to think about her hands the more the sweat pours out. What if someone needs her to pass them something? The thought only makes her more nervous. She wipes her hands on the top of her jeans and can feel the wetness on her thighs.

She can still hear the rants of the eight grade class bully, Billy Flynn calling her "Palm Springs." Having your calves spanked by Sister Mary Elizabeth paled in comparison to having the entire class laugh at you because Billy pulled another prank at your expense.

"Hello? HELLO?" Maive hears a shrill voice and looks up to see the four women staring at her.

It dawns on her that both Sister Mary Elizabeth and Billy Flynn have nothing on these bitches!

"How long have you and David been dating?" Nose asks.

"About eight months now."

"You're older than he is, right?" Anorexic asks.

"Yes I am, but I don't think it makes a difference."

The women share disapproving glances with one another.

"Have you met his family?" The frumpy one asks.

"Yes, I have. They seem like nice people."

"What did they think when he brought YOU home?" Janet asks.

Her question, like a bad smell, lingers in the air. She wonders if she should lie and tell them everything is fantastic with the Adelsteins or tell them what they long to hear. Maive glances up at the four of them and feels their gazes penetrate her soul. She suddenly feels like the dog from the pound sitting next to a bunch of pedigrees. She knows exactly what Janet intends with her question, but wants to see if she will actually come out and say it.

"I don't understand what you mean." She plays with the charm on her necklace.

"You know!" Janet says, looking around the restaurant as if someone might be eavesdropping. "It's not like you're JEWISH!" She blurts out the word.

"Well no I'm not, but…"

"Have they invited you to their summer house?" Anorexic asks.

"David did, yes." A brief smile covers her face, remembering the weekend.

"Was the family there?" Nose job asks.

"No, not that time, but…"

"I see!" Janet says. "So you haven't been there with the family?"

"No, but David did mention something about…"

"One summer I spent almost every weekend with them. The Adelsteins are the best! Did David tell you we were practically engaged at one time?" Janet takes a sip of her water-downed chardonnay.

David hadn't, but he did tell Maive that all Janet ever talked about was getting married and it didn't seem to matter to whom.

"What do they think about you doing hair?" Frumpy asks.

Maive knew they couldn't resist. "Mrs. Adelstein sees me for color!" She answers proudly.

"Really? Ethel sees YOU for her hair?" Nose asks.

Although Maive feels as though coloring Ethel's hair for free is one of the many prices she pays for dating her son, she isn't about to say anything negative to these girls.

"Is that the only education you have, Raven?" Frumpy asks.

Maive realizes there isn't going to be a follow-up call from any of these girls so she doesn't bother to correct her for calling her Raven. "Yes, I went to school for a cosmetology license."

"So you went to school for what, twelve months?" Nose adds.

It is actually only nine months, but twelve sounds better, so Maive doesn't say anything. The waitress approaches the table and Maive is momentarily relieved. She feigns a smile even though she wants to cry and listens to the waitress auction off their orders.

"Beef Fajitas with extra cheese?" The waitress asks and Janet nods.

While Janet's entrée doesn't sound kosher to Maive,

she isn't about to question her. She sure would love another margarita or six, but the waitress is already tired of them. She can't say she blames her. When Anorexic ordered the teeny martini with the pimento to be extracted from the olive, even Maive raised an eyebrow.

"Grilled salmon?" The waitress looks over the top of her glasses. Frumpy raises a finger.

"Chicken fajitas?" She asks, not even looking at the women this time.

Nose takes the plate and immediately hands it back to her. "No condiments! I told you no condiments!"

"I'll have the chef make you a new one." The waitress rolls her eyes.

"Plain lettuce? This must be for you." She hands it to the anorexic one.

"It's not plain lettuce! There are vegetables, too." She grabs the plate with a look of disdain.

"And the soup must be for you." She hands it to Maive.

Without asking if they need anything else, probably out of fear that they will, she walks away.

"N.A.S.A. we have a problem!" Frumpy blurts out.

"I think you mean Houston." Maive smiles.

Frumpy rolls her eyes. "It's the same thing!"

"Is that waitress for real? It's so obvious SHE doesn't have a college degree from Penn like I do!" Janet gloats.

"I knew she wouldn't get my order right." Nose whines.

"What do you expect? She's only a waitress!" Frumpy says.

"She's not getting a good tip, that's for sure!" Anorexic adds.

"It took her forever to get our drinks." Janet rolls her eyes.

Maive feels sorry for the waitress, but decides this isn't the audience to explain how hard it is to wait on tables. In fact, the only thing these bitches will probably ever wait for is the right moment to tell their boyfriend they expect nothing less than three carats.

The women pick at their food and engage in a conversation exclusive of Maive. She tries holding back her tears, but she's no match for this group. She hopes David will understand.

"Would you excuse me, please?" Maive gets up from the table. "I think I am coming down with something and it will be best for me to leave now." She grabs her coat and purse.

"Now? We just got our food!" Janet looks at her.

"It just hit me. I'm terribly sorry." Maive opens her wallet to leave money.

"It's such a shame that you have to leave, Molly. We were just getting to know you!" Janet forces a smile.

Speechless, Maive nods to all of the women and leaves the restaurant.

In lieu of taking a taxi she walks to her apartment and takes a moment to reflect on the evening. Her heart is beating like an animal escaping death or a young woman who has just been badgered by four bitter girls for taking one of their own. She takes a few deep breaths to try and calm herself and then bursts into laughter.

Proud of herself for taking a stand or at least a walk away from the table, Maive feels trepidation about telling David about the evening, but knows he will understand. Still, she can't understand why David would associate with someone like Janet. He is nothing like her! His mother, Ethel probably introduced them with intentions of David marrying her and now Maive has come along and ruined her vision. Ethel just needs to get to know her better. Once she does, she is certain that the two of them will bond. But there will be plenty of time for that because she and David are going to be together, forever!

She sings the song *At Last*, by Etta James, all the way to her apartment, thinking about David and how much she loves him. She rushes upstairs to call him and say goodnight, but gets his answering machine instead.

Same Evening
Upper East Side Of Manhattan
Apartment Of Debbie Adelstein And Daniel Weismann

Beaming from ear to ear, David can hardly wait to break the news to his family. "I am so glad we are all here together because there is something I want to tell you."

"Pass the salad." His mother, Ethel interrupts him.

"I am planning on…"

"Is that mango?" His father, Adam interrupts him. "My goodness! I don't think I've ever seen such beautiful mango." He reaches for the platter. "Dan, where on earth did you find mango this time of year?"

"It's Brazilian! I bought it at a small market. They're only available between September and February." Dan educates them.

"Mom, Dad, Debbie, Dan, I want you all to know that I am going to ask Maive to marry me." David blurts out the words before anyone else can talk.

All chewing comes to a halt and all eyes fall on David. Ethel's forced smile expands from ear to ear, while his father looks down into his food and shakes his head. Debbie hits Dan in the arm and the two of them lean in closer.

"Did you hear what I said? Isn't it terrific news? I've never been so happy!"

"What do you mean you've never been so happy? I can't believe you're saying something so insensitive." Ethel shakes her head at him.

"Really, David! Haven't your mom and I provided a good life for you?" Adam stares him down.

"Of course you have! What I meant to say is how happy Maive makes me."

Ethel clasps her hands. "David, I'm glad that you have brought her up. While we can appreciate the fun you are having, we don't think this relationship will ever amount to anything of significance."

"I don't understand. It's already significant to me. I want to marry her."

"In our family we always look out for one another and Daddy and I are only looking out for you now in regards to this matter." She taps him on his hand.

"I love Maive! I want to spend the rest of my life with her." David raises his voice.

"David, your mom and I know what is best for you and a hairdresser isn't the best choice." Adam takes a bite of food.

"What do you mean? You told me that it didn't matter who I married as long as I was happy." He looks at Debbie and Dan, remembering the phone calls that ensued and the excitement that buzzed through the house when Dan had asked for his sister's hand in marriage.

"But you are happy! We're all happy!" Ethel moves her hand towards everyone sitting at the table.

"Where would Maive fit in with our family? She's so different from us."

"If you will just give her a chance I'm sure you will love her the way I do."

"What more is there to know about this girl that we haven't already seen?" Adam helps himself to another piece of bread.

"Calories in, calories out!" Dan winks at Adam.

"You've always got my back, don't you, Dan?" Adam puts the bread back in the basket.

"You've never seen the real Maive! She's shy when she's around you." David looks at his parents.

"David, if someone can't be themselves around us than what more is there to know about them?" Ethel wipes the corners of her mouth. "Debbie honey, how about I take you shopping this weekend for your trousseau? We can spend the night at the Waldorf. A real girlie weekend!"

"I'd love that, Mommy! You're so good to me!" Debbie beams from ear to ear.

The familiar pit forms in David's stomach. He looks at his parents eating their dinner and then over at Debbie and Dan. They talk amongst themselves about dinner plans for next week and another date to see a Broadway show.

No matter what he says they won't hear him. Their ears are deaf unless you are talking about something that pertains to them, their mouths are closed unless they are talking about themselves, and their eyes are blind to anything or anyone that they simply do not care to notice.

He looks down at his full plate of food and feels

nauseous. "I think I better go."

"You haven't eaten a thing! I went and made all of this food and now you're going to leave?" Debbie glares at him.

"I don't feel well." He stands up from the table.

"Can you believe him, Dan? I cooked his favorite dish and he isn't even going to stay!"

He walks towards their apartment door fighting back tears, but manages to say something to his sister. "You know, Debbie, not everything is always about you!"

"David!" Ethel raises her voice. "Is this the kind of effect Maive has on you?"

David shakes his head. "What does Maive have to do with Debbie being so spoiled?"

"What's that supposed to mean?" Debbie grabs Dan's arm, tears beginning to form in her eyes. "How can he say something so hurtful?"

"Mom and Dad have always treated you differently than me." He opens the door to the apartment.

Ethel begins coughing loudly and soon it turns into choking. She stands up from the table grabbing her chest, pulling on the strand of pearls hanging around her neck. The string breaks and black pearls scatter across the hardwood floor. "My heart!" She manages to say, as she gasps for air.

"Call an ambulance!" Adam yells, as he runs to her side.

Dan, never without a phone, pulls out his cell and dials 911 and then checks Ethel's pulse.

David stands at the doorway watching everyone in

his family crowd around his mother. This is his fault! He has done this to her! He goes to her side and reaches for her hand. She struggles to breathe, as she pulls her hand away from him and holds it out towards Dan.

Within minutes an ambulance arrives.

David stands in the corner of the dining room by himself and watches his mom be placed on a stretcher. He takes the elevator down with his family and stands on the curb, as Ethel is loaded into the ambulance.

His father steps inside the ambulance and calls out to Dan, "Come on, son! It will help to have a doctor along." Dan looks over at David and shrugs his shoulders and then takes his place next to Ethel.

"I'll follow behind you in a cab." Debbie calls out to Dan and then snubs David as she turns towards her doorman and has him hail her a cab.

As much as he loves Maive he can't bear to be the cause of his mom's pain. She has done so much for him, he can't disappoint her now. Maive will find someone else, someone more deserving.

He returns to his apartment and does the right thing, or at least the one his family expects him to do. His tears ruin four drafts of a letter, before he finally comes up with an excuse as to why he can no longer see her.

Dear Maive,

Please believe me that I had no intention until the very last moment of ending what we had together. You are such a warm, sweet, beautiful person. I can't believe that I'm letting you slip out of my life. The eight months we had together were among the best of my life (and you know I've had a pretty good life thus far).

I also know that I have no right at all in bringing up education and careers as an excuse, but we are too inherently different in our thoughts and backgrounds for it to work out in the long run - even with a lot of give and take. It should not have to be "for better or for worse" – just better.

As a result of knowing you I have become a better person. You opened my eyes to a facet of giving and understanding that I did not have before. Thank you for that.

As I wipe the tears from my eyes and try to think past the next day, I know that I will always miss you and I promise that I'll never take for granted what a special time we had together.

I know that the person you eventually end up with will be the luckiest guy around. You have so much to offer and I hope he appreciates you as much as I have.

Please find it in your heart to forgive me and please don't think of me in a negative light. You were my first love and it's so difficult to say goodbye.

Love Always,
David

Present Day
A Strip Club
New York City

Another Thursday night at the club and Desiree peruses the crowd looking for the usual suspects. She spots one of her banana peels (a.k.a. a wealthy older gentleman with one foot in the grave, and the other on a conveniently placed banana peel) and she raises one eyebrow in earnest.

Staying focused is what has grossed her over three hundred thousand dollars a year, that and knowing where the money is. Most of the girls she dances with also work at clubs in the Bronx, which she thinks are a complete waste of time. After all, time is money and money pays for her time, it's as simple as that.

When she sees a new girl named Chastity dancing for a bachelor party she can't help but roll her eyes in disgust. What a waste of time they are! They always want to corral about five dancers and not pay a dime. They're probably the same type of men who read the *Victoria's Secret* catalog and leave the pages sticky.

Desiree looks at Chastity doing her best to coerce money from them and wants to slap her. It's so fucking simple, but the stupid bitch doesn't get it! Chastity doesn't know her worth. She's too afraid, too timid to ask for what's rightfully hers. Desiree was once like her when she first started dancing some sixteen years ago, but those days are gone, along with empathy for anyone who is stupid enough to get caught up in this rat race. Poor Chastity thinks a night at Morton's is equal to a poke in her pussy. There are times Desiree would like to take her aside and tell her that cute face and tight ass of hers are worth far more than a steak, but hey, nobody ever did Desiree any favors, so Chastity will have to learn all on her own.

She glances around at the array of beautiful women dancing in the club tonight.

Natalie is a girl who likes to pull her g-string to the side and expose herself to the customers. What a loser! She doesn't get it most of all. These men are here to pay for the possibility of seeing something and she's showing it to them for free.

Sherry is a Mexican girl who does surprisingly well for a plump girl. It must be because some men prefer an ass shaped like a portobello mushroom and giant tits they can immerse their wretched faces in.

Ruby is a black girl with the lightest skin she's ever seen. She tells all her customers there's nothing better than mocha and then does a flicking motion with her tongue.

It's a battlefield in here. There's always somebody younger, prettier, with a better body, or a bigger boob job, but Desiree has one quality none of the others have and that's apathy.

Most of the dancers get too caught up in the politics of the club, with the lives of their customers, with each other, with the manager. These girls aren't smart enough to realize the club needs them. There's no point in kissing up to people who are beneath you. You've got to save those kisses for the regulars. The ones whose wives are grateful they get it somewhere else. The way Desiree sees it, she's doing those women a favor!

Being unpredictable is another important aspect of succeeding in this business. One day you're the innocent school girl and the next night you're the four-inch heel fuck-me girl in leather. It drives men absolutely wild, not to mention to the brink of destruction. And there's nothing more orgasmic than seeing a powerful man rendered powerless.

How ironic that half the men who grace the door of this cesspool are as attracted to the dancers as the dancers are to each other. The laughs the girls all have behind the customer's backs can be heard on stage at times and Tommy the manager has to run down and tell them all to shut up.

Desiree has seen a few girls making out in the restroom before and quickly found the exit. The girls are pretty, but as long as there are vibrators she finds no physical need for a man or a woman to touch her, unless there is something monetary to be gained by it.

Desiree sways to the music like a pendulum on a finely tuned clock and then moves slowly around the metal pole, letting her long black hair kiss the dance floor.

"Take it off!" A hefty man in a cowboy hat yells.

She instantly stops moving and walks away from

the pole. She's been doing this way too long to put up with some out-of- town country bumpkin who doesn't know how to treat a lady.

She leans over to the side of the stage where the banana peel who calls himself Teddy is sitting and blows him a kiss. His valet pulls out the chair directly across from him, so Desiree motions to the dancer named Sherry to come and take her place.

"Hey, Theodore! How's it goin' tiger?" She purrs, as she sits across from him.

"You're...Ech! Ech!" He coughs and then spits into a bag his valet holds for him. She patiently waits for him to finish his thought.

"You're a sight for tired old eyes my lovely."

"You're a sight, too!" She coos and then leans over exposing her full breasts to almost the nipple and squeezes him on his right cheek.

Theodore takes a hit of oxygen and then a large swig of bourbon. "Join me for...Ech! Ech! Ech!"

"Dinner?" She finishes his thought.

He nods in agreement.

Glancing around the club she doesn't see anyone half as worthy of her time. It's either Teddy the geriatric, the hick, or the bachelors. Teddy is by far the most harmless, not to mention the wealthiest, but she usually prefers her banana peels a little less ripe.

"Why, Teddy, I'd love to!" She gets up and sits next to him.

Teddy pulls the valet closer and whispers something in his ear. The over-pumped steroid freak hands him a stack of hundreds and moves out of the way.

Teddy turns to Desiree and hands her one of the bills.

"Is this an appetizer, Teddy dear?"

"Yes, I…Ech! Ech! Ech!"

She feigns patience, but doesn't know how much longer she can put up with his hacking. She rethinks for a moment about the hick. He might have some money and just be overzealous. She glances over at him and catches him pinching the waitress's ass. Yuck! Nothing repulses her more than some loser who takes advantage of the poor girls pushing cocktails. He's obviously cheap as hell and not willing to pay for what really counts.

"Let's not waste time talking." She whispers. "Let's order some dinner and canoodle a bit."

Teddy shoos away the steroid freak with one wavering spotted hand and Desiree moves in closer and rubs his leg lightly. He takes another hit of oxygen and hands her two more hundreds. She glances down at his watch and smiles. At this rate the old fart will be out of oxygen, out of hundreds, and she'll be able to hit that after-hours club.

David Adelstein

He smells the sea air, hears a gull in the distance, and feels water lapping on his toes as the waves crash on the shore of East Hampton. The gorgeous blonde lying next to him softly rubs his arm. He glances over at her perfectly toned body with large breasts and smiles at the way they glisten in the sun. He cups them in his hands and begins to caress them. They are firm yet soft to the touch, like freshly baked challah rolls. "You need some more oil, sweetie?" He grins from ear to ear.

"What?"

"I want to make love to you right here, right now." He whispers, softly nibbling on her ear.

"Now? What's gotten into you?" A nasal voice answers him.

"You've gotten into me, baby!"

"First of all, David, it's not Friday night and second of all, I'm getting my period! And what the hell are you doing to that pillow?"

Startled, he sits up in bed and sees his wife Stacy staring at him. Her long black hair hangs over one sleepy eye and little bits of spit exit her mouth as she speaks through her night guard.

"Sorry, Stace! You're just so ravishing!" He rolls over on his side.

"I know! It's all those exercise classes I do." She rolls over in the other direction, bringing her night mask over her eyes.

David stares at the wall next to his bed wishing himself back on the beach. Ten minutes pass and still no beach. He hears his wife snoring and nudges her with his elbow in her bony back. If she exercises anymore there won't be anything left of her. With all the money she spends on classes she could have had a nice boob job by now. At least they would both get something out of that!

He sighs heavily and stares up at the ceiling. How much longer does he have to do this? How many more days can he go through the motions? No matter what he does he does it wrong and his wife doesn't miss an opportunity to tell him so. Sometimes he thinks the only reason she married him was for her Vera Wang place settings.

Her snoring becomes unbearable. It's more like a big sow as it eats from its trough than a woman with huge tonsils. He has to get out of here! The guestroom should be his room, as much as he sleeps in it these days.

As he heads towards the bedroom door he stops and looks back at Stacy, who is still wearing her night mask. He turns towards the closet door on his left and opens if half way before a loud creak stirs her in the bed. She rolls her head from side to side and then sprawls out across the bed and begins snoring again.

David squeezes his arm into the closet and feels for the shelf with his sweaters. He counts up to the third one and tugs slightly. He reaches his hand under the soft pile of cashmere and searches for the magazine. His fingertips touch a flutter of pages, but he can't get a grip on it. Leaning slightly forward, he grasps the magazine between his fingers and clutches it into his hand. As he pulls it towards him he loses his footing and bangs his knee on the door before both he and the magazine fall onto the hardwood floor.

"What…what's going on?" Stacy sits up in bed and whips her night mask off onto the floor.

David grasps his knee into his left hand and clenches his teeth, while reaching for the magazine with his right one. He pulls it towards him and places it under his thigh, right before Stacy turns on the bedroom light.

"David! What the hell are you doing? How am I supposed to take care of the kids tomorrow if I don't get some rest?"

"I couldn't sleep. I have a lot going on at work right now." He folds the magazine over and gets to his feet.

"What are you doing on the floor?" She rubs an eye to get a better look.

"Sit ups! Thought they would make me tired, but turns out they made me more anxious. I'm going to go work on this account." He glances towards the folded magazine.

"What account is that? I didn't know you were working on anything new. Just the other day you told me you were bored to death at work."

"New investment opportunity came to my

attention. I have to keep abreast of things, look at some pie charts. You know, check out all of the peaks and valleys." He looks at his wife who is looking confused. "It's a top company, one of the Big Ten. I want to make sure I'm absolutely convinced I like what I see before I blow a big wad on them." David walks towards the bedroom door trying to keep a straight face.

"Why don't you call your mother and get some pills from her?"

"You know she'd never part with them! She refers to them as her children. Besides, I don't need pills."

"Whatever, David!" Stacy reaches her hand into her bedside table, grabs another mask and then rolls back over to sleep.

David walks downstairs and goes into the guest-room and reacquaints himself with the latest issue of *Playboy's Big 10 College Girl's Nude* edition.

Maive Henry

She stares up at the ceiling and lets out a heavy sigh. Why can't she take a pill like the rest of the world does? One Ambien and she would be good to go! Maybe she'll ask Dr. Fine for a prescription, at least then she will be able to take lack of sleep off of her list. Let's see, at last count there was lack of a man, lack of money, lack of joy, and lack of a life!

Glancing over at the stack of books sitting on her bedside table, she looks through the titles hoping one will spark an interest. *A Woman's Worth*, *You Can Heal Your Life*, and *Dark Side of the Light Chasers* are all terrific, but each one of them has been dog eared, highlighted, and read so many times, you would think she would be better by now.

There must be something on television to put her into a sleep coma. Flipping through the channels, she finds *Pretty Woman*, *Happily Ever After*, and *Made of Honor*. This can't be happening! Where are the vengeful man-hating movies when you need one? They should have a channel that plays them twenty-four hours a day. Maybe she'll write a letter to the cable company and suggest that.

She needs to talk to somebody, but Dr. Fine will kill her if she calls at this hour. No doubt Desiree is still out at the bars looking for her newest victim. Besides, her advice is about as good as one of those phone psychics. Maive should know, she's spent a fortune on them! She could call her mom, but the last time she dialed her in the middle of the night her entire family showed up at her door demanding an intervention.

Oh, hell! She should call the airlines and put an end to this charade! If she weren't traveling back to New York City for a hair show she wouldn't be having all of this anxiety. Why is this always happening to her? What at first seems like a good idea soon winds up being a disaster.

What if she runs into one of David's family members or friends? As much as she loves New York City she can't stand the thought of seeing one of them. But what are the chances? It's not like any of them will be anywhere near her hotel. They probably melt if they breathe air that isn't from Park Avenue.

All of this thinking is making her hungry. Maybe the pie her neighbor, Mabel, brought over is still in the fridge. She walks into the kitchen and flips on the light switch, but it doesn't work. "Damn! How can a house be so fickle?" She shouts as she walks over to the counter and makes a note to call the repair man.

The house had been described as charming by a local realtor, but Maive later learned this is realtor lingo for small. She has grown to like every crack that needs spackling and every floor that creaks and originally they had been her reason for buying the property. She thought the various projects would be a great way to put her energy into something constructive instead of obsessing over David. But before long a few months turned into years, until finally her vivid imagination of seeing David pulling up into her driveway and professing how he couldn't live another day without her forced her to seek counseling.

At least she has her dogs! But at the rate she is collecting them she'll soon make the five o'clock news like the old woman down in Lauderdale did last week. Well, she's not that bad and besides, that elderly woman was hoarding cats. Maybe she should get a cat. They are cute and cuddly and pee in their own box.

What a ridiculous notion! Where would a cat sleep? The dogs already hog the bed and probably would not take too kindly to a feline. And the markings! She's already had to re-carpet the Florida room two times because the four male dogs can't figure out who the alpha one is.

She feels a brush of fur against her leg and looks down to see Buster standing next to her. "Hey, Bussy! You hungry, too?" He wags his fluffy white tail. "Don't tell anyone else." She hands him two slices of turkey after eating one herself. "A chunk of cheese and a pickle will be good with that. And some potato chips, too!" She finishes off her feast with a chaser of three Oreos and finally climbs back into bed.

Hopefully Dr. Fine will be able to see her this morning and diminish her anxieties before she gains four hundred pounds. If that happens, the only person in the world who will be interested in seeing her will be Jerry Springer.

She can hear the announcer now. "Be sure to tune in next week when we show you what can happen to a woman after she's been rejected." The camera will pan to Maive lying in her bed because she's too fat to get out of it. All four dogs will be lying under her, squished.

These horrible eating habits have to stop along with this ridiculous notion of David showing up for her. It's been long enough! She needs to move on and meet someone new. But what if she meets a man she likes, he asks her out to dinner, and he sees her eat? The thought makes her more anxious. Anxious and hungry!

There's no way she can do a good job of coloring her first client's hair. She might turn the poor girl's hair black instead of blonde. What a disaster that will be! Imagine the poor girl coming in for a touch-up a few weeks before her wedding and having her entire head the color of shoe polish! She can't possibly face a girl half her age and hear every detail of her wedding. She should have been married by now. Married to David! She bursts into tears.

Who cares if she misses one client? The girl will have to reschedule. There are more important things than making a living. Things like feeling sorry for yourself! Her boss Rudy will have to understand.

Pressing the number two on her phone it suddenly dawns on her that a gay man is second on her speed dial. The only thing more depressing is that her mom is number one. She sobs even harder at the realization of how pathetic her life has become.

Rudy Filona

"Oh, dear God! That can't be my phone ringing! Someone better be dead or dying to wake me at this hour."

Still in a haze from last night's escapades, Rudy reaches for the phone and is pleased with himself when he finds the most delicious creature lying next to him. While he appears to be passed out, he's in his bed none the less.

He picks up the phone and whispers into the receiver. "This is Madam Rudy! Who the hell is this and why are you calling me at this hour?"

"Rudy, it's Maive. I'm sorry to call you so early."

"Early? Honey, it's treacherous! You know I go out every Thursday night for disco fever."

"I know! I'm sorry. I wanted to let you know I'll be a few minutes late this morning."

"Did you get lucky, girl?" He laughs his sinister laugh and poor Maive begins to cry uncontrollably. "Sugar, what is going on with you?" He sits up in bed and lights a Merit.

"Oh, Rudy! It's David again!"

He rolls his deep brown eyes and takes a long drag on his cigarette. "Listen, princess, you've got to stop letting that bastard ruin your life!"

"I know, Rudy, I know, but we had something

special. I don't understand how he let it slip away."

"Maive honey, it's been almost five years! And he didn't let it slip away; he pushed it like a crack dealer in the ghetto!"

"But he loved me! I know it. I need closure, that's all."

"Darlin! How much more closure do you need? Christ! The only thing more closed is your legs! Honestly, Maive! I have a hard time believing that some man has been worth such a commitment to celibacy, unless of course he had a huge cock. Hell, not even if he had a huge cock!" He glances over at the hotty sleeping next to him and smiles.

"It's not sexual!" She cries harder.

"Maybe you should talk to somebody. Why don't you call Dez? She knows how to get over men."

"Rudy, please! Call Desiree?"

"Yes, girl! She told you about my salon when you were wanting out of New York City didn't she?"

"She did do that, but when it comes to men, the only way she gets over them is by dating another one. You can't heal when you do that. You only continue to attract the same kind of relationship. At least that's what all of my self-help books tell me."

"Heal schmeel, darlin! You've gotta be like those Lee Nails!"

"Lee Nails?"

"Press on, honey! Press on!"

"I try to press on, but it's so hard. I don't know what to do."

"Well, call my therapist then." He tries consoling

her, but his hangover is raging and he wants nothing more than to roll back over and fall asleep. He heads into the kitchen to make carrot juice instead. Drinking one glass a day keeps his sperm tasting sweet; all his lovers compliment him. Besides, he's been drinking it for ten years and hasn't needed glasses yet.

"I've been in therapy since we broke up and I am trying to get in to see Dr. Fine today. I'm calling you because I need the morning to re-group."

Even though it's the middle of the night and Maive's first client isn't until ten o'clock, Rudy is not about to say how ridiculous it is that she comes in late.

"Okay, doll, but don't cry too much. It will give you wrinkles!"

"And what if it does? I'm sure you can give me the name of your plastic surgeon and he can take care of them for me!"

"Now you know Miss Rudy hasn't had any work done!" He opens the cupboard where a small mirror is kept glued inside one of the cabinets and wonders if it's that obvious. He makes a mental note to fall off the Botox for awhile.

Maive manages a chuckle. "I'll only be about an hour late. My first client is a…a bride to be!" She breaks down again.

"Calm down, doll! Your turn will come! Every pot has a lid, girl!"

"Every pot has what?"

"A lid! Everyone has a match! Now go cry yourself a river, immerse yourself in the pity, and then get yourself together because you've got a busy day. Don't you worry about the bride, Maive. I'll take care of everything."

"Her mother is coming with her."

"No problem! I can handle more than one woman, Maive. I should have been straight, the ladies love me! I'll get the old battleaxe some coffee and let her rub up on me while I talk to the daughter about her wedding."

"You're too much, Rudy! Don't you think those old gals know you're gay?"

"Even if they do they can't help but want a piece of me. Everybody wants a piece of Rudy's booty!" He laughs and hangs up the phone.

He walks back to his bedroom and breathes in the air of the room, which smells undeniably of sex. Not just from the act itself, but from the décor. The walls are a vibrant red and mumble the word "sex" while the leopard print settee at the end of the bed and the large canopy overhead scream it. To Rudy the bedroom is a statement of oneself. It should let a person know exactly what's on your mind and Rudy doesn't want there to be any mistake in reading his.

The best designer on Sanibel Island did his place. Not a woman, for Christ's sake! The only good designers are gay, everybody knows that! But it can be quite difficult to draw the line between a professional relationship and a sexual one. Rudy desperately tried to maintain a professional air with his designer Marquis and felt quite satisfied that all he gave away was a hand job.

In all of the drama Rudy has almost forgotten

about the morsel lying in his bed. He stares at the sweet face lying on his goose down pillow and eyes him up and down. A muscular tanned leg peeks out from under his black and red checkered duvet, like a tempting appetizer before a gourmet meal.

You got to love youth, no inhibitions whatsoever! Rudy himself would never be caught dead lying like that. Cuteness might see his pimpled ass and run for the door! Rudy prefers to keep himself covered in his Dolce and Gabbana robe, until he reveals the goods. The latter being after he turns out the lights. Known for his candor, he is also no fool. He knows he's not the prettiest queen around, but he does have two bulges that keep em coming back for more – the one in his pants and his wallet.

As Rudy climbs back into bed he takes another look at the young man sleeping so soundly. Good Christ, he's brought home a baby! The delectable young creature appears to be about twenty- five years of age, fifteen years his junior. As Rudy tries to recall the bar where they met it occurs to him that he doesn't even remember the young man's name.

Hmm…Alan. No! Dick. No, that's what he got! Peter. Stop thinking sexually! What the hell is his name?

"Hey, gorgeous!" The handsome young creature rolls over and smiles.

"You want some coffee?" Rudy asks the tanned pretty face with a six-pack stomach, engulfed in his Frette sheets.

"I'd love some, but first I want some of you again."

He sits up, pulls Rudy towards him, and kisses him on the mouth.

Rudy is immediately repulsed by the odor coming from the young man's body and mouth. Suddenly the charm of this hotty has worn off, along with his cologne. He backs away and knows the only thing he wants to do are his sheets, in really hot water.

"What time is it?" The young man sits up and looks around for a clock.

"Time for you to go!" Rudy walks towards his bedroom door.

"Can't I at least get some breakfast?"

"Breakfast? This ain't no Denny's! You'll find a place two miles up the road. Here's twenty dollars, have a feast!" He grabs money out of his wallet, throws it on the bed, and leaves the bedroom.

The young man hurries to get dressed, putting on white briefs and blue jean cut-off shorts.

"Step it up, sister, I haven't got all day!" Rudy yells from the front door.

He emerges from the bedroom carrying his white tank top and work boots. "What about coffee?" He looks up at Rudy with big blue eyes.

"My machine's broken." He lies.

"Call me!" The young man walks through the door.

"I would, if I could remember what to call you!" With that said he slams the front door and rolls his eyes in disgust. What was he thinking? First thing he's got to do is lay off those flirtini martinis and construction workers right off the job.

Coffee! He needs coffee!

"Hmm...would you look at that!" He leans in closer to the microwave bolted under the kitchen cabinets. The reflection staring back at him reveals a fever blister the size of the disco ball at The Flame, his favorite dance club. "Damn herpes!" He pokes at the blemish on his face.

He walks across the plush white carpet in his living room and heads towards the bathroom where evidence of his antics from the night before lie everywhere. Candle wax has melted on the marble around his jacuzzi tub and full glasses of whiskey sit waiting for someone to drink them.

"I want a bathroom I could spend all day in." He had told his designer, Marquis.

"You mean something fit for a queen?" Marquis had asked.

"You read my mind." Rudy had answered.

Rummaging through his medicine chest, he finds a straight pin behind a can of shaving cream, runs it under hot water, and then punctures the blister until pus oozes out. He reaches for his toothbrush to bite on knowing the next part will sting. Dousing the open wound with rubbing alcohol, he clamps down hard on the plastic. He waits a few moments for the liquid to dry and then takes his Lancôme concealer and covers the blemish until it's no longer visible.

"You're too pretty to sleep with construction trash!" He tells himself in the mirror. "But he was a delight!"

Snickering, he runs both hands through his highlighted brown hair and notices a few grays popping through at the roots and makes a note to have Maive color them and then give him a toner to diminish a bit of the brass.

He walks out into his living room and prepares himself to start another day. Opening the green and gold brocade curtains that puddle onto the floor, he stares out the windows overlooking the harbor and watches the moon dance on the water.

Arranging a few pillows on the living room floor, he sits in lotus position, takes a deep breath, counts to ten, and then takes another. He begins to meditate until his ohms turn to snores and he falls over on the living room floor.

Hours later the phone rings and wakes him. He marches over to the telephone and screams into the receiver. "Leave me alone! I'm trying to center myself!"

"Is that you, Rudy?" His housekeeper, Maria, asks on the other line.

"Hi, girl! When are you coming by today? I've got a million and one things for you to do, starting with my linens."

"I call in sick."

"Sick? Are you out of your fucking Mexican mind? I need you to get over here right away!"

"My car no work."

"Oh, for fuck's sake! There's a bus on every corner!" He looks out his window and watches a man jog by on the beach.

"Bus too dangerous."

"Do I have to come pick you up again?"

"Yes, Mr. Rudy, or I no come."

"Alright, meet me on the corner in an hour. I don't want to have to come up there."

The last time he picked her up he was late, due to his run-in with her neighbor, the hottest Mexican guy Rudy had ever seen. He had propositioned Rudy with the line, "I give you something you never forget." Rudy, never one to say no, had quickly followed him behind a dumpster. He woke up later with a knot on his head, his wallet gone, and a memory that would stay with him forever.

Maria has worked with Rudy since he moved to Sanibel. He found her ad while he was shopping in Fort Myers. He goes there whenever he needs supplies for the salon or when he's feeling hungry for delicacies he can't find on Sanibel.

Maria's not the best maid, but certainly not the worst. Perhaps the one thing Rudy likes most about her is her lack of interest in his lifestyle. She has seen more trash coming and going from his place than the trucks hauling garbage to the dump and yet she never treats him any differently.

There are days when Rudy thinks she'll have had enough of him and he'll never see her again, but in the meantime he opens his dresser drawer, pulls out a bag of pot and a couple of shirts he hasn't worn in awhile to give to Maria's husband.

Dr. Teresa Fine

Half awake, she hears her phone ringing. "Must be one of the crazies!" She says to her husband and then rolls over in bed and reaches for the telephone. "Hello?"

"Dr. Fine, its Maive. Maive Henry."

"What can I do for you, Maive?"

"Well, I know you said to call you at home if I ever needed to see you outside of my appointment and today I need to see you."

"Is it something urgent? Has something happened?"

"Well sort of. I keep worrying about my trip to the city."

"The city is so much fun! You're going to have a great time!"

"What if I run into those princesses again?"

"The princesses! I see. Let me take a look at my book. Give me just a moment, won't you?" Dr. Fine puts one foot on the floor and slowly pulls herself out of bed. Last night she stayed up late to watch the first season of *The Sopranos* on disc and drank too much red wine. She sees her bright red appointment book lying on the dining room table and opens the page to today's date. "Can you come in around noon?"

"Noon? I can't do that, Dr. Fine. I have to work

today and then I'm catching a plane. What if I see one of those people again? I don't know what I will do!"

"You need to face your demons, Maive."

"But you've never met David's mother, Ethel. Dr. Fine, what if I run into David?"

Dr. Fine thinks about Dr. Melfi and wonders what her response would be if Tony Soprano were to ask her the same question, but her mind is too foggy to think straight. "You'll stand tall, stand proud, and smile. Or not! You might walk right up to him and slap him across the face, but whatever you do you'll do with conviction."

"I guess its wishful thinking on my part." Maive sighs.

"Wishful thinking will get you into trouble."

"Can I see you first thing this morning?"

"Perhaps we can do something in an hour."

"You're the best, Dr. Fine! You can come see me for free color if you want."

"That won't be necessary, Maive. I believe you have already done that in your past and you were completely annoyed by it. There's no need for you to give your services away for free any longer."

"You always know exactly what to say to me, Dr. Fine. I'm so glad I found you!"

"I'll see you in an hour, Maive." Dr. Fine hangs up the phone and crawls back into bed.

"Who was that?" Her husband, Harry, asks.

"The Princess."

"The Princess?" He asks.

"Yes! One of my clients always has an issue with

these awful women she calls princesses." She punches her pillow a few times to try and find a comfy spot.

"Who knew you would attract such royalty for patients!"

"What are you talking about, Harry?"

"Isn't your patient, Rudy, a queen?"

"Harry!"

David Adelstein

Twenty-five floors above Madison Avenue, in the offices of Advantage Edge Advisors, David Adelstein sits at his desk twirling his Mont Blanc pen. He gazes out his window, while the new hire, Larry Goldstein rambles on about some account.

Little pieces of conversation go in and out of David's ears, as he imagines himself aboard a Swan sailboat making his way towards Tortola. His brown hair is whipping in the wind, like the jib on the bow of this beautiful boat. His legs and arms are tanned and he's wearing one of his old t-shirts, cut-off shorts, and Sperry's with the small tear in them. He has left behind his wife, two homes, a collection of suits, and all the material garbage he feels is as heavy as the anchor attached to the sailboat.

The warm Caribbean sun beats down on his face and he catches the reflection of the turquoise water in his Revo sunglasses. A dolphin jumps out of the water in front of him and he smiles at the first friendly face he has seen in years. Free! Free at last! Living the life he has always wanted.

"My feeling is we should take the passive approach on this one. You know, let them come to us." Larry says.

David hears the word passive and the beautiful

imagery is shattered in an instant. He sits up straight in his leather chair. The word passive reminds him of aggressive, which reminds him of his wife, Stacy.

"Passive? Nothing, and I mean nothing, gets done in this business by being passive, Larry. We absolutely have to take the aggressive approach. Call them and say we have another offer on the table and must have their commitment by two o'clock this afternoon."

"Okay, David, but I thought…"

"Larry, when you start to think, the competition gets the edge. You have to act."

Larry visibly shrinks. "If you think so, David."

"Now tell me where we stand with the Blackwell account."

"Well…" Larry begins, but David's already back on the boat.

Something's got to give. How long can a man pretend to be happy when he's as miserable as hell? All he does is work, work, and work to pay for things that don't matter. He thought having one gigantic house would appease Stacy, but then she insisted they get a summer home and now she wants a ski house, too. How many places can a person sleep at once? How many cars can a man drive? There are days when he stares at the mirror in the washroom at work and doesn't recognize the man staring back at him. It's as though he is wearing a mask. He yearns to remove it, yet he can't. He doesn't know how.

"Mr. Adelstein?" His secretary, Mary, buzzes him.

"Yes, Mary?" David asks, jarred from his thoughts.

"Your wife is on the phone."

"I'm in the middle of something, Mary. Can you please tell her I'll call her back in five minutes?"

"She says it's urgent."

Stacy Kornberg-Adelstein is exactly what David's parents had envisioned for him, but quite the opposite of what he had seen for himself. Their initial meeting with one another had been awkward and he had only agreed to see her to appease his mom. He found Stacy mildly attractive, but a little too Jewish, and her voice was reminiscent of his sister Debbie's first go at the violin.

Within a week of their first date he received a call from his sister Debbie, which of course had been prompted by their mother. Throughout his life the two women had manipulated David into getting their way. Their tactic was quite simple and never failed them. The phone calls ensued each day, first Ethel then Debbie, wearing him down like a nail file, until he finally succumbed to whatever they asked of him just to get some peace.

David watches the flashing red light on his phone. It's almost as if Stacy's call has a certain rhythm to it. Nag! Nag! Nag! Stacy is obviously calling with her complaint du jour. He unbuttons the top of his shirt before pressing the button on the phone. "What is it, Stacy? Are the kids okay?"

"The kids are fine. Why is it ya never talk to me when I call? I always have to tell that girl it's an emergency."

"Her name is Mary." David tells her for the hundredth time.

"Whatever! Why haven't you called me back?"

"I just got into work." He glances at his watch. "It's not even ten o'clock in the morning."

"I know what time it is, David! P.S. just because I stay home doesn't mean I don't have a life, ya know!"

David rolls his eyes and looks up at Larry. "Can you excuse me for a moment?"

Larry nods apologetically and leaves David's office.

"I'm sorry, dear. I've been very busy."

"Well I'm busy, too! I've got contractors here ripping up our kitchen. Do ya know how hard it is to have these filthy workmen around every day? I can't believe I have to put up with this! I told them a hundred times to use the toilet in the basement and that smelly one who smokes the cigars still uses the upstairs bathroom. I want ya to tell him he's not allowed."

"What's the big deal if the guy uses the bathroom? Have Cecilia spray it with some Lysol."

"I'll tell ya what the big deal is! You get on a train every morning and get to drink your coffee, read your paper, and I'm stuck here in the suburbs dealing with things I shouldn't have to. I swear, David! Sometimes I feel like ya don't appreciate me!"

Now he's done it! He can hear the tears working their way up into a sob. "You're right, sweetie! Sometimes I can be so insensitive to all of the work you do around the house. I know I have you to thank for the way things are in my life. I'll talk to him when I get home from work."

"Now! I want ya to tell him now!"

"I'm in the middle of a meeting, honey. I promise

I'll take care of it when I get home."

"And another thing! Don't forget to pick up my earrings today. They're the ones with the two carat emeralds and tiny diamonds on either side."

Damn earrings! She's been harping about them for three months now. Like David isn't aware of which ones he's supposed to buy for her. She's only circled them in the *Tiffany* catalog, written down their identification number, and made the wallpaper on his computer a picture of them.

"The ones at Macy's, right?"

"No, Tiffany's! How many times do I have to tell ya this?"

"I'm just kidding, Stace! I won't forget."

"Well ya forgot to stop at the store and get milk last night after I asked ya four times. What makes ya think you'll remember my earrings?"

"I told you I had a late meeting with clients. The milk sort of took a back seat to their five million dollar investment."

"Are you belittling me? It sounds like you're talking down to me, David. I don't like it when ya take that tone with me! Like your job is far more important than raising these two children."

Shoulders tense, David tries changing the subject. "Honey, I've got to get off the phone and call Tiffany's. You don't want me to screw up the earrings, do you?"

"Of course not!" Stacy quickly changes her angry tone to a happier one. "By the way, David, it's Friday and I didn't get my period yet!" She sings the last part.

David cringes, as he remembers his sexual dream

which had quickly turned to a living nightmare.

"Hey, you! My husband wants to talk to ya." Stacy yells in the background.

"Got to go, dear! My other line is ringing."

"Wait! My parents want to take us to Bermuda in the fall. Make sure ya clear your calendar!"

David looks up at the picture of Stacy and his two kids Josh and Lily, sitting outside his parent's summer home. For the past four years he's always carried his family in his thoughts, but there are days when he would rather not give his wife any thought at all.

Ethel Adelstein

Sitting at her plastic surgeon's office, she flips through the latest *People* magazine searching for the perfect chin. Every now and then she tears out an image and places it in her pocketbook.

"Ethel Adelstein! Is that you? Well, I see we have more in common than a membership at the club!" Gabby Feinstein looks at Ethel over the top of her oversized Tom Ford sunglasses.

Ethel straightens her spine and swallows hard. She didn't expect to see anyone at her surgeon's office at this hour, not to mention someone she knows. The last thing she needs is Gabby, a name never suited a person more, telling everyone she saw Ethel at the plastic surgeon.

"Gabby! So good to see you!" She gives her the sweep with her brown eyes, taking in every aspect of Gabby's face again. This time she is certain that nose of hers has been done. Last year she looked like the witch from *The Wizard of Oz,* and certainly not Glenda.

"So tell me, Eth! What have you had done? And why on earth are you here at Dr. Glick's, when your son-in-law is a plastic surgeon?"

"Oh, Gabby! I'm not here for myself. I'm here for..." She thinks quickly. It's better to give up someone else than herself. "David's wife, Stacy. And my darling son-in-law, Dan, could never operate on family, something to do with ethics."

"That's right! Barbara Bernstein's son is a doctor and he won't even write his own mother a prescription. Can you imagine? What's the harm in a Valium?" Gabby flails her arms as she speaks.

"Well I wouldn't know about Valium! I never touch the stuff." She makes a mental note to refill her prescription.

"I didn't know Stacy needed any work. These kids today are having so many surgeries done. And so early!" Gabby lines her Largemouth Bass lips with red liner.

"Well I think Stacy is quite beautiful, but she thinks it might be time for a tummy tuck, so I thought I would surprise her and pay for it myself."

"That's so nice of you! I've been trying to get my own daughter in here for years. She moved out to Oregon last year and blew up like a puffer fish. Her legs are as big as tree trunks! I would love for her to get liposuction."

"Well Dr. Glick is the man to see! Or so I hear." Ethel turns her attention back to the magazine.

"Psst…Ethel! Do you think Marilyn Schoenstein has had something done?"

The nerve of Gabby! Marilyn is one of Ethel's closest friends and although she has had more surgeries than Ethel can count, she isn't about to tell Mrs. Gab-A- Lot.

"Actually, Gabby, Marilyn has had about as much work done as I have, which is nothing. We have denounced plastic surgery. When you get to be older you should learn to respect your right of passage and accept who you are. There is a real sense of peace in that."

"You are so inspiring, Ethel! I wish I could be more like you. Unfortunately, the only peace I want to find is a piece of my fat thigh lying on the operating room floor."

"Oh, Gabby! That's so disgusting!"

"Not as disgusting as my thighs!"

"Ethel! Ethel Adelstein!" The nurse calls out into the waiting room.

Ethel raises a pinky and follows the woman into the back room where older women are transformed into younger versions of themselves.

"I have asked you a hundred times not to call my name out in the waiting room, now I am telling you! If you ever do that again I'll not only have you fired, I'll bring charges against you!"

"I'm sorry, Mrs. Adelstein! I can't remember every patient who comes through the door and their specific requests." She chomps on a piece of gum.

"Well you should remember me! My son-in-law worked under Dr. Glick during his residency and I have graced the door of this place more than anyone. I probably pay your salary!"

"Yes, ma'am!"

"Now where's Dr. Glick? This conversation is giving me a headache, which in turn will give me wrinkles. Tell him I need Botox, Restylane, and I want him to take a look at my chin again."

Stacy Kornberg-Adelstein

She hangs up the phone with David and glances down at her engagement ring. Turning the three carat sparkler from side to side, she admires the way the sunlight creates a rainbow prism as it catches each facet of her ring. She had hoped for David's grandmother's yellow diamond ring, but apparently she wasn't worthy of it and only received her gold wedding band instead. Next anniversary she's going to ask David for a canary diamond eternity ring and put this simple band in the back of her jewelry box.

On the counter in front of her is her list of things to do. She reads it for the fifth time to make sure she hasn't forgotten anything.

Tennis lesson
Mani/Pedi with Janet
Lunch with Janet
Gym
Make calls for party
Call Mom and ask about her luncheon
Order take-out
Run on treadmill
Bath
An hour of news
Bed

She sips her hot tea from Starbucks and exhales. A crumb of cereal lies next to the floral arrangement in the center of the table. She presses a nail over it and rushes it over to the sink with the diligence of an emergency room attendant. While at the sink she takes the yellow dish sponge and wipes around its stainless surface again. Out of the corner of her eye she notices a smear on the toaster, so she takes out a schmatte and spritzes it with Windex.

Suddenly she finds that all of the appliances need polishing, which sends her into a manic cleaning frenzy. First the refrigerator gets sprayed. She wipes it until she sees her reflection in the brushed silver and then glances over at the Viking stove and sees a few tiny fingerprints, unmistakably Joshie's. She wipes them away and then turns to examine everything again.

A sparkle as magnificent as her diamond engagement ring stares back at her, but all she can do is burst into tears. "I hate you! I hate you!" She screams, as the tears fall down her long, thin face.

Caught up in the perfect town, in the perfect home, with the perfect husband, she blames her mom Dorothy, the psychologist for how non-perfect her life really is. For as long as she can remember all her mom ever did was talk about when Stacy got married and how happy she would be. She hadn't realized until now that her mom was talking about her own happiness, not Stacy's.

Originally from the Island, meaning Long Island, Stacy had her Bat Mitzvah, graduated at the top of her class, and continued her education at N.Y.U. where she received her Master's Degree in early childhood education. Before accepting a teaching position at a local school she took a year off to travel abroad and returned home a different girl. The change frightened her mother so much that she broke out into hives for an entire month.

"Stacy, honey, why don't you go to temple? They are always having socials for bright young people like you. You should give it a chance. You never know, you might meet a young man to marry!" Her mother had suggested.

"Mom! Do you really think marrying a Jewish boy is all that matters? Shouldn't it be about love?" Stacy recalled saying.

"The only true love that can ever exist is with someone of your own kind. You have to stick with someone who understands us, someone with the same background. We're such a small minority, you know." Her mother told her for the hundredth time.

When a trip came about for Stacy's father, Roy, to attend an academic conference in Paris, Dorothy couldn't pass on the opportunity to shop on the Champs d' Elysse. In her absence Stacy was expected to take Bubbe to Temple.

Being at temple was the last place Stacy thought she would see the man of her dreams, but she did meet Ethel Adelstein, who insisted that Stacy call her David. She took his number with no intention of calling him, until her mother ran into Ethel at the club a few weeks later.

"Do you want to end up like Aunt Alice?" Dorothy

raised her voice at Stacy.

Stacy didn't! Aunt Alice had gone against her mother's wishes and married a Polish man. He wound up leaving her with two children and a pile of debt after meeting someone fifteen years younger than himself. Alice was so devastated by the loss she found solace in food and now weighed at least three hundred pounds. Stacy shuddered at the thought of being alone, broke, and fat.

She dialed the number with her mother standing next to her. When David's answering machine picked-up instead of him she was relieved. He sounded nice enough, her mom said he was handsome, not to mention rich, which would make her parents ecstatic. Most importantly he was Jewish and that alone would appease them. Perhaps he was the change she so desperately needed to get over her last relationship.

Overjoyed by the prospect of Stacy meeting a nice Jewish boy who came from a good family, Mrs. Kornberg made sure she went out of her way to push Stacy towards David. She and Ethel gravitated towards one another at the club and soon sailing trips were arranged on the Adelstein's boat. With both Dorothy and Ethel at the helm, the relationship was sure to stay on the proper course.

Stacy found David rather handsome, and all of the accouterments that came along with him even more so. The Adelstein's charm was rather refreshing, especially when presented aboard their forty-five foot yacht called Contagious. She could tell his family was quite smitten with her when they began making plans for both families to get together over the holidays.

A part of her felt giddy at the prospect of marrying into such a vast amount of wealth. Certainly she had never wanted for anything growing up, but her family wasn't even in the same league as the Adelsteins. David had such big plans for the future and appeared to be on the right track, since he had chosen a mentor several years his senior who appeared to be guiding him along the gilded path of success called finance.

Within six months of dating, David proposed to Stacy, proclaiming his commitment to her over an extravagant dinner at Daniel in New York City.

Stacy is well aware that there isn't one Jewish girl who wouldn't trade places with her. Probably even a shiksa or two. Well maybe not a shiksa! David is far too Jewish for them and besides, they would have to contend with a Jewish mother-in-law, something no shiksa would understand.

As she looks around her kitchen she thinks about all of the work that went into making it just the way she wanted it. The architect, the contractor, and her team of designers. The tiles on the backsplash and the chandelier over the kitchen table were imported from Paris and the tile floor costs more than some people make in a year. There are probably a million people who would love to have her kitchen and she doesn't even cook.

"What's wrong with me?" She asks, knowing full well what the answer is.

Desiree

Freshly showered, she sits in front of her vanity table brushing her long black hair. A cappuccino just brewed from her new machine warms her body, along with the silky robe against her skin. The only thing that comforts her more are the seven one hundred dollar bills she moves between her fingers.

She rolls her head from side to side, stretching every muscle. She closes her eyes and takes a few deep breaths, letting thoughts of the prior night drift away, much like Teddy's caressing of her breasts, which seemed to her to be more like a cat batting at a ball.

It's best not to bother herself with the trials and tribulations of her on-the-job stresses. Everybody has them. If it wasn't dirty old Teddy feeling her tits, it would be some lecherous boss at an office pretending he didn't mean to grab one as he reached across his desk for a letter and "accidentally" touched her breast instead. At least Teddy is smart enough to know he has to pay to get near her.

She exhales loudly and then breathes in again. A slight smile forms as she thinks back on a special time in her life. A tree-lined cobblestone street comes into view, followed by brightly colored duplexes, each one belonging to a close friend or relative. Wherever she looks there is someone who cares for her. She's a child again. The last time she felt at home.

As quickly as the image comes, it is shattered when her mother's face intrudes on the happy memory. She yanks the Maison Pearson brush through her hair, remembering their move into a new neighborhood and how unforgiving it had been for her.

The frustration of having to put on her old face when she has become so accustomed to her new one takes a real toll on her, and she barely goes home for visits anymore.

Her poor father! Sometimes she wished he would leave Texas and come live with her in New York, but she knows he will never leave her mother. It would figure that the old bitch would conveniently get Alzheimer's and forget every evil thing she ever did to her.

She moves in closer to the mirror and notices a few tiny lines forming in the middle of her forehead. "Oh, my God! I've got to call Dr. Glick!"

Opening the drawer to her vanity she takes out her Mont Blanc pen, a gift from that Danish fellow she fucked last summer, and writes down a few things on a piece of paper.

Wine
Cigarettes
Condoms
Brow-lift appointment

Looking down at the pen, she suddenly becomes disgusted at how callous the Danish man had become in not realizing her worth. "Cheap fucker! You were a complete waste of my time!" She slams the pen on the glass top with such force, hair pins fly off the vanity in every direction and a small piece of glass chips from its surface. "God damn it!" She yells, rubbing the rough glass with her perfectly manicured nail. The sharp edge cuts her index finger and blood drips in small splats onto the vanity top.

She runs into her bathroom and searches through the cabinet filled with perfume samples, condoms, and the potion from the herb lady down in the East Village who swears it makes your pussy tighter. She finds a band aid behind a douche bottle, takes it out of the cabinet, and walks over to a chair to sit down.

Clothes from the night before are lying on the chair, concealing a hot iron she has plugged in. While holding the band aid in one hand she sits down with the help of the other and her robe falls to one side, exposing her left thigh. The point of the iron burns her delicate olive- colored skin. She looks down at the bright red spot and begins to panic. In a matter of seconds she could be maimed for life.

She throws on a blue linen dress, flip flops usually reserved for pedicures, grabs her black Chanel bag and keys, and runs to the door of her apartment. She undoes the three locks and slams the door behind her.

Rushing down the two flights of stairs and onto the street below, Desiree stands on the curb for no more than thirty seconds when three cabs approach her and argue over who is going to pick up the Goddess.

"Will one of you smelly fuckers open a door and take me to the hospital?" She yells at them all.

A small round man who barely speaks English and didn't understand her complete annihilation of them all opens a door with a pleasant smile and closes it behind her.

Desiree favors her right side, keeping all one hundred and fifteen pounds of her five foot seven-inch frame off of her left. Time is of the essence, so she directs the man to the nearest hospital, which is five blocks away. As much as she's worried about the burn scarring, she still waits for change from a five dollar bill and a fare of four dollars and fifty-five cents. She hands him a quarter and slams the door behind her.

Ignoring the woman standing behind the admitting counter, she rushes right through the doors marked: STAFF ONLY.

"I need to see a doctor right away!" She yells down the hallway.

People in uniform pass by her, pushing gurneys filled with patients brought in by ambulances.

"I need to see a doctor!" She yells louder.

The admitting nurse storms through the door with a policeman and gestures towards Desiree. He walks over to her and grabs her by the arm.

"Let go of me, you animal!" She tries pulling away from him.

"Miss, you're going to have to come with me."

"I said let go of me!" She frees her arm and pushes him aside.

A handsome young doctor hears the commotion and sees a very striking woman looking bewildered and panicked. "Can I help you, miss?" He walks over to her.

Desiree looks at his name badge and sees that he is an internist. Why in the hell can't he be a plastic surgeon?

"Miss? Are you okay? Do you need to sit down?"

This one will get the Southern charm. "Thank God! Will ya please take a look at my side, Doctor? I've sat down on a very hot iron and I'm afraid I might need to have surgery. I absolutely cannot get a scar! Will ya please take a quick peek? I'd be forever grateful." She smiles and flirts with her eyes, using her best Southern accent.

"Sure!" He nods to the officer and admitting nurse and they walk away. "Come in here for a moment and I'll take a look." He walks her towards an area filled with patient beds and pulls a curtain aside.

Desiree sits down on the bed and lifts her dress, exposing more than her left leg.

"Where are you from?" He searches on her small thigh for a third degree burn, but only sees a red blotch.

"Texas. Fort Worth, Texas. I'm only here visitin' a friend. The city is much too rough for someone like me." She twirls long strands of hair between her fingers.

"Well I'm happy to tell you this should heal just fine." He points to the nickel size burn.

"But I know my skin! It will scar and then I'll have to have plastic surgery to make it look better."

The doctor is amazed at her obsession over such a trite wound, but he has seen it before. He did his pre-med training in L.A. "I'll tell you what, I'm going to write you a prescription for a special antibiotic cream and it should heal in no time."

"Do ya really think it will help?"

"Absolutely!" He smiles with sincerity and Desiree feels he might be telling her the truth. She takes the piece of paper from him and gives him a smile in return.

"You're too kind! I do appreciate ya seein' me like this." She bats her eyes at him.

"It was my pleasure! I know you said you were visiting here, but…"

Desiree knew this was coming! The stupid fuck is going to ask her out. She smiles and waits patiently for him to finish his thought even though she could make it easier on him and do it herself.

"Maybe you would honor me with your company for an evening out." His nice smile turns to a sheepish one.

The urge to reach over and slap him crosses her mind. On second thought he might be good for a script or two of Xanax. "Why, I'd love to! Why don't ya give me your card and I'll call ya."

"Terrific! You can reach me here most days or at this number right here." He points to phone numbers on his card.

"I'll call ya soon!" She walks towards the double doors.

"Hey! I didn't get your name." He calls out.

She tucks her long hair behind her ear. "MaryAnn." She rolls her eyes when she turns the corner and mumbles, "Loser!"

Ethel Adelstein

Making her way down the hallway of a hair salon, she pulls out her cell phone and presses number two. The phone rings three times before someone picks up.

"Good morning, David Adelstein's office! This is Mary speaking, how may I…"

"Mary dear, this is his Mom. What took you so long to answer the phone? Another donut break?"

"No, Mrs. Adelstein, I was taking shorthand for David. Would you like to speak to him?"

David hears Mary on the phone with his mom and immediately begins making large gestures with his hands. He flails them back and forth like a man bringing an airplane to the gate and then he points to his chest and then towards the window.

Mary has become versed at sign language, even though it was not a prerequisite for the job. "I'm sorry, Mrs. Adelstein. Here I am asking if you want to speak to him and he seems to have left his office."

"Honestly, dear, how are you ever going to stay in that job if you can't keep track of one person? Tell David I called." She hangs up her phone.

"Hi, Mrs. Adelstein! You can have a seat over here." The color assistant pulls out a chair.

"Tell Annabelle I need to see her before she mixes

my color." She talks to the mirror, while holding her cell phone.

"Yes, Mrs. Adelstein. Would you like some coffee while you are waiting?"

Ethel holds up a finger to the assistant, halting her from speaking and stares at herself in the mirror while talking on her phone. "Hi, Debbie honey, it's Mom! I'm missing Zoe so much I was hoping to come by and see her today. I have an hour free from three to four and then I'm meeting some friends for a show." She hangs up her phone and leans in closer to the mirror, examining her eyes and then her teeth.

The assistant walks away to get the colorist, rolling her eyes. "Annabelle, that woman who has had way too many surgeries is here to see you."

"That's half my clientele!" Annabelle laughs.

"Mrs. Adelstein!" Becky sticks out her tongue.

"Thanks, Becky! Try to be patient with her. I know she's a handful." Annabelle leaves the color room and heads towards Ethel.

Ben, one of her co-workers, stops her before she reaches her. "Are you doing Ethel Adelfuck's hair?"

"Oh, my! Is that what you call her?"

"She's a cunt! Do yourself a favor, honey. Fuck up her hair and send her packing!"

"She is a bit difficult, but I ignore her." Annabelle starts to walk away.

He grabs her by the arm. "A bit difficult? Can you say cheap, condescending, and rude? And those are her good qualities! She'll run you ragged, be in your chair every other week for a re-do, and hand you a ten dollar bill like it's an option at Google." He raises his hand in the air and then marches off in the other direction.

Annabelle approaches Ethel with caution. "Hello, Mrs. Adelstein. How are you today?"

"I'm fine, dear." She eyes the colorist up and down.

"Becky told me that you wanted to talk to me about your color."

"Yes I do, but I would also like a coffee. That girl asked me if I wanted one, but never brought it."

Annabelle sighs. "Becky!" She calls out to her and Becky comes running over. "Can you please get Mrs. Adelstein a coffee?"

"A cappuccino!" Ethel talks to the mirror. "Two sugars, extra foam, and make sure it's hot!"

"Let's take a look at your roots, Mrs. Adelstein." Annabelle combs Ethel's hair.

"The color didn't last long." Ethel sneers in the mirror.

"It's been six weeks."

"I know how long it's been! It seems to me that it should have lasted longer. When I went to my last salon it didn't fade this fast." Ethel dials her phone and then looks up at Annabelle.

"You're almost a hundred percent gray, your natural color is dark brown, and you have your hair colored California blonde."

"What's your point? My schedule does not permit me to come here every six weeks and do my hair. I have a life you know, trips to take, parties to plan." She turns away from Annabelle and talks into her phone. "I need to order some food for my annual cocktail party. Yes, it's the same number of people as last year and I don't want you sending me so much food this time. What do you mean, I won't have enough? I don't care if I run out! People shouldn't be so presumptuous when they come to a party." Ethel looks up at Annabelle, who is sitting on the chair next to her. "Aren't you going to mix my color?" She motions with her hand and Annabelle gets up from the chair. "No, not you! I'm here at a salon. Call me back when you get a price for the party." She hangs up her phone.

A waiter comes over with a cappuccino and puts it in front of Ethel.

"This doesn't have enough foam!" She pushes it away.

He puts it back on the tray and walks away and then returns with the same cup of coffee two minutes later.

"That's better!" She takes it from the tray and takes a sip.

Annabelle exhales loudly as she brings Ethel's base color and sits it on a tray table. Becky stands next to her, waiting to put a towel around Ethel's neck to keep the color from getting on her clothes. "Try not to choke her with it!" Annabelle whispers in Becky's ear and the two of them burst into laughter.

"I'm going to need a lunch menu." Ethel looks at Becky.

"Yes, Mrs. Adelstein. I'll get a waiter over here right away."

"And when you wash my hair this time make sure you give me a good scrub. Last time it was flimsy, like you weren't even cleaning my head. You should use your nails!"

"I'll do my best, Mrs. Adelstein, but I don't have any nails." Becky looks down at her color-stained fingers.

Ethel looks at Becky's hands and cringes. "Use your nubs then!"

"I don't think you need highlights today." Annabelle covers her roots with color.

"What on earth are you talking about? Once you put the color in it is going to look dark. I have to have highlights!" She looks up at Annabelle.

"When you first came to me you told me you wanted to keep your hair color subtle. I believe you said, 'Not too blonde.' You are already five shades lighter than your natural color, that's why the maintenance is so much."

"Maintenance, shmaintenace! I want it blonde like these women here." She points to a group of women posing for a Scandinavian tourism ad in a magazine.

"We would all like color like that, it's natural!" Annabelle and Becky smile.

"For the price I pay to come here you should have no problem making it as "natural" looking as possible. I'll give you one more try, Annabelle, and then I'll have to go elsewhere."

"Alright then, we'll make sure you're nice and blonde when you leave here today." She turns to Becky and whispers, "Go mix me some bleach with one hundred and thirty volume peroxide, please."

"Don't we usually use foils and ten volume on her?"

Not today we don't!" Annabelle smiles at Becky and then winks at Ben, who is watching Ethel from a safe distance.

Maive Henry

While Enya plays on her stereo, she pours herself a cup of hazelnut coffee, adds some cream, one Sweet 'N Low, and sits the box of tissues on the kitchen table in front of her. After hanging up with Rudy she had mustered up the energy to take a shower, but then put her nightgown back on.

Facing the brown box wrapped in a periwinkle bow, she takes a few deep breaths and then slowly opens the top and the scent of lavender and dried rose petals escape. She brushes the flowers aside much like David had done to her and stares down at its contents. Cards, photos, and tickets to the theatre lie on top.

She sifts through the memorabilia until she comes across the letter. It looks so benign sitting there. By the looks of it, no one would ever know it had served as the weapon which shattered her heart. She takes it out of the envelope and reads it, probably for the thousandth time, and the words pain her all over again. Especially the part about how they are too inherently different.

"Like you and your hideous family are the better and I'm the worse!" She yells at the yellowed pages.

The ache in her heart over losing David immediately turns to rage at the person she feels is responsible for their demise. How she had fantasized about telling Ethel off now that she had endured a few years of therapy and had finally gotten up the courage, at least on her therapist's couch.

Aside from Ethel giving birth to David, Maive had decided there wasn't much to like about her. Everything about her was exaggerated; her dress, her jewelry, her complaints, but mostly her sense of entitlement. Maive often thought that Ethel had missed her calling and would have made a terrific actress. Playing the victim and using her infamous passive-aggressiveness, which was actually more aggressive-aggressive, were two tactics that worked beautifully to ensure that Ethel got her way. If they didn't work, "I sure would hate to be disappointed" did every time. Maive had watched it work on David and his sister Debbie and she had even fell prey to it herself.

Still, she couldn't understand why she had been good enough to color Ethel's hair, but not good enough to date her son, especially when Ethel seemed genuinely giddy about finding a new hairdresser.

Maive knows there will always be a stigma when it comes to her profession, but usually when people meet her they dismiss those ridiculous stereotypes altogether. But not the Adelsteins! They weren't able to get passed them.

Is being a colorist that bad? Surely there has to be other professions that are far worse. And what the hell does it matter what someone does for a living as long as they aren't hurting anyone and they're happy? Will other men reject her because of what she does for a living? The thought is too great to bear, and that's why it's easier to be alone.

She can't handle meeting another David, only to have his parents come along and interfere. The Adelsteins had shown her that no matter how talented she was, no matter how hard she worked, no matter how nice she was to other human beings and animals, no matter how she looked, and no matter how much she loved their David, she would never be good enough to love in return.

The letter, his last communication to her, was proof.

How she wishes she had it in her to be more like Desiree. She has got to be the most vapid person she has ever met. There is definitely something off with her. Maive often wonders what happened to her to make her so bitter. Bitter as she may be, she does manage to always land on her feet. She never lets a man keep her down. How does she do it, and more importantly, why can't Maive? After all, it's not like she and David were together for so long. Why is she so hung up on him?

She puts the letter to her nose and hopes there might still be a hint of Armani cologne on the pages, but it only smells like mold. Mold in the closet? Great! She puts the letter back in the box.

Maybe she should marry the fix-it man. At least she wouldn't have to pay him for the disaster this house is becoming.

"It's about that time, boys! Mommy has to get to the head shrinker lady before I imagine you're talking back to me or I start barking." The dogs all look at her and howl. "For real this time! Look! I'm putting away the tissues." She walks towards the kitchen and grabs some potty bags. "Come on, guys! Let's go for a walk. I've got to get to work now. A bride needs me!" She makes a face and rolls her eyes.

For Maive the word bride is synonymous with David's sister, Debbie, since it was one of the only times she had been included in an Adelstein family gathering. "Little Debbie," so sugary and sweet, like one of those dessert cakes that are really bad for you, was dressed in head to toe tulle and marched down the aisle with that perma-grin on her face to the tune of a fifteen piece orchestra.

Her fiancé, Dan, ultimate schmoozer and gay as a picnic basket, waited for her at the end of the aisle flanked by his parents.

Maive wonders if perfect Dan ever came out of the closet. Literally! It seemed to her that he had spent more time in there than at his own reception. The coat check boy was a looker and had a rather nice build, but still, at his own wedding! If Debbie were more human, Maive would have felt sorry for her. But as far as she could tell it had been a match made in heaven or hell, since Ethel the devil had set them up.

If Maive ever gets married she is going to elope and have only one photo commemorating the day. The last thing she needs is someone like Rudy looking through her photo album fifteen years later laughing at her hairdo.

She sighs.

Who is she kidding? If she ever gets married she'll march down Main Street and have the biggest party ever. But first she needs to get a date!

Rudy Filona

"Hey, bitch! You sleeping?"

"Fuck no! I snorted so much blow last night, I can't shut my fucking eyes! Why do you sound so far away, Rudy?"

"I'm on my cell phone, girl, sitting at the Lighthouse Cafe eating breakfast. I have to open up early for a few clients, which is where you better be within the hour, Billie."

"Give me a fucking break, Rudy! You're the one who turned me on to the shit. I swear to God! It's fucking crazy! My eyes are huge! How come you're opening up and Jennifer isn't?"

"None of your fucking business, Mary! Don't you think I know how to run my salon?" He chews on a piece of toast.

"Of course you do! You work all the time."

"If you must know, I told Jennifer I'd open this morning. I'm doing Maive a favor."

"Why isn't that silly bitch at work?"

"Poor thing is still whining over that loser in New York." He pulls out his cigarettes and the waitress shakes her head no.

"Oh, for God's sake! She needs to get laid. She's so dull. I don't know why you hang out with her, Rudy."

"I love her! She's fabulous! Besides, everybody

has their shit. Look at you!" He throws money on the table, walks outside, and lights his cigarette.

"What's that supposed to mean?"

"Honey, please! Do I have to spell it out for you?"

"I guess you do."

"Well alright then. Take last night for example. I bet you were so fried you got laid." He puffs on his cigarette and gets into his car.

"As a matter of fact I didn't!"

"What about pussy? Did you get any of that?"

"You're one sick mother fucker, you know that?"

"You're the bitch who goes both ways!" He puts his car into gear and drives home.

"That was one time and I was totally wasted."

"Give me a break, Billie! You'll do anything!"

"That's not true! You're the one who will do anybody."

"Girl, you know I stick to my own kind!"

"I've got to go, Rudy. My eyes are killing me. I think I might have some Visine left from the last time we went out."

"You better find something for those circles too, bitch! I know you're going to have 'em!"

Rudy hangs up the phone as he reaches his garage. He opens the door to his apartment and tosses a few items into a gym bag. He takes one last look in the mirror and sprays himself with cologne.

"Do you have the day off, Rudolph?" His neighbor, Mrs. Randall, catches him closing his door.

"No, just getting a workout in before I head to the

salon. I've got to stay in shape, you know." He uses his best butch voice and flexes his muscles.

"I do envy you young people, so energetic, so attractive. In my day I turned heads, too!"

"In your day? You're still the most beautiful woman on Sanibel."

"Oh, Rudolph! You're the sweetest young man. We've got to find you a nice girl!"

"You keep looking, Mrs. Randall! In the meantime, I'll be home early if you still want me to help you move that piano."

"I had my son-in-law do it, dear, but please come by for a toddy and talk. I have something to tell you about the new widow that moved in."

"Scandalous! I look forward to my return." He raises his shoulders and looks out over the top of his sunglasses at her.

Rebecca (Billie) Lane

Pacing back and forth like an expectant grandparent in a maternity ward, she puffs on her Virginia Slims menthol cigarette and tries to calm herself. Her brown eyes fill with tears, but she does her best to fight them back. A drink, a Valium, she needs something to take the edge off.

Beneath the surface of her peroxide blonde hair, what's left of her brain tells her this is insanity, but her heart speaks in a volume she cannot control. It tries to move on and meet someone else, but no matter how hard she tries, she always ends up back where she started. Or worse, spending the night with someone she doesn't care about, pretending he is the man she really wants.

Why does he have to be so handsome? Charming? Funny? Oh, face it! Just so damn sexy! She wonders if it is because he is essentially unavailable, or is she really in love with a gay man?

She's always falling for the wrong type! Her first husband sold more drugs than a pharmacy, her second husband cheated on her with her next door neighbor, and now Rudy.

Getting away from Oklahoma and coming to Sanibel would be a "spiritual awakening" for Billie, her Aunt Ginny had promised. What a hippy! The only awakening Billie has had since she's been here is that she's totally fucked up!

She stares in the mirror over her bathroom vanity and makes faces. Her lips are still stained bright red from the night before and black eye liner is smeared under her saucer shaped eyes. Her pocked skin looks like the surface of a pizza with burnt cheese. "You're one twisted bitch, Billie!" She speaks to the mirror.

She rubs a chipped red fingernail over the right side of her face, feeling the dimples on her skin. Her complexion has bothered her since high school, but her parents never had the money to fix it.

"Get some fucking dermabrasion!" Rudy told her over drinks the other night.

She had called a doctor and made an appointment despite the enormous pain she feared it would cause. Is she crazy to listen to a gay man? To care so much about what he thinks? Probably, but if it means getting his attention for only a moment, the pain and the expense will be well worth it.

Hanging out together all the time and getting completely bombed has its good points. Rudy is totally comfortable around her and she has seen him naked several times. It's no mystery to her why the boys like him so much, but she wants her chance with him, too. She is convinced that if they sleep together, he will never be interested in men again.

She steps into the shower and washes her petite frame with the rose scented soap that reminds her of Rudy. She bought it in a specialty shop in Paris while on a trip there together. She was certain that Paris would be the place she finally made love to him. As it turned out, she ended up on the plane home alone after Rudy met some Bohemian fucker and stayed an extra week to shack up with him.

But they were way beyond that now. She knows he is attracted to her on some level and has the same burning desire she does. He just isn't consciously aware of it yet. His verbal insults or the way he calls her a filthy whore are things she is willing to let slide. Besides, he is only joking, which everyone knows is a form of flattery, even downright flirting.

Although she fantasizes about telling him how she feels about him, she wonders how he'll respond. What he'll say. What he'll do. She has seen Rudy turn on people with the viciousness of an attack dog so she hasn't done it yet.

Time. Time is the key to winning him over. She needs to be there for him through the good and the bad, even if it means hearing his stories about the latest trick he screws. She hates hearing about them! But if it means late night calls from him, she will listen with the attentiveness of a faithful girlfriend for as long as he wants to talk.

If he says, 'Why can't you be more like Maive' one more time, she is going to lose it! Fucking Maive! God damn goody-goody who still harps on and on about some fucking bozo in New York who doesn't give a shit about her! Be more like Maive! Please! And what the hell does he mean by that anyway?

Maive needs to go! Maybe she is the one standing in the way of her and Rudy's relationship. He isn't real with Maive. How can he be? She is so straight-laced and boring she probably thinks coke is the "real thing" you drink. There is no way he has more fun with her! Maive gets drunk on two glasses of wine and doesn't even smoke. Christ! She might as well be a Mormon.

Billie tries her best to push male clients Maive's way, but she never looks at any of them. If she can marry the bitch off, it will be one less person to deal with. Bad enough she has the faggots to contend with, let alone the prude!

Be more like Maive! Maive can't fill out this black shirt like she does. Look at these girls peeking out! Wait till Rudy gets a load of her in this thing. She pulls on her leggings revealing camel toes and then slips on her boots.

Her tiny eyes squint in the mirror as she puts a blue colored contact in each one. She usually wears a frosty blue eye shadow in the corner of her eyes and finishes them with black liner, but today her eyes are big enough so she opts for mascara only. She lines her lips with a mauve liner and then fills them in with a shade of frosty pink lipstick. She takes one last drag on her cigarette and throws it into the toilet.

Billie believes no woman is completely dressed until she douses herself in perfume. She chooses hers according to her mood. Today she opts for a scent called Vamp.

She pours black coffee into her favorite mug, the red one with white lettering that says, "All this and single, too!" lights up another cigarette, and heads to work.

Desiree

The sun shines brightly as she exits the hospital and walks towards the nearest grocery store to have her prescription filled. She wishes she wore her sunglasses to cover her face. Some people might find the sun worth worshipping, but to her it only means wrinkles.

She takes in the world around her. People carrying shopping bags from local markets, couples strolling arm in arm, and dog walkers attached to five leashes bring a rare smile to her stoic face.

Smells of fresh bread, coffee from the kiosks pulled up to the curb, and piss stained sidewalks permeate the air. In the span of five blocks she has heard no less than seven different languages. Actually eight if you count the man who yelled, "Get the fuck out of my way!" in a heavy New York accent.

One of the reasons she likes it here so much is for its diversity and the way all of the different cultures co-exist. The Village has its charms, like the tarot card readers, Indian food, and the potion woman. Hair extensions are cheap there too, but Park Avenue is her favorite neighborhood by far.

Park Avenue, that reminds her. She stops at a magazine kiosk and picks up an array of magazines and newspapers and a pack of Marlboro Lights. After packing the cigarettes against her leg she pulls one out and puts it to her lips.

The man behind the kiosk trips over a stack of new magazines trying to light it for her. "You beautiful lady!" He grins from ear to ear.

"Thank you! How are your wife and kids?" She asks, making sure he knows she hasn't forgotten the plastic coated picture of them he keeps hanging from a ceramic Allah.

"Very good, thank you! My wife is due any day. I hope for boy this time."

"Well you should really hope the baby is healthy, but I suppose since you already have two girls I can understand why you want a boy. Best of luck to you!" She waves behind her back as she walks away.

She can feel his eyes watching her tiny ass twitch from side to side. Turning slightly, she looks back over her shoulder and yells, "You're a nasty man!" She then begins her immediate search for a new kiosk.

Kiosks are like cabs and cabs are like men, there's one on every corner. No need to fret over one that pisses you off or isn't available, cause in a matter of seconds another one will surely show up.

A sudden pain in her side reminds her that grandma is coming to visit, so she decides to look at the healthy snacks aisle in the grocery store after dropping off her prescription. She stocks up on fat free chocolate goodies, three bottles of Evian, and some Midol. Staying fit used to be much harder until the entire population joined the calorie and carb conscious diet. Now when her time of the month comes, she can eat her cravings away with an entire low-fat cake and not feel guilty.

Grateful the line isn't long this time of day, she puts her items on the conveyor belt and waits for the clerk to ring them up. Running into a potential suitor could be a deal breaker, since her items reveal a weakness. Revealing a weakness is detrimental in her line of work, unless of course a man shows his to her.

"Somebody's got a sweet tooth!" The twenty-something pimple faced check out boy says.

She ignores the comment and shoves a bite of a Slim Fast bar into her mouth.

"Why don't you let me take you out for dessert? I know a great place!"

"Are you addressing me?" She takes off her glasses and stares him down.

"Yeah! I was saying…"

"You must be joking!" She rolls her eyes and then puts her glasses back on.

"You don't have to be so rude!" He mumbles under his breath.

"Me, rude? You're the one paid to work here and wait on customers, not harass them. Now bag my things and don't say another word to me or I'll go to the manager and have you fired!"

He shoves the groceries in a bag, hands it to her, and quickly turns to the next customer in line whispering something under his breath.

"You have a nice day, too!" She turns and walks out of the store, talking as loudly as possible. "A person can't even go into a store anymore. Fucking animals! They're everywhere!" She takes a sip of water and heads towards her apartment.

Her favorite pet store is up the street on the left and she can't help but stop whenever she passes by. "Hello babies!" She taps on the window at the four Pug puppies. "You're such cuties!"

A man in his thirties stands next to her, eyeing her up and down. "They are cute, aren't they?"

She ignores him, which pisses him off.

"What? You too good to talk to me?"

She continues to ignore him and he finally gives up, muttering bitch under his breath as he walks away. She stares ahead at the puppies as though the man was never there at all. It would be so much fun to have a puppy, but her hours at work are too long.

Work, fuck!

She glances down at her watch. She's got to get a work out in today, but now there may not be enough time if she is going to make her date at eleven. Damn! Why didn't she bring her cell phone? Her trainer will probably try and charge her if she cancels a session. If that happens, she'll find another trainer, since trainers also happen to be like cabs, kiosks, and men.

The waxing! She can do that after her date. It certainly won't be necessary beforehand. She's already questioning his potential, since he asked her to lunch at Macy's. But hey, you never know, he did have an expensive tie on. If he's a complete waste of time, she'll complain of cramps. That should turn him off!

For the first time in her life Desiree is glad she wore flats as she races towards her street. She reaches the gray building and opens the door. As she's walking in her neighbor is walking out, so she looks down in her purse and pretends to search for something to avoid eye contact with the young girl.

Desiree walks into her kitchen and pours a glass of red wine. She lights another cigarette and puts a Barry White cd on her stereo. She sips on her wine, takes a long drag on her cigarette, and begins to sway back and forth to the music. She kicks her shoes across the room and unbuttons her dress, slowly taking it off her shoulders before turning towards the mirror and shaking her ass. Practicing her dance moves when she's alone has proven to be quite effective for when she has to show them off later to a hundred screaming losers at a club.

She looks back over her shoulder and licks her lips and then slides the dress down her thin back. She lets the dress float down to her ankles and then slips out of it, one leg at a time. It's taken years to make this move look graceful.

Standing in her matching leopard print bra and g-string panties, she admires her perfectly sculpted body. In all of the excitement she forgot that she left the house in such a sexy outfit. This explains why the doctor was so hard when she left him.

As she stares at herself in the long mirror attached to her bedroom door, she thinks the hot pink bra and panty set might be a better choice. Digging through purple, silver, black, tangerine and yellow matching bra and underwear sets, she finally finds it. The hot pink set always works on the men at the club so maybe it will charm the potential sugar daddy she's meeting for lunch. She hasn't figured out why the outfit gets such a response from the crowd. You'd think it would be the black one. Men always like black lace.

She pulls the thong up her tightly toned legs and over her round, firm ass, thanks to lipo and hours of personal training at the hottest gyms in Manhattan. After she does a spin in the mirror she admires her body again and knows exactly why men pay so much to see it.

Desiree touches her surgically enhanced size D breasts, puts her elbows underneath them and then squeezes them together until they touch. A white tag sticks out from under the bra so she pulls it from the garment and sees it's a size 34 B. That explains why men like it so much!

As she parades back and forth in front of the mirror, she reaches over and touches the floor occasionally and then gyrates her small hips in slow circular motions, smiling at the way she looks. "If I were a guy, I'd want to fuck me!" She says to the mirror and then takes a sip of wine.

Running a hand up her right leg, she lets her fingers delicately touch the lips protruding through her panties and feels herself getting wet. She glances around the room for her vibrator and sees it lying on the side of her pillow.

As she walks towards her bed she sees her burn in the mirror and stops to look. "Fucking maimed!" She yells. "Who the hell is going to want a lap dance from someone who is maimed?" Desiree throws her wine glass at the mirror. The glass shatters and red wine runs down the length of the mirror and onto the hardwood floor.

She rushes into the bathroom and looks through the tote bags from Barneys and Bergdorfs until she finds the concealer usually reserved for late nights out. The cream is thick and cold as she taps it lightly on her shriveled skin with a Q-tip, applying it until the imperfection is gone, at least for the moment.

She walks back into her bedroom, opens her closet, and looks over her wardrobe choices. Of course! The Gucci wrap dress will show off her tiny waist and when she leans over the plunging neck line will reveal her pink bra. It will be fun to see how many times he stares at her chest during the meal.

How should she do her hair today? She looks at her selection of wigs, scarves, and hats. It would be so much easier if men thought women were sexy being bald, but they're obsessed with a long head of hair instead. It's just another one of those double standards where bald can be rather charming on a man, but certainly not on a woman. She reaches for a long, white scarf and wraps it around her mane of hair in a loose bow.

She puts her gold strappy heels on and looks into the mirror for one last inspection.

"You better work!" She laughs, as she sprays her neck, arms, and crotch with Boucheron.

Grabbing a fifth of vodka from the kitchen, she tosses it into her purse and slams the front door behind her.

Maive Henry

The four dogs make their way towards the sandy path at the end of her street. Each one takes a turn spraying the sea grass on either side of the path.

"Good boys!" She calls ahead to them.

The four dogs run towards the water, while Maive sits on a massive gray rock overlooking the ocean. The waves roll lazily against the shore and then crash into the rock. She sees a sailboat out in the distance. It looks like a Hinckley. Funny how she never would have known that, had she not known David. He was so into boats. She wonders if he still is.

She closes her eyes and lets the gentle breeze cool her face, just like it had that day on the Long Island Sound.

She was holding the tiller of the boat in one hand and her camera in the other. The sun was hot and David had covered her body in sun block before they set sail, insisting she not burn her delicate skin. His nose was covered in zinc oxide and when a small bit had smeared his glasses he had taken a corner of his ratty old t-shirt to wipe them off.

When they rounded Jessup's Neck and headed towards Shelter Island, David took over the tiller and moved the boat into the wind. The sails flapped as he grabbed Maive by the arm and pulled her to his side, kissing her passionately.

"Here, David?" She asked softly.

"There's no better place!" He kissed her again, pulling a blanket out from under the galley to lay it on the teak flooring of the boat. He took off his shirt and shorts and stood naked, holding out his hand. "I want to make love to you, Maive."

They kissed again and made love three times over the next two hours, interrupted once when a yacht sailed by, the crew catching a glimpse of the two of them half dressed.

"You two on your honeymoon?" The captain yelled.

"Yes! David yelled back and Maive wished it were true.

It had been a perfect weekend and one she cherished like it had happened yesterday.

The two hour drive from Manhattan to the Adelstein summer home on the North fork of Long Island had gone quickly, as David pointed out places along the way, relaying stories from his childhood and telling Maive about the Gold Coast.

Maive had suspected that David came from money, but she had no idea just how much. Once she saw the house on the water with two motor boats, a forty-five foot sailboat, and another one which was simply a smaller version of the larger one, all suspicions were confirmed.

The landscape was breathtaking and she had never seen so many different hues of green and blue before.

She could recall a hundred paintings that had tried to capture the beauty, but not one could measure up to what she saw at that moment.

The house itself was pale yellow in color and sprawled out across three lots of land. David referred to the house that had been there before as a tear down. Nearby houses were similar in size, which only reminded Maive of David's favorite catch phrase, "birds of a feather." It suddenly made sense to her, the setting Dan up with Debbie and keeping it in the family thing.

Who was Maive to think she and David had a chance? Did love actually conquer all? She knew only time would tell, so for the weekend she let her worries about the future slip away into the four hundred thread count sheets and the bubbles from the jacuzzi at the water's edge.

As dusk filled the countryside, lightening bugs danced around one another in the light of the moon and crickets bid each other goodnight. A thousand stars twinkled in the sky and the smell of fresh air permeated her nostrils, which was a welcome scent after breathing in the stale air of the city.

It was her fondest memory of David, and he was the most relaxed she had ever seen him. He was truly in his element and unfazed by all of his family's wealth. She guessed that when you grew up with that kind of money it became a part of you, like your skin or your hair.

"You rotten people! Why couldn't you have accepted me?" She yells at the sea.

In the distance she sees two dolphins playing in the surf. They jump in and out of the waves for awhile and then swim side by side back out to sea.

She wishes she had a companion, but not just anybody, someone really spectacular! The next man she meets will be the kind of guy who has her running to the phone when it rings, hoping it is him. Her heart will beat a million miles an hour when she's with this man, anticipating each and every moment of newness. She will welcome the point where she can finish his thought and has a drawer full of her personal items in his apartment or maybe even a key. When she meets this man she will let go of all reason and give in to her heart, because it will know that it is finally home.

"Huh!" She sighs. "Like that's ever going to happen!"

While watching Dunkin and Sammy play their favorite game of tag, she slips off the rock and takes off her sandals. The sand is cool between her brightly colored toe nails. As the wind whips through her long blonde hair, a chill fills her body. She places her arms around her waist to try and warm herself, and for a second they're David's arms that night on the beach.

Four years seem to have slipped through her fingers and at the same time dragged like one of the last days of school before summer break. Most days she gets by without even a thought of him. Today however, the most trivial thing is bothering her.

Out of nowhere all four dogs come running towards her.

"Guys! Stop it, fellas! You're going to get me wet!"

Water flies off their coats as the two larger dogs spray her long white gown. Cricket and Buster run in circles around her feet, wanting to get in on the fun, too.

Five hundred yards away, Benjamin Koppel is leaving the 7-11 after making an early morning escape from another one of his late evenings out and notices the blonde vision playing with her dogs on the beach. He thought he knew everyone on the Island. She's obviously a tourist or new to the area.

He runs a tanned hand through his curly dark hair and smoothes out his linen shirt before hurrying his pace. As he gets closer it becomes obvious that she's wearing a nightgown. Benjamin isn't used to seeing women so real, so unaffected by their surroundings. Even at the gym they're overdone with their hair perfectly coiffed and make-up dripping off of them as they pretend to work out.

"Ah, shit! Stupid coffee!" He yells out, as the steaming hot beverage he is carrying douses the front of his khaki pants. He stops to assess the damage and is disappointed to see he can't possibly approach her because she'll think he pissed his pants.

"Let's go, boys! Mommy's got to get ready for work. Somebody's got to pay for your food." Maive tells her clan as they head towards the grassy path, oblivious to the man right behind them.

Benjamin wants to call out to her, run up and introduce himself, but his pants are ruined and she'll think he's a complete moron if he chases after her. Instead, he stands there helpless as he watches her walk away.

Her long blonde hair blows in the morning wind and her white gown, now soaked from those mangy dogs, reveals small, perky breasts. Within seconds she's over the small hill and out of his sight, but the vision of her beauty will stay with him the rest of the day.

Katrina Emery

"I'll have the vital boost, please." She orders from the health bar at the gym.

"Do you want that with sea kelp or without?" The guy asks her.

"With, please!"

While waiting for her drink she notices three women staring at her. They're eyeing her up and down and whispering to one another. She zips her jacket to try and conceal her breasts, which are protruding from her black leotard. She turns away from the women and attempts to make small talk with the juice guy as he mixes her drink. "Who do you think is the best trainer here?"

"I can't say, they're all good."

She leans over the counter and motions to him with her pointer finger to come over to her. "Let me ask you another question. If you were going to get personal training, who would you use?"

"Randy, definitely Randy!" He answers her chest.

"Thank you for your help."

As she exits the juice bar one of the women taps her on the shoulder. "Didn't I see you at Bergdorf's salon last week?"

"No, I think you have mistaken me for someone else."

"You were seeing my colorist."

"It wasn't me!" She turns to walk away.

The woman touches her shoulder and stops her. "I never forget a face, but your hair is different. It wasn't blonde the day I saw you."

Katrina nervously touches her hair, tucking pieces behind her ear. "I've been a blonde my whole life so there's no need for me to get it colored." She smiles and exits the juice bar.

She takes the flight of stairs to the locker room and heads into a stall to get undressed. She carefully pins up her hair and steps into the shower. The warm water cascades down her thin frame, washing away the stress of that insignificant woman. She takes a few deep breaths to calm herself. She must stay focused!

Today she will audition for the role of a lifetime. Katrina made a promise to herself that she would not leave New York until she landed this part. It's time to rise to the occasion and step foot into the role she was meant to play. All of her studying and dedication will finally reap its reward.

After emerging from the shower, she carefully pulls her outfit from the plastic garment bag and runs a hand over it to inspect her new purchase. Surely this outfit will inspire her to perform way beyond expectations.

The maid in the locker room sees Katrina applying her make-up and comments on the dress. "What a beautiful outfit!" She smiles.

Katrina notices her teeth right away. Two of them are missing and one has a gold cap on it. "Thank you! I've never seen you here before. Have you been working here long?"

"Two weeks. I came from Mexico to make money for my family back home."

"A lot of people come to New York for the same reason. It must be hard to be away from them." She zips the back of the dress.

"Yes, but I buy them things they would never have."

Katrina smiles at the woman and then continues to get ready.

"You look like someone I used to know in Mexico." The maid talks to Katrina in the mirror as she studies her face.

"I don't know anyone in Mexico. In fact, I've never been there."

"Dios Mio! Such a resemblance!"

"They say we all have a twin!" Katrina smiles at the maid and then puts her lipstick on.

The maid walks away, talking to herself in Spanish.

Katrina takes one last look in the mirror and smiles. She heads upstairs and hails a cab. There's not one in sight so she is forced to take the subway, something she never does.

Stacy Kornberg-Adelstein

Ignoring the receptionist, Stacy walks to the back of Suzy's Nail Salon towards her friend Janet. She glances around at the women sitting in chairs and doesn't recognize any of them. Suzy must have done a mailing with a coupon.

"Hey, Stace!" Janet yells from a pedicure station. "I'm so glad you could come!"

"Janet! Oh, my God! You look great!" Stacy gushes and then takes an inventory of the jewelry Janet is wearing.

Despite the fact that Stacy heard Janet's name mentioned more than once in her courtship with David, when she met her at a Mommy and Me class, they instantly bonded. Two dozen gym, ballet, French, swimming, and karate classes later, they still meet for mani-pedis once a week.

"I couldn't get you a seat next to me." Janet rolls her eyes and holds her nose at the woman sitting next to her.

"That's okay! I can hear ya over here." Stacy walks over to a chair with a purse on it and throws it on the floor. "I finally got Lily into camp, Janet. Now I have to go buy trunks for her clothing. Hey, you! Do ya have the latest *Town and Country* magazine?" Stacy yells across the salon to a manicurist.

"Only one, miss, and the lady sitting next to you is reading it." The manicurist motions with her head towards the woman sitting next to Stacy.

"Mazel tov! I was beginning to think Talia would have to go without her. Everyone has signed up, you know! Did you know that famous actor's kid goes there?" Janet yells back to Stacy.

"Hold on a sec, Janet, I'm getting a call. Hello? Ya did? Is it Ralph Lauren? I can hardly wait to see it!" She hangs up her phone.

"Who was that?" Janet asks.

"My decorator. She's at a store right now and told me she found the best wallpaper for my library." Stacy glances down at the manicurist and says, "You're not filing them right! Do it this way!" She motions her hand back and forth.

The petite Korean woman doesn't look up at her. Speaking in Korean, she mumbles a few words to the girl sitting next to her working on a pair of jumbo-sized feet, and the two of them burst into laughter.

"Did I tell you what happened with Talia at school the other day?" Janet yells across the four women separating them.

"No, did she get into trouble? Did she get hurt? Did that boy kiss her again?"

"She got chosen to play the princess in the school play! Victor and I are so proud."

"That's great! Hey, are you on any committees this year?" Stacy looks through her Blackberry for messages.

"Class parent, art room helper, bingo night, and ride-your-bike-to-school day."

"You are so ambitious! I'm only doing class parent and green committee. Hang on a second, Janet." She answers her phone. "Hello? Hey, Cindy! What? No way! Tell me everything!"

"Who is it, Stacy?" Janet yells.

"Cindy Meehan." Stacy whispers loudly and then moves her fingers back and forth motioning that she talks too much. "Stop filing them that way!" She raises her voice at the manicurist. "I've got to go, Cindy, I'm having a nail disaster!" She puts her phone in its Burberry case. "I like them natural. This is hardly natural. Here, let me show ya!" She grabs the nail file with one hand and begins sawing away at the nails on her right foot.

The manicurist speaks in Korean again. When translated to English, it means, "If this stupid cow wants to file her own nails, let her!"

"There! Now they're perfect." Stacy hands her back the file.

"Hey, Janet, have ya heard about the new caterer in town? I'm using them for Lily's fifth birthday party."

"Of course I have! I went to Isabelle Weinstein's baby naming last week and she used them. Their food is amazing! Hold on a sec, Stace, now I'm getting a call."

Stacy sips on her iced latte and keeps a watchful eye on the manicurist as she trims her cuticles. "Is that thing clean?"

"Yes, miss!"

"Now when you paint them, I want a subtle shade of pink. Do ya have a subtle shade of pink?

For the first time since Stacy sat down, the girl looks up at her. "I'll be right back." She walks up to the front and returns with three shades of pale pink.

"What's this?" Stacy holds the colors up in the girl's face.

"You ask for pink. I bring you these."

"These are hideous! They look like something a hooker would wear!" Stacy sighs, marches up to the front in her bare feet and pulls out the color "Ballet Slippers." She walks back, slams it on the station, and declares, "This is more like it! The girl I usually see always knows what color I like. Where is she anyway?"

"What's her name?"

"Nicole."

"You mean Nancy? She quit."

"I told you to get chocolate! What do you mean, they didn't have it? Did you go to Balducci's like I asked you to? I knew it! You take the cake back and then go to Balducci's. They'll have exactly what I'm talking about. What do you mean, you don't have time for this? She's your mother!" Janet shoves her Blackberry into her purse and walks over to Stacy on her way to the nail dryers. "Can you believe that idiot? Can't even get a cake right! And I'm not about to go out of my way to get his mother one."

"Men can be difficult." Stacy tries to appease her.

"Not your husband, he's perfect!"

"David? Perfect?" Stacy laughs.

"He gives you everything you want! And your house is perfect, too!"

Stacy smiles, knowing her friend is right. Perfect

is something she strives for, even if it means putting on a good front, especially for Janet Stein-Shapiro who David dated in college and who Ethel Adelstein never stops talking about. "He's just been lucky."

"Lucky? Every time I go over to your house I see something new. And you guys are always going away somewhere. You even have a live-in! I had to beg for a cleaning lady that only comes once a week." Janet's phone rings again.

"You have a live-in, too! What about that girl from Jamaica you hired a few months ago?"

Janet answers her phone. "Hi, Ma! No, I'm not going to go. I told you this last week. I'll talk to you later!" Janet hangs up and places her phone on the table next to her. She yells over to Stacy. "What were you saying?"

"That girl from Jamaica who works for you. What's her name?" She turns to the woman sitting next to her and reads the magazine over her shoulder.

"I couldn't keep her! She refused to get on her hands and knees and scrub the marble floors."

"That's ridiculous! You paid her what, two hundred and fifty dollars a week and let her live with ya? The least she could do is be grateful! Can I see that magazine, miss?"

The woman looks up at Stacy and rolls her eyes at her.

"How rude! Janet, have you ever?"

"That's what I said, Stace, but you know how the hired help is these days. They act like they're doing you a favor if they do anything at all."

"Mine was sick last week. So sick she could barely keep her food down. I wanted to barf too when I saw what she had done to my bathroom." Stacy looks down at the woman's toes and lets out a loud gasp when she notices they're painted neon orange.

"Listen to you! You're still upset about it. What did you do?" Janet asks, as she looks through her phone messages.

"What could I do? I asked her sister to come and get her. I wasn't about to touch her! She was totally incoherent and throwing up everywhere." She looks down at the woman's toes and then motions with her finger towards her throat.

"Everywhere?"

"You wouldn't believe it, Janet! She has her own bathroom off the room we keep her in and she threw up in one of ours. Some people just don't know their place in the world." She glares at the woman with the magazine.

"That's awful! Doesn't she know where she belongs?" Janet puts down her phone and flips through a magazine. She rips out an article in *Vogue*, which shows movie stars in designer wear walking down the red carpet.

"Apparently not! I suppose just because she's been with us since both kids were born she feels she's part of the family. It never ceases to amaze me how people think they belong when they really don't." She turns and looks right at the woman and waits for a response.

"I know exactly what you mean! I had this nanny

one time that kept talking on her cell phone while she was watching my kids. The nerve of her! It's one thing if I need to make a call, I'm their mom and I'm not getting paid to watch them!"

"And p.s., after throwing up all over the bathroom, she ends up being sick for an entire week! It really put me out. David insisted we pay her even though I said we shouldn't. There's only one thing I can't stand more than bad taste and that's someone who inconveniences me." Stacy glares at the woman until she finally puts the magazine down and gets up to leave.

"Maybe you should fire her."

"I would, but she's so cheap, I keep her. Besides, if she weren't there when the kids got home from school, I wouldn't be able to go to my tennis and golf lessons." She flips right to the wedding section and looks at all of the couples.

"You have to keep her then. Besides, it's not like she's not making out in this, too. I mean, she gets to live in your house. Hey, how is Ethel? I haven't seen her in awhile."

"She's terrific! She and I are so close." Stacy lies, giving her best fake smile. She knew it was just a matter of time before Janet asked about her nemesis. How Janet likes Ethel is beyond Stacy's comprehension. For some reason, Janet thinks Ethel is the next best thing since Botox, despite the fact that Stacy does whatever she can to convince Janet otherwise.

"I had such fun spending summers with the Adelsteins. They're just like family to me!" Janet looks over at Stacy and waits for a response.

Stacy ignores the comment. "What would you think if someone bought Talia a hamster for her birthday without asking you?"

"I would take the creature back or put it in the backyard!"

"But you can't! Let's say she is already attached to it."

"Who would do such a thing?"

"Ethel! She bought Joshie a hamster for his birthday. Mind you, he's a little too young to be taking care of it so I'm the one who has to do it!"

"What about your maid?"

"She won't do it! In her country they probably eat them!"

"Stacy, I'm sure Ethel is just trying to be a good grandmother. She would never do anything to intentionally upset you."

Stacy picks up the latest copy of *Star* magazine and flips through the pages. Another attempt at getting Janet to see what an evil monster Ethel is has been foiled. She only hopes Janet will change the subject before she has to excuse herself to the bathroom and throw up.

"You are so lucky to have her as a mother-in-law and Debbie as a sister-in-law. The Adelsteins are the nicest people!" Janet genuinely means it.

Stacy moves uncomfortably in her chair and feels her skin starting to get hot. It's bad enough she has to spend holidays with David's overbearing family; she doesn't want to spend the afternoon talking about them.

"Ow! What are you doing?" Stacy screams.

"I am sorry. I use credo knife for your feet. Very calloused." The manicurist says.

A woman's voice interrupts the conversation. "I believe you're sitting in my chair."

Stacy glances up and sees torn blue jean shorts, a t-shirt that's most definitely a poly-cotton blend, and a turquoise ring on an obvious home manicured hand. "Excuse me?" She asks.

"My purse was sitting there. I went to get waxed and you took my seat."

"Is that what that was? I thought it was one of the worker's lunch sacks."

"No, it was my purse. How can you take someone's chair?"

"I'm sorry. Do you pay rent here? Are your initials carved on it?" Stacy looks over at Janet and the two of them laugh.

The young woman grabs her purse off of the floor and walks up to the front of the salon.

Stacy picks up her phone and calls Janet, who is sitting under a nail dryer.

"Hello!" Janet answers, laughing the entire time.

"We have to go now!" Stacy whispers.

"Because of that twirpy blonde girl with the bad handbag?"

"No, it's something else." Stacy motions with her head towards the manicurist.

"Is she that bad?"

"The worst!"

"Let me ring you on your phone. I'll pretend I'm

the sitter and tell you to come home."

"Forget it! I'm gonna tell her she stinks."

"You can't do that!"

"Watch me!" Stacy closes her phone and pulls her feet out of the water. "You can stop now!"

The girl looks up at Stacy, shaking her head.

"That was a completely unprofessional pedicure. I mean a total disaster! I'm not going to pay for a thing." Stacy stands with her hands on her hips.

The manager comes running over and talks severely to the girl in Korean and she runs into the back room crying.

"I'm so sorry, miss! You will come back, yes? I give you a free service today."

"You should train your people better. Customers pay good money to trust that you will take care of them. I would hate to tell everyone ya don't do that here."

"No, miss! I give you free service today and next time you come, free back massage for ten minutes."

"Well, I guess I'll give ya another try." Stacy walks over to Janet who is putting her shoes on. "Did ya sign Talia up for another gym class?"

"Of course! Did you sign Lily up?"

"I like taking the classes because all my dear friends do, but one day when you weren't there the teacher actually asked me to stop talking. I'm paying over four hundred dollars for a class, which, mind you, I have done for both kids and she has the nerve to ask me to participate." Stacy takes her keys from her purse.

"Did you tell management?"

"Of course I did! I was so angry, I called that afternoon."

"What did they say?" Janet checks her phone for messages.

"They told me some garbage about how they believe in participation and I told them I am participating, I'm paying money for two kids to go to your stupid classes!"

"That's right! Who do they think they are, telling you what to do? Hey, you want to hit that sale at Prada? There's a cute bag I have to have."

"I can always do Prada. We have to stop at the Juicy store, too." Stacy checks her messages.

"I'll go with you, I love the way Talia looks in it. Hey, have you seen the new Tod's? I want to get a pair of those."

"Already have them!" Stacy gloats and holds up one foot.

"I'm so jealous! Those are too cute!"

"I got them yesterday, but I could use another pair. I can't stand schlepping clothes from our house here to the one out in the Hamptons. Sometimes it's such a burden to have so many properties."

"I don't mind so much except when I can't find someone to clean them."

"I thought you guys were selling that place out east?"

"We thought about it, but then I said to Victor, where are we going to go, the Jersey shore?" Janet laughs.

"Hey, how about we have lunch at that Italian

place?" Stacy looks at her messages again.

"Perfect! They have the best selection of salads." Janet calls out to the girl who did her nails. "Hey, you! I need to get going."

The girl rushes over to her and presents her with a bill.

"Put it on this and make sure you give yourself five dollars." She hands her a credit card.

"Five dollars? Are ya crazy? You'll spoil her! Give her three." Stacy nudges her in the arm.

Janet pays the cashier and turns towards Stacy. "You ready?"

"Most definitely!"

They leave the nail salon and Janet walks towards her Mercedes. "What was the deal with that manicurist, Stacy?"

"I don't know, you'd think I was speaking another language or something!"

"But Stacy, honey, you were speaking another language, she just didn't speak it!"

The two women burst into laughter and Stacy turns towards her Range Rover. She climbs into the driver's seat, puts on her blue tooth headset, and opens her purse to find a stick of gum. After opening the gum she presses the button on her window and throws the wrapper onto the street below. She can't tolerate garbage in the car!

Janet pulls out first and Stacy follows her to the mall for another afternoon of shopping.

Benjamin Koppel

He sits behind his desk in a worn, leather chair, pulling up the latest stock quotes while his client waits patiently for him to speak. Benjamin retired to Sanibel six years ago at the age of thirty-six, but still likes to keep his hands in the market.

As he gazes into the computer screen, a fly lands right in the middle of it. He makes an attempt to shoo it away, but it keeps landing on the same spot. "What the hell?"

"What is it, Benny?" His client asks.

"Nothing! I'll have that answer for you in a minute." He takes a tissue and licks the end of it and then rubs it over the smear on his computer screen. A piece of tissue sticks to the screen, blocking his view of the numbers. "You still with me, Jer?"

"All day! What the hell is taking so long?"

"Just want to make sure I give you the right information, that's all." Benjamin walks into his kitchen and quietly tries to move four pots from the sink to locate the sponge. He's got to get a maid, preferably one he doesn't find attractive.

After wiping the sticky goop off the screen, he dries it with a corner of his shirt and decides he shouldn't eat anymore Crunch-n-Munch while working. Rambling off numbers, he listens to Jerry's voice become shaky.

"I should have dumped this shit when you told me to. This damn market is making me go bald."

"There's always Rogaine." Benjamin laughs.

"I'll be damned if I give another corporation any of my money. Last night I sat with mayonnaise on my head for two hours because I read somewhere that it's good for the follicles."

Benjamin looks out his bay window and sees a small dog running on the beach. He stands to attention and glances from side to side, searching for an owner. Maybe it's her, the Goddess on the beach this morning who was wearing a white nightgown that clung to her every curve.

"Koppel? Koppel? For fuck's sake! I'm asking you a question here!"

"Sorry, Jerry! Someone was at my door. Damn kids are always trying to sell me something!"

"What are your thoughts on dumping some of those low end stocks?"

"I think you should sell them, but not just yet. I don't want you to worry, Jer. One day you're up, one day you're down."

"I tried telling my girlfriend that and she suggested Viagra." Jerry laughs despite his concern about the market.

"That's the way, Jer! You gotta keep a sense of humor. Money comes and money goes. It will turn around again."

"You know, Koppel, if you weren't so damn good at predicting this shit I'd have dumped you along with some of those stocks years ago."

Benjamin smiles. "Alright then, have a good one, Jerry! Enjoy that big boat of yours."

"Hey, when you coming down for a sail? My girl here says she has a friend or two for you."

"You are living the good life, aren't you, Jerry? I'll take a rain check for now. You enjoy for me, will ya?"

"You know I will, Koppel! You know I will!"

Benjamin hangs up the phone and heads back into the kitchen to make a sandwich. He stands with his head inside the refrigerator, hands clasped in front of him, hoping for a miracle. A twelve pack of beer, a bottle of seltzer, one jar of mustard, a lifeless piece of bologna lying on greasy deli paper, and a slice of Swiss cheese with mold around the edges stare back at him. Maybe if he scrapes the mold off of the cheese and adds some mustard he can make a snack. There must be a half eaten bag of chips around here somewhere. Where did he eat those last?

He throws a dismissive hand up and reaches for his wallet on the kitchen counter. He shuffles through the bills and is happy to see he still has plenty of money after last night's outing.

No stranger to topless bars, Benjamin has frequented them since college and isn't about to stop any time soon. He calls it a necessary recreation and knows many men who feel the same way. The club is filled every time he goes there, so that's proof right there.

They know him by name at the club, which is something Benjamin finds to be a plus. While other men chose to remain anonymous, Benjamin finds being a regular always gets him the best seat and the prettiest girls. Due to his deep pockets, the girls swarm around him and make a fuss over who will get to have his company for the night. Benjamin's reputation as a big spender precedes him, but he's also quite particular about which panties he drops dollars in. He likes to pick a favorite girl for the night and hope to see a return on his investment.

He's also no dummy. The ladies like him as long as he is spending the cash, and, quite frankly, he would rather go to a topless bar and know exactly what he's getting right up front then suffer through another blind date, only to wish he were at home eating a crusty TV dinner and watching some garbage reality show.

There is the rare occasion where he actually thinks about settling down, but after an inventory of all the women he knows who will gladly give up their single status to marry him, he feels he will be doing just that, settling.

Years ago he did the Jewish dating circuit. Internet sites, luncheons, dinners, dances. After all, it had been ingrained in him from an early age that his mother would prefer him to marry a Jewish girl. At this point, however, she will be elated if he marries anybody as long as it isn't a man. Of course, if any more time passes, she might accept that as well.

Benjamin had hoped the incessant chatter about a wife would stop the day his sister Sarah married Michael Silverstein. Mike is okay as brother- in-laws go, but a bit square. Sarah is happy, though, and that is all that matters to Benjamin.

While doing his requisite visit last week with his

mom and Aunt Kitzy, he had heard the speech again. Bad enough he has to put up with Aunt Kitzy's cooking, let alone the guilt they shove down his throat to go along with it.

"Don't you give up on meeting that special someone!"

"Ma, I'm not even looking for anyone."

"Well, you see, that's when you'll find her! And don't you worry if she isn't Jewish. I'll learn to love her just the way she is! If she happens to be Jewish, that will be a plus."

Benjamin smiled at her like he always did as his mom went on auto pilot, naming all of her friends' children and who they had married. He gnawed on a piece of brisket and pretended to wipe his mouth as he put the charred meat pieces into his napkin.

"Have more kugel, dear." His mom piled another serving onto his plate.

She continued with her speech, taking intermittent sips of her gin and tonic as he fed the dog his second piece of kugel.

Right about now that kugel might be pretty tasty. Nah! Not even if he had to chose between it and his left hand. Now if you're talking the right hand he might have to succumb to the kugel.

Heading out his door he bends down and picks up his mail, which is scattered across his doormat. The bitter single woman next door is always getting his mail. Ever since she mistakenly received his subscriptions to *Penthouse* and *Playboy* last year, she has barely spoken to him.

A small purple envelope sits directly on top of the pile. Maybe it's from the men's club, a few free drinks or something. He tears open the envelope and pulls out the card and reads:

Just a reminder...

It's time for your haircut. Please call the salon at your earliest convenience to schedule an appointment with Rudy.

Benjamin runs four fingers through his dark hair. What do you know? It is time! He throws the stack of mail inside his entryway and heads towards the stairs to the garage. He turns off the solitaire game on his I-phone and dials the salon's number. A couple of thirty-something girls walk by and giggle coyly at him. He smiles in acknowledgement of them.

"Thank you for calling Rudolph's! This is Jennifer. How may I help you?"

"Hi, Jennifer! Benjamin Koppel here."

"Oh! Hi, Benjamin!" She gushes.

"I need to get my hair cut. When does Rudy have time for me?"

"Let me check, Benjamin." She places him on hold and then quickly comes back to the line. "Benjamin? Rudy says he can see you any time you need to come in."

"How about in an hour?"

"Perfect! We'll see you then." She hangs up the phone.

Benjamin shakes his head and smirks, another one

with a crush on him. Too bad her boss has one, too! If he didn't give such a great haircut he'd have gone somewhere else by now. He wonders if it's really so awful to let a few rubs up against him slide. He shrugs it off. Surely he has done worse!

He skips down the steps on the way to the garage, gets in his Porsche Boxster, and places the new U2 cd in the player. He glances up at himself in the rear view mirror and smiles sheepishly. He revs the engine and then peels out of the parking lot with his music blaring full blast.

Dr. Teresa Fine

"Let's discuss your trepidation about going to the city, Maive." She looks over the top of her glasses.

"I'm paralyzed, Dr. Fine! Wherever I go, whatever I do, it's David! David! David! Did you know I've read fourteen self-help books? Three times?"

"Okay, Maive, let's start with what brought this anxiety on."

"I was thinking about the city and how much I love it. How much I resent having to live here. I mean, I love my house, I love my job, but sometimes I feel like I had to come here, like I had no other choice." She looks down at the carpet.

"Maive, life is full of choices. You could have stayed in New York."

She looks up at Dr. Fine with a look of disbelief. "What? And run into those awful girls again? Have the humiliation of David writing me off being rubbed in my face?"

"Let's talk about those girls for a moment. I understand they upset you, but did you ever think that maybe they were trying to get to know you better?"

Maive rolls her eyes. "Dr. Fine, please! 'What did his parents think when he brought YOU home?' What else could they possibly mean by that other than you're not good enough?"

"Maive, sometimes I think you way over-analyze these things. Perhaps you put the emphasis on the wrong words. When you do that, you can change an entire thought completely." She motions with her hands.

"Well I SUPPOSE you MIGHT be right, but that still doesn't excuse the rotten way people associated with David treated me."

"Like who, Maive?" She looks up from her notes.

"Where do I begin? You have the notes! There's Debbie, Ethel, his aunt, his uncle, his brother-in-law, his awful girlfriends, and his dog."

"I didn't know David had a dog." She searches through her notes.

"He doesn't! I'm just saying that if he did, than the dog would have shit all over me, too. "

Dr. Fine refrains from laughing. "Maive, you are such a bright, intelligent, talented, gorgeous young woman. I am sure those girls were jealous of you. I would bet that you probably threatened them."

"Well I wasn't toting a machete, Dr. Fine! Why on earth would they be threatened by me?" She lets out a heavy sigh.

"Unchartered waters."

"Do you have to use a sailing metaphor?"

"David?"

"He was an avid sailor. I can barely make it to the beach anymore. Just this morning I had a memory about him. Do I have to stay locked up in my house?" She burst into tears.

"No, Maive, you have to start living life! You are the only one keeping yourself from moving on. Why do you torture yourself with these memories? It's been almost five years! Why not start living in the present?"

"I want to, but then something reminds me of David and I get angry. A part of me wants something really bad to happen to him. I feel horrible when I think things like that. I actually feel guilty. Dr. Fine, I think Ethel's horrible influence has affected me!"

"Maive, guilt is such a wasted emotion."

"Not in David's family. They breathe it into the air! I think Ethel has it pumped into the ducts of their home. It's on an automatic mister, like one of those air fresheners." She sinks down in her chair.

"I doubt that, but I understand what you're saying. Some people thrive on guilt. In fact some people don't know what they would do without it. Perhaps that is what young David's problem was. One of the many, I mean." She takes off her glasses.

"What do you mean?"

"It's the relationship he has with his mother. Like a bond of sorts. She only shows him love or affection when he appeases her, so he has come to know that if he disappoints her she will shun him. It's quite sad, really, but not uncommon. Many mothers make this mistake and far too many children have become victims of this type of abuse."

"Am I supposed to feel sorry for him? Feel sorry for her? Because I have to tell you, Dr. Fine, it only makes me hate her more."

"Hate is such a strong word! I understand you're angry about what David did and I know you think his mother is inappropriate, but you have to remember that relationships aren't always what they appear to be. Sometimes people pay a pretty hefty price for the love and acceptance of someone else. Try and look beyond the surface, beyond the mask."

"Ethel's should be sold at Halloween. The stores would make a fortune!"

"Alright, enough about the Adelsteins! What is going on in your social life? Have you met anyone? Given anyone a chance?"

"Yeah, right! I'm convinced there are no princes left in the world." She rolls her eyes and blows on a stray piece of hair hanging in her face.

"Maive, a man doesn't have to be a prince, you know. I think you have read way too many fairy tales."

"I was always fond of fairy tales. Good versus Ethel. I mean evil. Good wins out in the end." She raises a finger in earnest and smiles at Dr. Fine.

"Perhaps winning could mean something as simple as letting go and meeting someone who reciprocates your feelings. You know you might want to consider joining a group or doing an extracurricular activity." She searches through her drawer for a brochure. "For instance, I happened to pick up this pamphlet a few days ago on knitting classes."

"Knitting? That's all I need! I can hear Rudy gasping now. I just want to get on with my life, Dr. Fine. All I need is closure. I need to hear David tell me himself why he broke up with me."

"The letter, Maive, that's what the letter is about. In his own way, David told you that it wouldn't work. Granted he should have told you in person, but my thought is that he probably really cared for you and didn't want to hurt you anymore than he already had."

Maive shakes her head. "When did life become so complicated, Dr. Fine?"

"At birth!" She says, laughing.

Maive smiles slightly. "When I was a kid, partners were chosen for their ability to make you laugh, share their chocolate, and keep a secret. Now people judge you if you don't carry a Prada bag, wear a David Yurman bracelet, or lack a degree from an Ivy League school."

"Most kids have that sense of innocence about them. But you know what? You don't have to lose it."

"Oh, come on, Dr. Fine!" She grabs her purse and reaches for her keys.

"Just because there are people in this world who judge others by the way they dress or by other means, doesn't mean you have to fall prey to it. People who act that way are very insecure. Why would you want to associate with someone like that?"

"I don't know." She applies gloss and wipes the excess on a tissue.

"I think that's something you need to consider for our next session, Maive."

"What's that, Dr. Fine?"

"Did you really love David or did you love the idea of the fairy tale life you think the Adelsteins live?" Dr. Fine looks over at Maive who is staring off into space. "You know, Maive, maybe you thought if you won the Adelsteins approval, than it might actually be okay to be a hairdresser and all of the other labels you have put on yourself."

"You think I put labels on myself?"

"We all do! The problem with labels is sometimes we believe them when they aren't true. Sometimes we buy into what other people label us as well, and it can affect us a great deal. Perhaps David and his family were meant to be nothing more than a lesson for you."

"What kind of lesson is that, Dr. Fine?"

"A lesson in self-worth."

The drive from Dr. Fine's office back to her house goes quickly as she thinks about her session. Did she really love David or love the idea of the fairy tale life more? She stares off for a moment, thinking about the possibility and then immediately shakes it off.

Of course she loved David! He was so attentive, coming by the salon and bringing lunch to her, sitting through dinners with her and her desperate single friends as they droned on about what bastards men were. He always made her laugh, and bought the music to the shows he would later take her to so that she would have a better understanding of the story. He was always thoughtful like that. One time she was home sick from work and he brought her matzo ball soup and fed it to her in bed. And the way he held her! She was certain he would crush her at times. His kisses were so passionate. It was as though the world didn't exist when she was in his arms.

She didn't need the Adelsteins approval! The whole idea is ludicrous and she is going to tell Dr. Fine the next time she sees her. Approval! She doesn't need anyone's approval.

When she pulls into her driveway, the dogs hear her car and rush towards the front door. She can hear paws scratching on the door. "Hold on a sec, Dunkin!"

While scanning her list of things to do before leaving Sanibel, the name Desiree with a question mark beside it is written at the bottom of the list. Perhaps passing up a visit will be for the best.

Although the two of them couldn't possibly be more different, the connection with Desiree had proven to be invaluable. She not only helped Maive find her first apartment in New York City, she also helped her make the transition to Sanibel by providing her with Rudy's name.

She will always be thankful for Desiree's help; thankful, but cautious. If it's one thing she has learned about Desiree, it's to keep a distance, and sometimes keeping a distance means having an unlisted number. Maive has her own drama and she doesn't need to be caught up in Desiree's as well.

The last time they spoke, Desiree told Maive she had found God. Having encountered more than one person who claimed to love the heavenly father more than any mortal man, Maive felt this new-found devotion to the Lord could be far worse. Especially in Desiree's case, always trading one set of addictions for another.

Maive gathers her bags and keys and then walks over to her dogs and gets down on the floor. "Goodbye, babies!" She kisses each dog on their head and then rubs their faces until their hair is all disheveled. "See you guys on Monday. I'll miss you! Mabel is going to take great care of you!"

All four dogs let out a loud howl.

"Come on, guys, she's not so bad!"

They howl again.

"She means well!"

More howling.

"Well, she's the best I can do! It's either her or Dr. Veck, and you know what happened last time you were there! Dunkin still has a scar on his nose from when he tried to dig you guys out of the kennel." The four dogs run into her bedroom.

Maive makes the short drive across town in her Volkswagen Beetle. She pulls up to Rudy's salon and recognizes four of the five cars in the parking lot.

"It's showtime!" She says, and then grabs her purse and heads inside.

The Salon

"Well here she is! I told you girls she is okay." Rudy pats an anxious client on the shoulder and walks towards Maive.

Twenty minutes late and focused intently on her clients, Maive completely bypasses the handsome gentleman sitting in one of Rudy's chairs and walks towards her station.

"You get that awful man out of your system?" Rudy whispers in her ear.

"For the moment."

"Be careful with Lillian, she's on the warpath today. Apparently her gardener quit." He rolls his eyes and heads back to his client, Benjamin Koppel.

Benjamin notices the gorgeous blonde who just walked in and can't take his eyes off of her. He follows her every step as she walks to the back of the salon.

The woman sitting next to him can't help but notice. "Careful, fella! You keep staring like that and you're liable to hurt your neck!"

Benjamin picks up *GQ* magazine and flips through the pages.

Billie stands at her station arranging her combs and brushes. "Hey, Maive!"

"Hi, Billie!" Maive turns slightly and then greets her first customer.

"I fixed one of your client's hair last night. Well actually she's my client now." Billie speaks loudly.

Maive walks back towards Billie. "What are you talking about? You don't color hair."

Billie speaks louder so that all of Maive's clients waiting to have their hair done hear her. "Well I do it better than you apparently. It was awful, Maive! She came into the salon in tears. I had to fix it!"

"What is her name?" Maive folds her arms.

"I don't know! What does it matter? I can't believe you did that to someone's hair!"

Maive looks around uncomfortably. Her clients are all staring at her and shifting in their chairs. She walks closer to Billie, who is applying another layer of lipstick, and whispers in her ear. "If there is a problem with a client, I would appreciate you speaking to me in private." She turns and walks towards her clients.

"Why, so nobody finds out what a horrible colorist you are?" She yells.

Maive ignores Billie and greets her clients. "Hi, ladies! Good to see you all this morning."

"I was here first!" The tall, bosomy blonde named Frederica Chevoy tells her. "What's the matter with pock face today?"

"Frederica!" Maive gasps.

"Last time you made my streaks perfect! I want you to do exactly the same thing again." Frederica purses her lips in the mirror.

"Excuse me, but I think I was here first." Lillian Wintree interrupts.

"I beg your pardon! I have had a standing

appointment with Maive since she moved here." Frederica talks back to her.

Maive walks over to the one client who has only kind words and a cup of coffee for her everytime she comes for her color. "Good morning, Doris! I see you're right on schedule to get these roots done."

"When I start to look like a zebra, I know it's time!" She laughs. "If it's not too much trouble, Maive, do you think we can sprinkle my hair with a few light pieces?"

"Doris, let's give it an all out thunder storm!"

Maive goes into the color room and asks her assistant Julianne to mix her some balayage. Lillian and Frederica, still yelling at one another, haven't even noticed Maive is no longer standing next to them.

"I am not in the mood! I've already lost one staff member today, and I'm not about to play second fiddle to some tart in bad shoes!" Lillian snaps at Frederica.

"Bad shoes? I'll have you know I paid over four hundred dollars for these!" Frederica shouts at her.

"You mean you overpaid! Didn't your mother ever tell you that class can't be bought, dear? Oh, and by the way, you might want to re-think the highlights since the boobs are already overdone." Lillian grabs the newest *Vanity Fair* magazine and turns her back on the girl.

Frederica rolls her eyes, but manages to get one last dig in. "My boobs may be over done, but they get a standing ovation every night. I'll bet your buttoned up husband has seen them at least once." She sips some of her tall latte with skim milk and takes a bite of her apple Danish.

Lillian ignores the comment since the girl isn't worth her time, but mostly because she's probably right. Through the years she has learned to ignore her husband Jeffrey's wandering eye and late nights out entertaining clients. Besides, she has fourteen beautiful three-plus carat rings, five tennis bracelets, a place in Aspen, a place in Italy, a brand new Jaguar every year, and carte blanche with the credit cards to make up for his lack of fidelity.

Looking the other way is something she learned to do a long time ago, after her initial desperate attempts at trying to keep him interested failed miserably. When a tummy tuck, face lift, two liposuctions, and her own breast augmentation didn't keep his focus, she finally resigned herself to playing second fiddle to his extra-curricular activities.

"How are things going, Mr. Koppel? Have you been keeping up with the Dolphins?" Rudy does his best to act butch for his manly client.

"Things couldn't be better, Rudy, but this isn't football season so the only dolphins I've been keeping my eye on are the ones swimming in the ocean."

Rudy laughs an uncomfortable laugh and quickly changes the subject. "Hey, Billie! Since you're not doing any clients right now, why don't you make yourself useful and get Mr. Koppel some coffee."

"Who is that stunning woman?" Benjamin asks.

"Billie? Dear God! You must be as blind as a bat!" He turns towards the receptionist. "Jennifer, bring Mr. Koppel your glasses!"

"No, not Billie! That blonde over there." He

motions with his head towards the back of the salon.

Rudy looks back at Maive's clients, but they're all blonde. He spots Frederica and figures he must be talking about her, because the other two are old hags. "Name's Frederica Chevoy. A real looker, yes, but she doesn't come cheap." Rudy rubs his fingers together.

Benjamin looks back and doesn't see Maive. She suddenly appears from a room carrying a bowl of something.

"I'm talking about the girl in the black suit."

Rudy turns and looks back again, but doesn't see who he is referring to. Then all of a sudden it dawns on him. "Maive? Our Maive? That's who you're asking about?" Rudy chuckles.

Although Rudy thinks Maive is one of the most beautiful women he has ever met, he had assumed that Benjamin was the sort of man who would prefer Frederica's type. And of course Rudy is right, but there is something about Maive that draws Benjamin towards her.

"She's so familiar." He says, and his mind drifts off. All of a sudden it dawns on him that she is the vision from the beach. "It's her!"

"What? Who's her?" Rudy looks around.

"That woman! I saw her on the beach this morning walking some dogs."

"That would be Maive! She loves those dogs. I'd love to introduce you to her, but she's down on men these days." Rudy throws his hand in the air.

Billie returns with the coffee and bends over, exposing two large breasts ready to spill out onto the marble countertop in front of Benjamin and Rudy. She overhears their conversation and can't help but add a comment. Sure she'd like to marry Maive off, but she doesn't deserve Benjamin Koppel. "She's a big dike!" Billie says.

"Takes one to know one, honey!" Rudy snaps at her. "Scram, Billie! Go drum up some business for a change!"

"Is she really gay? I mean there's nothing wrong with that."

"No! Straight as they come, or don't, for that matter. She went through a really bad break up, but it was over four years ago."

"Yikes! How come I've never seen her here before?"

"Because you usually come late at night and she's gone by then to take care of those mangy mutts."

"Well I think I'll start coming during the day more often."

Rudy smiles, all the while thinking about how he can get Benjamin interested in someone else. He certainly doesn't want to lose a client over this and the chances of Maive going for a guy like him are out of the question. Not only has she sworn off men, she's sworn off Jewish men in particular and Benjamin has mentioned to Rudy that he goes to synagogue with his mother.

"I've got this client I think you should meet. She's about 5'10, gorgeous brunette, successful, a doctor. She's always looking to meet men like you."

"Not interested! I can't date someone smarter than

I am." Benjamin laughs and so does Rudy, not knowing what else to do.

"Will you please introduce me to her? I can be pretty smooth with the ladies. If you make the introduction I can take it from there." Benjamin looks up at Rudy and waits for an answer.

"Alright! Alright! But I warn you, she bites! Rudy turns in Maive's direction and yells across the salon. "Maive honey, when you get a second can you come here, please? My client would like to talk to you about his color."

Billie glares at Maive. Maybe she can trip her on the way over to Rudy's station.

Maive answers without looking back. "Sure, Rudy! I'll be there in a minute."

"What the hell did you tell her that for? She's going to think I'm some fruit!" Benjamin is miffed, but so is Rudy, at the fruit comment.

"Listen! Maive is not going to just waltz over here and meet you. The only way to get her attention is to talk about hair color or those dogs of hers." Rudy rolls his eyes.

"Who the hell is this guy who screwed her up so bad?"

"David Adelstein! I've been hearing about him since she moved here from New York City. I know every detail about the jerk and I've never even met him."

"What is he, a serial killer? Married?"

Rudy shakes his head no.

"Come on! What's his problem?"

Rudy decides to lay it on the line the best he can without coming right out and saying anything that might offend his client. "They were madly in love, she wanted more, and he broke it off with her rather abruptly because his family didn't approve of her."

"How could they not approve of her?"

Rudy feels his skin starting to sweat under his favorite Versace shirt. "Different backgrounds, different religions, different everything." He turns quickly to grab some gel off of the marble counter.

"Well, that's a shame! I know about these differences you are referring to. It's more common than you think. When I was growing up my best friend fell in love with a girl who wasn't Jewish and his parents offered to buy him a car if he ended the relationship."

"That's ridiculous! What kind of car was it?"

"Does it honestly matter?"

To Benjamin it might not, but to Rudy it could.

"Well, all I know is that David's family didn't believe Maive was good enough for him. You know, being a hairdresser, not formally educated, and from no money. I personally believe that it had nothing at all to do with the fact that she isn't Jewish."

Benjamin turns around and looks Rudy right in his deep brown eyes. "It rarely does!"

Rudy perks up, feeling like there might be hope for Benjamin and Maive after all.

"What does this guy do for a living besides break lovely women's hearts?"

"Something to do with finance." Rudy puts some gel in his hands and then runs his long, slender fingers through Benjamin's hair. "Give me just a second, will you? I'll go fetch Maive."

With a comb in one hand and a paint brush in the other, she puts her full lips together to blow long strands of hair out of her face and hands her brush to Rudy. As she makes her way towards Benjamin, he watches her every move and thinks his heart might pound right out of his chest.

She places one hand on his broad shoulder and begins combing his wavy, dark hair. "What is it you are thinking of doing to your color?" She asks to the mirror.

Benjamin stares into the mirror and watches her comb his hair, unable to speak. Her arms are long and toned and the cut in her blouse reveals a cleavage he imagines running his hands over. She is even more beautiful than he had imagined, and her perfume wafts into his nostrils and then directly to his blood stream.

"Is it these few gray hairs that are bothering you?" Her eyes meet his.

Benjamin is quite fond of the gray hairs and feels like they make him look distinguished. "Yes! I was thinking about covering them up." He lies.

"Really? They're quite distinguished looking."

Touché!

"I don't think I'd do anything to your hair. It looks fine to me." She smiles politely and waits for a response.

Benjamin sits paralyzed and in a state of utter awe. He stares at her blankly, like some boy who just got his first glimpse of naked bodies in a *National Geographic* magazine.

"Well, if that's it, then I have to get back to my clients. They have more than a few gray hairs to worry about." She whispers softly in his ear.

Her breath on his ear wakes his friend below and he quickly shifts to one side of the chair in an attempt to put him back to sleep.

"Thank you for your honesty and your time." He blurts out as she walks away.

"It was my pleasure."

"It was my pleasure!" Billie mumbles under her breath, while looking at the paper.

Benjamin feels his confidence rise again along with his friend down below. Her pleasure! Of course it is. This isn't going to be so tough.

Maive walks over to Frederica who has been patiently awaiting her magic hands and motions with her head towards Benjamin. "There's a live one for you, honey!"

Frederica glances over at Benjamin, who is staring at himself in the mirror. "I think I've seen him in the club before."

"That figures! He looks like a real player and reeks of cologne."

Rudy Filona

"I'm taking lunch, Jennifer. Tell my clients they can kiss my ass!"

Jennifer looks up from the appointment book with a phone in both ears. She lifts up a finger signaling him to wait a minute, but Rudy throws his hand in the air dismissing her altogether and opens the door to his salon.

"Mrs. Finklestein wants to come in now." She covers the phone and whispers.

"Tell that old bitch to fuck off!" He whispers back. "She's a cheap old thing!"

"Rudy says if you hurry over he will see you before he takes lunch." Jennifer smiles snidely at Rudy.

He gives her the finger and walks out the door. His hunger for money overpowers his hunger for lunch so he stands in front of his shop and smokes a Merit. His cell phone rings and he chuckles as he answers it, certain that it's Jennifer. "Yes, darling?"

The voice on the other end of the line laughs. "It's me, fucker!"

"Miss Thing! Is it really you? Girl, I thought you dropped dead!"

"Me? I'm too evil to die. I called to let you know I'm fine and to ask you when you're coming to visit me."

"I can barely hear you." He yells into the phone.

"It's this cell phone. I need to get a new one. I

asked you when you are coming to see me."

"Oh, Dez, you know I'd love to, but I can't leave the salon. The old girls need me too much. Why don't you come here?"

"Please! Sanibel? I sort of picture that to be the equivalent of hell. Which reminds me, did I tell you I've found GOD?"

"God? As in Our Father?" He takes a drag from his cigarette to keep from laughing.

"No, dear Rudy. G.O.D., as in Gobs of Dough!"

"Uh huh! I know that's right! You always find your way to the hive, don't you my busy bee?"

"Always, Rudy! Always!"

"Who's your latest victim, honey?"

"Victim? Victims, Rudy! Victims!" She laughs.

"You are so nasty, Miss Thing!"

"One of these days I might surprise you and fall in love!"

"Girl, you're always in love! Come to think of it, we both are. With the dollar!" He laughs.

"You know me too well."

Rudy listens intently, chain smoking his lunch as Desiree relays her stories about all of the sugar daddies she is meeting. He keeps looking down at his Tag Hauer watch, a gift to himself after he stayed in business a year, wondering when old lady Finklestein is going to show.

"Rudy?" Billie calls to him from the doorway of the salon.

"What is it, Missy? Can't you see I'm on the phone?"

"I'm sorry! I'm going to the store and wanted to know if you needed anything."

"If I need something from the store, I'll get it myself. Now leave me alone! I'm talking to someone." He turns his back on her.

"Who is it?" Billie walks over to him.

"Someone flawless!" He shoos her away with his hand.

"You're so nasty, Rudy! Who were you talking to like that?" Desiree asks.

"Some girl who works for me that follows me around like a lost puppy dog."

"Probably has a crush on you!"

"Get the fuck out of here! Hey, did Maive tell you she was coming to the city this weekend? She's attending another tired old hair show. I told her if she wanted to see a show, she should head over to Chelsea. Poor thing! She's staying at the Sheraton. If you get a chance, give her a call. Maybe you can show her how life is meant to be lived."

"I haven't seen her in so long. How's she doing?"

"That tale is too long to tell and I don't have the patience anymore." Rudy coughs loudly in the phone.

"That sounds pretty! You should lay off those Merits; they've been known to cause cancer."

"When did you go to med school, girl?"

"Rudy stop! I'm concerned about you."

He spits on the ground. "Well, don't be! I was out late last night, that's all."

"Do tell!"

"There's nothing to tell. I don't even remember

his name!" But he certainly remembers his breath.

"You see, that's the kind of attitude Maive needs. If it's one thing I've learned, Rudy, it's that a girl can get over any man. Would you like me to talk to her?"

"She won't listen! She needs to find out for herself that she's been wasting her time thinking about that creep from New York. Hang on a second, honey. My latest victim just pulled up. In an Aston Martin, no less!" He puts the phone in his pocket and walks towards his next client. "Well, hello, Mrs. Finklestein! How you been, lady?" He kisses her on the cheek and opens the door for her. "Jennifer will get you into a smock. I'll meet you at my station in uno momento."

"Rudy? Rudy, where the hell are you? Quit schmoozing with that old battleaxe and talk to me!" Desiree yells into the phone.

Rudy takes his phone back out of his pocket. "Sorry, doll! I gotta go. My bread and butter just showed up for her appointment."

"You've never eaten bread and butter in your life."

"So true! Okay, my martini and foie gras just showed up. Hey, you still seein' that garmento with the big dick?" Rudy takes one last puff of his cigarette before throwing it on the ground.

"Are you referring to Gary?"

"Yeah, that's the one! I don't know why I never remember that, it does rhyme with fairy!" He laughs again.

"Yes, we're still seeing one another, but I'm getting tired of his same old speech. You know the one! 'I swear, babe! I'm going to leave my wife.' He hasn't done it yet so I'm pursuing other options."

"Well I hate to say I told you so, but I did tell you he'd never leave his wife and he hasn't left yet. He's got too much money invested with her."

"But he says he loves me!"

"Love, schmove, honey! You're a queen like I am, so go after another pawn."

"But it's not fair! These men need to know how much they are hurting women when they screw around with them and don't make a commitment. I wish there was some way I could teach him a lesson."

"Move on, sugar! There's plenty of dick out there for everybody. I gotta go! Call me later." Rudy extends his right hand, makes a circular motion and then drops the cell phone into his pocket and walks in his salon.

"Good Lord! What the hell did she do to her hair?" He asks Jennifer, as he smiles at Mrs. Finklestein, now taking a scarf off of her head.

"Rudy, darling!" Mrs. Finklestein calls out to him.

"Hey, gorgeous! Who the hell got a hold of your hair, Edward Scissorhands? You go away for a month and this is what happens?" Rudy picks at her hair with his hands like she has bugs and then yells at Jennifer. "Call my next client and see if she can come later."

"Yes, Rudy!" Jennifer answers, already dialing the number.

"Is it that bad, Rudy?" Mrs. Finklestein asks.

"Bad? Bad would be good. Your hair is a disaster! Now sit down and let me work my magic on you."

Katrina Emery

Walking up and down the aisle at Barneys, she stops to look at a Nicole Miller blouse and glances around for someone to help her. Two sales girls catch a glimpse of her, but turn their backs and walk away. Since she's been in New York, other women's jealousy is as common as a leering look from a man. If it weren't for her strong will she would have fallen apart years ago.

She doesn't need Barneys. She'll go to her favorite store instead. Bergdorfs is always a welcome sight. From the moment you enter the store it takes you in and envelops you in glamour. A girl could spend all day there! Maybe she will treat herself to the Gotham salad served in the café. She heads for the nearest door and into the first taxi she can find.

When she gets to Bergdorfs, she goes directly to the designer department and finds the Alberta Ferretti collection. The magenta dress is still there. She grabs her size and hands it to the girl standing behind a register. "Can you have this wrapped, please?"

"Yes, of course! Is there anyone helping you today?"

"Not today!"

"Will there be anything else?" She eagerly smiles at Katrina.

"No, that's it."

"This is such a lovely dress! Are you wearing it to a special occasion?" The salesgirl tries making small talk.

"The most special I can think of." Katrina smiles from ear to ear.

"Here you go! If you need anything else, please give me a call. I am more than happy to help you." The girl hands her a card.

Of course she is! The frock costs over sixteen hundred dollars! Little does the salesgirl know, but Katrina will be returning it at a later date and say the fit isn't right. All she has to do is make the return when this one isn't working. She can't believe they haven't caught on to her yet. She was only in here a week ago returning the outfit she bought for her last audition.

"Why don't you write down the hours that you work so I can make sure I shop when you are here?"

"Great! I would love that!" She jots down the information on the back of her card.

Heading back to the beauty department, Katrina peruses all of the counters and finally selects mascara from Lancôme.

"You get a gift with a purchase if you spend twenty-five dollars or more." An elderly woman smiles at her.

"Maybe just a little lipstick! And some blush." She reaches for a deep red lipstick.

"That color will look divine on you. Your skin tone is just gorgeous!" The older woman presents her with a blush in a deep plum color.

"They're both perfect! I'll take them."

She pays for her purchases, crosses the street, and makes her way to Victoria's Secret. She adores La Perla, but prefers to save those goodies for under the sheets.

On her way to the store, she passes a construction site where five men are sitting on a wooden plank attached to some scaffolding, reminding her of five blackbirds sitting on a fence. The difference between the two is that blackbirds have a pretty melody when they open their mouths, while these imbeciles do nothing but squawk rude remarks at her. As if their comments are going to land them a date!

"They didn't grow em like that when I was younger." The rather large one in a white t-shirt hits his scrawny friend in the arm.

"Did you see the rack on her? Jesus Christ!" The scrawny one waivers back and forth, trying to catch his balance.

She smirks to herself, slyly thinking how men are nothing more than boys who wear bigger clothing. Some wear a uniform, some wear jeans, and some wear suits, but they all follow their penis.

She enters Victoria's Secret and goes right over to the satin bras and panties and begins to look for her size.

"Can I help you, miss?" A voice startles her from behind.

She turns to see a rather bulky looking girl with butchered dark hair, chomping on a piece of gum.

"No, I'm fine." Katrina waves her away.

"You sure are!" The girl whispers in an audible tone. "I'll be right over there if you need me." She points to the register, salutes Katrina, and walks away.

Katrina quickly grabs a bra and panties and looks at the thongs. She's very aware of the girl watching her so she heads upstairs and looks around some more. After killing about ten minutes she returns to the register with a few teddies and is relieved to see the girl isn't there any longer. She pays for her items and leaves the store.

"Hey, baby! I knew you'd have to come out here sooner or later." A voice says behind her.

Katrina glances back and sees the girl smoking a cigarette. She rolls her eyes at the aggressive bitch and walks away.

"What? You think you're too good for me?" The girl calls out to her.

Katrina raises her hand and hails a cab. One pulls over to the side of the curb in a matter of seconds and Katrina turns back to the girl and yells, "Way out of your league!"

Benjamin Koppel

It's been one week and one day since Benjamin found out who the lovely creature on the beach was. Last night he left the island to go out to one of his favorite topless joints and came home after a half hour. Every face pales in comparison to Maive's, and the only thought that seems to occupy his mind as of late is when he will see her again.

Combing the beach every morning for the past week looking for her and those mangy dogs hasn't panned out, and it's too soon for another haircut. He's running out of options. There must be something he can do to see her. He could go by the salon and buy a fancy shampoo.

His rational mind, the one that goes two miles out of his way to save five cents on a quart of milk, tells him this is ridiculous, but the part of him that longs to see her makes the trip across town and pays fifteen ninety-five for a bottle of shit that doesn't even compare to his favorite Herbal Essence. At least he finds out she has been out of town and will return later today.

He decides that when he sees her, he's going to march right up to her and ask her out. Enough of this pansy-ass fucking around! When the hell has he ever been afraid of a woman? This babe should be no exception! Except this one doesn't trust anyone. Face it!

She doesn't trust your kind, Koppel.

He glances up at his reflection in the kitchen window and admires the haircut Rudolph gave him. Although it's perfect, he could go back to the salon and ask for more to be taken off the back. That way he would get to see Maive. No, that won't work! He'll come across like some pain in the ass mamby-pamby who whines about everything. She'll think he's too persnickety, too needy, and too obsessive. He needs something else, something that will get her attention. But what?

"God, if you're listening, it's Benjamin Koppel. I know I don't talk to you that often and for that I'm sorry. I'm real busy, that's all. Ah, hell! I'm not busy. I need something that will help me prove to this woman that I'm different. Do you think you could help me with this one?"

He's different alright, walking around his apartment talking to the ceiling. This is ridiculous! He grabs his keys and walks out the door. A few laps in the pool at the gym and a round of free weights will do him some good. Sitting around thinking about Maive is driving him crazy.

He gets into his car, opens the top, and blasts the radio. The song *Desperado* is playing and he quickly turns it off.

Mary Humphreys

"I'm done with that project you wanted, David. Do you need anything else?" Mary stands over his desk holding her pleather handbag in one hand and a stack of messages in the other.

"No, Mary. I'm finishing up here." He motions his hand over a pile of papers.

"Here are your messages. I alphabetized them for you."

He nods his head towards a corner of his desk and Mary places them there. She eyes David up and down, taking in one last look of him and his office.

His Ferragamo tie is tucked into his two hundred dollar shirt and she can tell he has taken off his Gucci loafers because she can smell his feet. The man has the worst foot odor!

His hair is slicked back like the kid in that *Wall Street* film, only David is no Charlie Sheen! She's seen pictures of David where his hair is wavy and grease free, but he looks like a different person, much younger, much less encumbered.

There are lots of fancy leather books on the dark wooden shelves that surround him on two walls. A third wall is nothing but windows that overlook the bustling center of Manhattan. Two chairs sit directly in front of David's desk, while a conference table with six more chairs is located to the right of it. Mary could move in here tomorrow since his office space is bigger than her apartment, but the photos would be the first thing to go.

David's office is filled with them! Some are pictures of him with celebrities he has made investments for, some with presidents of companies, politicians, and a few of his family. Mary has spent hours in this office staring at the photos of his wife, Stacy, and wishing bad thoughts on her. She would do the same to his mother, Ethel, but there isn't a clear enough photo of her. Every single one of them is a profile or taken too far away to get a good look at her. Mary can practically hear Ethel directing the photographer on how to capture her. Mary would like to capture her too, only it wouldn't be in a photo, it would be in a pine box!

The Adelsteins are by far the oddest group of people Mary has ever met. If they were a fruit, they would be a prickly pear cactus reversed, sweet on the outside and prickly on the inside. There's something not right about them. It's almost as if they are from another planet. They're far too surreal to be real. And so nasty! Mary would give anything to tell them off, but they wouldn't care if she did.

All it takes is one phone call from them and she's diminished to nothing. She never thought of herself as having such low self-esteem, but she never came across such a narcissistic and aggressive group of people before, either.

Mary knows it's all about ego because she has attended several spiritual weekends and now considers herself somewhat of an expert on the matter. The Adelsteins are the kind of people who need to show you how important and rich they are. It's not enough that they have a lot of money, they have to wear showy clothes, buy mammoth homes, talk about all of the philanthropic work they do, all of places they go, who they dine with, and where they dine.

Even David buys into it. His walls of glory are living proof. Mary is convinced that deep down inside David there is another man dying to come out, he just hasn't had the courage to listen to him. Not yet, anyway.

"Is there something else, Mary?" David looks up at Mary for the first time that day and notices that she looks tired. He should give her an extra day off.

She takes a deep breath and exhales. "David, I don't think that I can..."

David's cell phone rings and he glances down to see who is calling him. "Shit!" He shakes his head.

Mary doesn't care who it is! This time she is going to quit. "David, I wanted to tell you that I can no longer..."

He raises a finger to Mary, signaling her to stop and answers his phone. "Hi, Stace!" He rubs a hand on his forehead.

Mary looks at David and feels that pang again. Poor thing! She can imagine what he must have been like as a boy, only wanting to please everyone, telling them what they wanted to hear. It was probably the role he was given since the day he was born. She has seen him be manipulated by his mother and now the tradition continues with that monster he's married to. David was obviously an avid student. Ethel must be so proud!

Mary shakes her head in pity as she listens to David kowtow to his demanding wife. It must be true what they say about men. They always marry their mothers. And there is no one more evil than David's.

"I'm sorry, Mary. You were telling me you could no longer do something." David hangs up his phone.

Mary glances around David's office. "I can no longer water your plants. I'm no good with them. I kill them all!"

David bursts into laughter. "Mary, we'll call a service! You really had me going there! I thought you were going to tell me you could no longer work here." He gets up from behind his desk, grabs his briefcase and walks Mary to the elevator.

"No, David! I love it here!" Mary does her best to smile as she and David ride the elevator together.

They reach the street and David turns to head towards his subway, while Mary turns to head towards hers. All of a sudden he turns around and calls out to her. "Mary, I know your birthday is this week and I wanted to give you the day off, but we're having a huge meeting and I really need you here."

Mary pauses before turning towards him. How can she think of quitting? This poor soul needs her. "David, I don't need an extra day off. I'll be here. You can count on me." She smiles and turns away.

David has no idea how such a small gesture like remembering her birthday keeps Mary coming back to work each day.

Katrina Emery

Overcome with nausea, she turns towards the tracks in Penn Station and pukes down the side of the concrete wall. Immediately relieved, she wipes her face with a tissue and then sprays some Binaca in her mouth. She hopes it's something she ate, but had better make an appointment with her doctor just to be sure. She'll call and cancel her date while she's at it.

Looking smart in her new dress with tailored jacket and high heeled black patent Chanel shoes, she clutch es her Louis Vuitton handbag in her right hand while swinging her shopping bags in the other. She pulls out her cell phone and dials her doctor's number as she heads back up the stairs to get some fresh air.

Just then one David Adelstein comes rushing down the stairs desperate to catch the 5:20 out of the city, while trying even more desperately to end a conversation with his wife. "I can't hear you anymore. I'm hanging up now. I'll call you back when I get out of the tunnel." He shuts his phone.

As Katrina heads up the stairs, David heads down them, oblivious to the gorgeous woman he is about to slam into. He glances down at his watch and sees he only has one minute to catch the train, so he starts taking the stairs two at a time. Just as he leaps down the last four, Katrina looks up and sees a man heading right towards her. He crashes into her and knocks her to the ground.

"Ouch! Oh, my leg!" She cries.

David looks towards the voice moaning in pain and for the second time today he notices another human being. Not just any human being, but one of the most captivating women he's ever seen. "I'm so sorry! I'm trying to make my train." He looks past her shoulder and sees the doors beginning to shut.

Katrina winces in pain, holding onto her leg. David glances up to see his train pulling away, while she looks up at the well-dressed man standing in front of her and can't believe her clumsiness has finally paid off.

"Are you okay?" David reaches for Katrina's arm and helps her back on her feet.

"Your train, you'll miss it." She glances over his shoulder.

"I already have."

"I should have been watching where I was going. I'm always falling or tripping over something."

"No, it was my fault. I was talking on the phone to..." He stares at the gorgeous blonde standing in front of him. Her nose is perfectly proportioned to her slender face, her lips are cherry red and voluptuous, and her green eyes are deep and dreamy. "I shouldn't have been on the phone." He manages a comment.

"This is New York. Everybody is on the phone!"

"Can I help you to the top of the stairs?" He extends a hand.

"That would be so nice of you. I was supposed to meet someone for dinner, but I'm not feeling well."

She speaks with a soft, breathy voice, each word weaving a tighter web around his groin.

"I feel awful! Were you meeting someone special?" Strangely, he hopes she says no.

"I was supposed to meet my boyfriend, but it's just as well that I can't make it. I think he's going to break up with me."

"What kind of man would break up with you?"

"A married one!" She answers. "I'm Katrina, Katrina Emery." She stops walking and extends her hand to shake his.

David grips it tightly in his palm like he normally does when he shakes someone's hand, but her hand is different. Soft, like silk. Fragile even, like a child's. "I'm David, David Adelstein."

"I'm so upset! He never told me he was married until recently." She bursts into tears, and puts her head on the shoulder of David's finely tailored suit.

At first he stands uncomfortably as this stranger seeks comfort from him, until he finds himself putting a hand on her back and softly caressing her shoulder. He takes in the smell of her perfume, an erotic musty smell, unlike the floral number his wife douses herself with. He can feel her breasts against his chest and he yearns to pull her closer and never let her go. The last time he felt this overwhelmed by someone it had been Maive. Shit!

"Listen, I'm really sorry I bumped into you and I would love to stay and comfort you since it was my fault I knocked you down, but I have to get home to my family."

Katrina looks up at him, puzzled. "Can you at

least walk me out to the street and help me into a cab? I'm not sure how wobbly my leg is going to be, and besides, the next train isn't leaving for another thirty minutes." She looks up at him with wounded eyes.

"Well, I guess it's the least I can do."

Katrina tries walking by herself. "My leg! I don't think I can walk up the stairs without your help."

David holds her hand and she leans onto his shoulder. Her suit jacket falls to the side and her dress gapes open, so David quickly sneaks a peek. Katrina notices David staring down at her breasts and smiles to herself.

She looks into his eyes. "Have you ever lived in the city?"

"Several years ago. Actually, it was more like another lifetime ago." He stares off and sighs.

"Another lifetime, huh? That sounds intriguing. I love it here! My neighborhood is so charming. I looked at over a hundred apartments before I found my place. It's above that great French restaurant on the corner of Sixty-third and Third Avenue."

They reach the top of the stairs and then ride the escalator together out into the busy rush hour streets of New York City. David waits with Katrina by the curb.

"Can you hold these for a moment, David?" She hands him her shopping bags from Bergdorfs and Victoria's Secret.

She takes out a compact mirror and lipstick. David watches intently as she traces her full lips with a light gloss and then taps them together. She purses her lips in the mirror and then dabs them a bit with a tissue. She glances over at David, who looks as though he is doing something wrong. "How do I look?" She asks.

"Wow! You look..."

"I look okay then?" She smiles.

He nods his head yes.

She throws her hand in a sweeping motion up towards the sky and beckons a ride. Within seconds a cab pulls over to the curb. Katrina turns towards David and coyly asks, "Can I ask you one last favor?"

"Sure!"

"I'm so hot from being in the station. Can you please help me take off my jacket before I get into the cab?"

He puts her bags on the curb and gently removes the beige jacket from her shoulders. The dress she is wearing is tight and molds her ass like a finely tailored glove. Her breasts are full and beckon to him like a mountain climber yearning to feel the peaks of Mount Everest. He opens the door to the cab for her and she climbs in sideways, her long slender legs parting slightly as she leans back on the seat. Her dress gives way just a bit and he sneaks a peek. She's not wearing any panties.

"It's been such a pleasure meeting you, David. I'm really glad I bumped into you."

He smiles in a daze as the beautiful blonde drives away. It takes David a few minutes before he realizes he is now in possession of her shopping bags.

David And Stacy

Every Friday night David and Stacy have dinner with another couple at their favorite Italian restaurant. Tonight is no exception.

Stacy looks in her bread knife to check her lipstick, while David stares off into space and thinks about Katrina. The waiter comes by and tells them the specials, describing chicken breasts that send David's mind wandering off into thoughts of Katrina's breasts and how amazing they felt up next to him. He swallows hard and moves to the left side of his chair, thinking about her soft, sexy voice and the way she said his name.

"Can I get the two of you something to drink?" The waiter looks at Stacy and David.

"Give me a glass of white." Stacy speaks to her knife.

"Whenever you get a minute, I'll have a scotch on the rocks, please." David turns and acknowledges the waiter.

"Honestly, David, ya don't have to be so nice to the help. It's not like they aren't getting paid to wait on us. I swear! That's half the problem, ya know. You forget you're paying these people. I see it time and time again! It's just like the contractors." Stacy puts down her knife and looks up at David. "David!

You're not listening to a word I'm saying. Where are you tonight?"

"I was thinking about some business." He polishes his silverware with his napkin.

"I talked to Janet the other day and she told me she was at a party where they used the new caterer. I want to use them for Lily's birthday party." She takes a sip of water and then chews on an ice cube.

"She's four!" David extends four fingers towards Stacy.

"I am fully aware of how old my daughter is! And she's not four anymore, she's almost five." She raises her finger in the air.

"All I'm saying is, do you really think we need to cater her party? It's kids, for God's sake! We can order pizza and cake." He wipes his plate with the napkin.

"Do ya think I'm gonna have a party with pizza and cake? What will my friends think?" Before David can answer she goes off on another tangent. "Don't ya remember Talia's party? They had horses and a clown. I already cheaped-out on the entertainment, I'm not about to skimp on the food." She waves her hands all over the place.

"But none of your friends eat anything. Why do we have to bother with a caterer?"

"Oh, my God! Ya just don't get it! Don't I always make sure ya have clean clothes? Food on the table?"

She is right, although David can't remember the last time she actually washed a load of clothes herself or cooked a meal. The waiter returns with the drinks and quickly leaves the table.

"Do ya realize Lily just now got accepted to the same camp as Talia? She almost didn't get in. What would have happened then, huh? How would I explain that to poor Lily? All of her friends going, but not her?"

"I'm glad you brought camp up. I think Lily is too young for sleep-away camp. I didn't go until I was seven."

"Are you joking? I loved camp! It was the best place in the world to be. I think Lily will get so much out of it."

"What does it matter if she waits another year or two?" He takes a large gulp of his drink.

"What am I supposed to do with her? Do you expect me to sit around all day and cart her from one place to the next? Huh? Answer me that! Am I not entitled to a summer, too?"

"What about Cecilia? Can't she help you? This way you can get some time off." He begins to back pedal.

"Why can't our daughter go away like everybody else? Why do you have to fight me on this, David? Don't you want the best for her?" Stacy begins to get weepy.

"Fine! Send her to camp, but please don't pick one that costs ten grand and is filled with a bunch of privileged kids being flown in on private jets. I'm sure you can find another camp that's just as nice with a little more diversity." He pulls out his phone and looks through his messages.

"Are you telling me that Lily isn't worth ten

thousand dollars? You spend that in a weekend on one of your golf trips! And p.s., diversity is so overrated! Why shouldn't Lily be entitled to the same privileges that you had as a kid?"

"I'm not saying she shouldn't. I'm saying that I think she is too young, that's all."

"I'm disappointed in you, David. I really am. I would have thought with your sister Debbie sending her daughter there, you would have wanted the cousins to be close."

"I didn't know Debbie was sending Zoe there."

"Where have you been, David? Zoe has gone there since she could practically walk! Debbie doesn't seem to have a problem sending her off to camp. As a matter of fact, I think your mother funds it." Stacy reaches for her purse and takes out her phone.

"Really? My mom funds it? Dan is more than capable of paying for camp." He puts his phone down on the table.

"Of course he is! All we ever hear about it is how much money Dan makes, but what everyone fails to mention is how cheap he is! Why should he pay for camp when your mother will?" She dials her phone.

"Who are you calling?"

"Amy. She and Lev should have been here by now." David opens his mouth to speak, but Stacy cuts him off. "How do ya think Janet and Victor afford the same things we do? He doesn't make that much money, does he? I mean you're the one with the M.B.A.! You'd think you would make way more than he does." She makes an ugly face and takes a sip of her wine.

"I'm sure Victor does quite well. Besides, what does it matter? I thought you and Janet were best friends?"

"We are! I can't talk to you about anything." She dismisses him with her hand.

David fiddles with the napkin in his lap and glances around the restaurant, wishing he were anywhere but here. He takes a sip of his vodka and listens to Stacy drone on about her day.

"Did I tell ya Cecilia didn't mop the floors today? I can't believe it! How many times do I have to tell that woman to do the same thing? And you think she is going to help with Lily?" She sees their friends walk in the front door. "Hey you guys, we're over here!" She yells across the restaurant.

David slumps his shoulders in embarrassment when everyone in the restaurant turns to look at their table. He lowers his head and reaches for a roll. It's firm, round, and warm from the oven. He squeezes it lightly and imagines that Katrina's breasts might feel similar.

"Should I fire her?" Stacy asks him.

He reaches for his bread knife to butter the roll. "What, honey?"

"For fuck's sake, David! Can't you listen to me? I've had a hard day! They didn't have my size at Barneys, Cecilia didn't clean what I asked her to, and everybody has more money than we do!" She takes another sip of wine and leaves a huge lipstick mark on the glass.

David shuts down like he always does when his wife goes off on one of her tangents. Their friends Lev and Amy reach the table and Stacy continues to scold David. "My parents are coming over on Sunday. What am I going to do about the floor?"

"We'll get it done, honey." He tries appeasing her as he stands to greet Amy and Lev.

"Well, I'm not gonna do it!" She rolls her eyes towards the ceiling, grabs her earlobes, and jerks them back and forth at Amy. "Looky! Looky!"

"Those are gorgeous!" Amy gushes. "David, you are too kind!"

David nods politely and sits back down. He likes Lev, but finds Amy utterly annoying. He's known her since high school and she hasn't changed a bit. Her hairstyle is still worn in the same bob, her clothes are as boring as her personality, and she gossips about everyone.

"Did you guys hear the latest about the Silvers?" Amy asks within the first minute of sitting down.

David was secretly calculating how long it would be before she talked about someone. This is a record!

"They're getting divorced!" She whispers. Before anyone has had a chance to say anything, she eagerly shares the details of their separation. "He cheated!"

Stacy lets out a gasp.

Both David and Lev act as though this isn't news at all, and David can't help but wonder if Lev is thinking the same thing he is.

"Poor Mitzi, she's so distraught! I think we should go over there tomorrow and cheer her up." Amy says.

David knows this means "get the details."

"Absolutely!" Stacy agrees. "A girl needs her

friends at a time like this."

David secretly wants to cheer for Fred Silver, who has taken more torture from a spouse than anyone should ever have to. Last summer, Mitzi forbade Fred from seeing his old buddy from college, saying it was frivolous spending, and then proceeded to book a trip for her and her mother at the Ritz in London for the same weekend. What David finds most appalling about Mitzi is her incessant need to put Fred down any chance she gets, regardless of who is in earshot.

Mitzi has gained at least ninety-five pounds since their marriage, and is always on some diet that miraculously allows her to eat anything she wants. On the other hand, Fred probably weighs one hundred and forty pounds wet. David guesses old Fred probably started looking at other women way before Mitzi put on the weight, but the second chin didn't help any.

"After all she did for him! She told me she practically put him through med school. It's probably some slutty nurse at the hospital, right?" Stacy sneers at the thought.

"No, worse! A hostess at that Thai restaurant in town." Amy turns up her nose.

"A hostess? Is she from Thailand? Ya know some men pay money to marry those girls! I hope the bastard wasn't sleeping with Mitzi at the same time he was sleeping with that slut. God knows what the girl has!"

David laughs to himself at the mere notion of Fred and Mitzi still fucking. Inside his head David hears the song *For He's a Jolly Good Fellow* and thinks Fred Silver's got a real set of balls! Without realizing it, he begins to hum the words. He looks up to see everyone at the table staring back at him.

"You're disgusting, David!" Stacy scolds him.

"I'm sorry! I was thinking about this retirement party we had at the office today. We all sang that song."

"You have such great timing! Could ya at least pretend to be sympathetic for poor Mitzi?" She turns towards Amy and rolls her eyes.

Poor Mitzi, ha! Once she's taken half of everything she and Fred acquired during their thirty years together, she'll be anything but poor. David's mind wanders off to his work associate Bruce, who left his wife of thirty-six years for a younger something flight attendant. Although she is fifteen years his junior and Bruce lost half of his financial worth, he still seems pretty happy. David thinks about the changes in Bruce. He has a smile that wasn't there before, a hunger for the day, and things that once stressed him out no longer do. He even dresses differently.

"So what do ya think, David?" Amy asks with a mouthful of bread.

David feels the sweat beads starting to form on the top of his forehead. If he says he doesn't know what they were talking about, his wife will berate him again. "Sounds great to me!" He answers.

The two women give each other a high five.

"You didn't hear a word they said, did you?" Lev whispers in his ear.

"Hell, no! I tuned her out the minute we got in

the car." David confesses.

"Well, congratulations! You just agreed to a weekend in the Hamptons with us, the Freud's, the Lowenstein's, and Mitzi and her kids."

David motions to the waiter to come over and orders another scotch on the rocks. While he waits for his drink, he looks at his wife sitting next to him and finds her gesture of talking with her hands reminiscent of a person shooing away enormous horse flies. The shine from her diamonds blind his right eye, so he glances away for a second and then turns back to take an inventory of some of the jewelry he has bought for her since they have been together.

Two David Yurman bracelets and one tennis bracelet on her right hand, a platinum Rolex with diamond bezel on her left, accompanied by a Hermes bracelet, and one three carat, perfectly round diamond engagement ring accompanied by a one carat trillion on either side. And, of course, the earrings he just bought her!

The only non-glitzy piece of jewelry she owns is the plain gold wedding band that was his grandmother's, and he knows she'll toss that to the back of her jewelry box the moment she gets a replacement.

This evening she's wearing the double strand of pearls he brought her back from India. He only remembers this because he also brought back a stomach bug and was sick for weeks, but she didn't care about that.

The Prada bag that siphoned a good part of his paycheck is tossed on the floor like a crumb from the table. Although she already had three others, David didn't fight her when she asked for another one.

"Need, schmeed! I want it!" She said, and that was the end of that. David wonders how many bags a person needs. After all, you can only carry one at a time.

She crosses her leg and Manolo Blahnik pokes him in the shin. He waits for an apology, but it never comes. Her shoes! She's got enough of those to open her own store! Every day she comes home with a new pair. "Whatever makes her happy" has been his mantra for as long as he can remember, but as of late it seems frivolous and thankless, especially when she's started buying Lily all designer items as well.

As his wife drones on about her problem with Cecilia to Amy, and how ungrateful the help is, her insatiable and sullen manner suddenly strikes him in the most frightening way.

He watches her movements, the way she never smiles, the exaggerated roll of her eyes, and the dismissive motion she gives with her hand towards the wait staff and him. He wonders when the girl who once held him in such high esteem began to disregard him altogether.

He thinks back on their time together, wondering when it all went wrong. He racks his brain for a memory, an incident that must have occurred. A chill goes up his spine and he finds himself buttoning his suit jacket and folding his arms. It suddenly dawns on him that there was no incident and the only memory he has is that his heart had been broken by someone else and he never loved Stacy at all.

David makes small talk with Lev, while the two

women act as though their husbands aren't even with them. At the end of the evening, they'll both be expected to produce credit cards to pay for salads their wives barely eat and entrees they dissect with their forks while moving the food from one side of the plate to the other.

Dessert will be out of the question. Just once, David wishes his wife would be unpredictable and order dessert. Something really fattening! Something that says, "I'm not a cliché." Dessert, he thinks, that's what is missing from his relationship with Stacy.

Stacy leans over towards David, holding onto Amy's wrist. "Ya see this, David? This is the bracelet I was telling you about. Wasn't it nice of Lev to get it for her?"

"Very nice."

"Nice? It's gorgeous! Look at the way the light catches the rubies! Could ya die?"

"Yes, I could." David says under his breath.

Stacy turns her back to David and the two women start gossiping about someone at temple. Talking about someone at temple seems sacrilegious to David, even though he doesn't consider himself an observant Jew. Although his family celebrates Rosh Hashanah, Yom Kippur and Passover, he realized a long time ago that his family based their beliefs on a cultural basis more than a religious one.

"Those shoes! Did you ever see anything like them?" Amy snickers.

"She's so "jappy!" I find women like that so offensive." Stacy says.

"Jappy?" David springs to life for the first time this evening. Although he has always hated stereotypes of any kind, especially anything Jewish in nature, he can't help but think his wife and Amy are two of the "jappiest" women he has ever known.

"I'll have the chocolate soufflé." He hears a woman's voice at the table next to theirs. "I usually make a mess, but what the heck!" The woman tells her friend.

It can't be! David's heart flutters. Maive always made a mess of dessert. He looks over his shoulder at the blonde woman sitting directly behind him and does a double take, but it's not her.

He turns back towards his table and half listens to Lev talking about the stock market and how much money he has lost. David's lost. Sometimes he thinks he's been lost since the day he lost Maive.

"Look at that chocolaty goodness!" The blonde sitting next to them gushes as the waiter places the dessert in front of her.

David glances back at her. Maive loved chocolate! He remembers it dripping down the front of her shirt at Café Lola. When she asked to wear his jacket he had been reluctant to let her, afraid she would make a mess of it. He had been such a jerk! What he wouldn't give now to see her in that jacket.

"What do you think?" Lev taps David on the hand.

Jarred back into the present David answers, "I try not to these days."

While Stacy complains to Amy about her lack of

jewelry and how she drives last year's Range Rover, David wonders how much longer he can stand to play the role of her husband. Every year she plans three trips for the two of them without the children. Their agenda is planned down to the last second, including reservations at all the trendiest spots and places she has to shop. He's been to some of the most beautiful places on earth, yet his memories of them are marred by a woman who only finds the flaws in them.

Stacy reaches for David's arm and his skin repels at her touch. He suddenly realizes that not only does he not love his wife, he can't stand her. There must be something he can do. Maybe he can talk to her about how he feels. Nah! That will never work! She doesn't listen to a thing he says, and if he even broaches the subject, she will whine or cry and it will end up costing him more money.

He looks around the restaurant and notices some of the couples sitting together. The wives talk incessantly while the husbands look off into the woodwork or down at their phones. They nod every now and then and feign interest, but most look completely disenchanted.

What is it that's missing? Is it joy? Passion? He searches his brain for the right word until he hears the unmistakable sound of pure delight, coming from the blonde who is enjoying the hell out of her chocolate soufflé.

"Dessert!" He blurts out the word.

"If you must, David! If you must! But don't complain to me when you feel like a tubbo later." Stacy laughs.

David looks up at Stacy and subtly shakes his head in disapproval. He may have been young, foolish, and only wanting to please his parents when he met Stacy, but that David no longer exists.

A bit of a grin forms on his lips and then transforms into a large, boyish one.

The lingerie! He's got the lingerie!

Desiree

She takes a swig from the fifth of vodka as the cabbie turns the corner and almost clips another car in the lane next to him. The speed of the taxi stimulates her body as she closes her brown eyes and pushes her black pumps to the worn floor of the cab. Aside from money and rich men, feeling totally out of control is the ultimate rush.

She takes a cigarette from her purse and puts it to her lips.

"No smoking!" The driver says, but she lights it anyway.

Going to the strip clubs to dance is not something she wants to do, but something she has to do in order to keep the lifestyle she has become accustomed to. If she drinks the right amount of booze before the cab pulls up in front of the club, the slight buzz will make stepping onto the catwalk in full view of the two hundred men howling like wild animals more tolerable.

"Do you have any kids?" The driver asks.

As far as she is concerned, it's a four letter word. "No!" She snaps at him.

"That's too bad. Kids are great! I have five of them."

She turns and looks out the window, desperate for him to stop talking.

"My youngest is going off to college next year. His name is Tracy, but I call him Trey." He smiles in the mirror and keeps talking.

She hears the name, puts her hands over her ears, but still hears him talking.

"Trey got into N.Y.U. My wife and I are so proud of him."

Her hands move down her face and to the back of her neck. She struggles to find her breath, so she rolls down the window for some fresh air.

"Trey told me just the other day that he is going to buy me a new car when he gets a job. My wife says all I ever do is talk about him. Trey this, Trey that."

She wishes she could lean forward and slap the driver. Why can't he shut up? All this banter about Trey! She has tried so hard to forget him. And what he did to her.

It was her first night at a new strip club in Atlanta. She had only been dancing for about an hour when a handsome man in a cowboy hat beckoned her to the side of the stage. "I'd love to be your boyfriend!" He smiled wide and then took out a wad of cash and put it in her g-string. "My name is Trey Perkins and I'm damn delighted to meet you!"

Some girls work for months before a sugar daddy comes along, so Desiree couldn't believe her luck. She agreed to stop dancing as long as he paid all of her expenses, despite a warning from another dancer.

It was love! He loved her. She was certain of it. They dated for three months, their affair growing more intense by the day, and Desiree could imagine spending the rest of her life with him. Getting pregnant was a complete surprise, as was finding out Trey was married and already had a family. The night he threatened to kill her, she left Atlanta and never looked back, except to call his wife from a pay phone in Manhattan to tell her everything.

The cab driver slams on the brakes as a delivery boy swerves out into the traffic.

"Jesus Christ! What the fuck is wrong with you?" Desiree holds her chest and exhales loudly.

"Sorry, miss! A boy almost hit my car."

"You see what happens with kids? They go and do stupid things like that!"

"Kids are many things. Not always perfect, but they fulfill you." The driver stops in front of the club.

"If kids fulfill you, then you must be one empty mother fucker." She throws him a five dollar bill and slams the door.

Red carpeted stairs meet her at the curb of the club. She steps over a pile of something that resembles lumpy soup and opens the front door. Darkness, the stench of stale beer, and cigarette smoke greet her. No matter what time of day it is, it's always show time in the club, so she dons a smile in case anyone is around.

Tommy, the manager and resident scumbag, comes out of his office zipping up his pants. Desiree looks over his shoulder and sees the newest hire getting off of her knees and wiping her face. The sight of him sickens her, but she knows how to work him, too.

"Hey, Tommy! You're looking handsome today. Did you get a haircut? Something looks different about you." The filthy pig slicks it back, puts it in a pony tail every night, and it looks as though he never washes it.

When he grabs her by the arm her first instinct is to slap him across the face and kick him in the balls.

"Thanks, babe! Someone just blew me! Maybe that's the look you see." He pours himself a whiskey on the rocks and swigs it down in one gulp. Desiree watches his pimpled neck swallow hard and she wants to vomit at the sight of him. He lets out a loud belch and then lights a cigarette and drags on it with wet lips. "Why don't you join me for a drink?"

"I've got to get ready." She sees the girl leaving his office.

"How come you never go out with me like the other girls do? You think you're too good for me?" He slurs his words.

It's true, she does think she's too good for him, but the fact that he notices isn't good. The last thing she needs is him having it in for her.

"Oh, Tommy, you're too good for me! I can never go out with you because I won't be able to work here and neither will you. I'll have to have you all for myself and before you know it, we will have to get married and have tons of babies."

The thought of one woman, day after day, repulses him, not to mention the word babies. "Get the fuck out of here!" He yells at her and pours himself another drink.

"Fucking slime!" She mutters under her breath as she clocks in and heads downstairs to see what Mom, the lady who takes care of all of the dancers, has to show her.

"Hey, Mom!" She calls out to the plump, black woman sitting on a metal chair.

"Hey, Dez! What's goin' on baby girl?"

"Just another night in hell!" Desiree opens her purse and takes out her cigarettes.

"I know that's right!"

"I ran into that fucking prick, Tommy, upstairs. He's so gross! Asked me why I never go out with him." Desiree puts a cigarette between her lips and Mom lights it.

"Cause you're smart, that's why. Stupid new girls that come in here! I try to warn them about that no good bastard, but they don't listen to Momma."

"Well, they should! Hey, did you get those new accessories you were telling me about?"

"The girl is coming back in an hour to show everybody else, but I did manage to pick out something special for you." She hands Desiree a silver bra and panty set with a silver and hot pink boa.

"You're always looking out for me, Mom. I really appreciate it!" Desiree hands her a twenty.

"I thought you were taking some time off, Dez?"

"I was, but that boyfriend of mine is acting up again so I figured I will play it smart and look out for myself. Besides, there's more than one gullible fish in the sea."

"Tell Momma what kind of fish you want honey."

"Why, a GOLD fish, of course!" Desiree laughs.

"Well this place is a fuckin aquarium!"

The two women burst into laughter when Desiree pretends to cast a fishing line.

Benjamin Koppel

Early Sunday morning Benjamin makes his way back home through the winding roads that overlook the shore of Sanibel Island. The sun is beginning to burst through the vast expanse of blue sky, and vibrant shades of orange and yellow look as though they are kissing the water.

Sweating profusely from a vigorous workout at the gym, he reaches into his duffle bag for a towel to wipe his face. He dabs the sides of his cheeks and talks to himself in the rear view mirror, pondering this David fellow and what he could have done to Maive to make her hate men so much.

Someone should tell this girl that the break up had nothing to do with her. Damn mothers! Speaking of mothers, he didn't call his this morning. He takes his eyes off of the road for only a moment and reaches into the glove compartment for his cell phone.

When Benjamin's eyes meet the road again he sees a small white thing in front of his car. He slams on the breaks and his car screeches to a halt, but only after a loud thud is heard. "Oh, shit!" He opens his car door and runs out to see what he has hit.

There on the black tar road is a small, white dog howling in pain and bleeding from his left leg. "Damn it! Hang in there, buddy!"

He runs back to his car and grabs his phone and dials 911. After asking an operator to help him find the closest veterinarian, he runs back towards the dog, now whimpering in pain. "No, you can't die! Hang in there, fella!" Benjamin bursts into tears. "Little guy, can you hear me?" He softly caresses the head of the motionless ball of fluff.

An older woman with three dogs in tow comes over a sand dune and screams in horror. "Buster! Oy vay! What have you done to poor Buster?"

Benjamin gets up and walks towards the woman screaming at him. Just as he is about to speak, a white station wagon pulls up behind Benjamin's car and a tall, thin man wearing glasses emerges.

"Hi, I'm Dr. Veck. I was on my way home and got a page."

Benjamin points to the front of his car and walks back towards the dog. "This poor guy came out of nowhere!"

Dr. Veck walks to the front of the car and sees Buster lying on the pavement. "Ah, jeez! It's one of Maive's."

"Maive's?" Benjamin walks to the side of the road and heaves. This is not what he intended when he asked God for help.

"What were you going so fast for, you blazing idiot?" The woman with the three dogs yells at him. "What kind of fool drives so damned reckless? You should have your license taken away! You dog murderer!"

"Calm down, ma'am! I wasn't being reckless. He came out of nowhere."

Mabel Hempstead knows this is true just as she knows it is her responsibility to take care of all four dogs while Maive is away. "You're right, honey! I don't know what I'm thinking. He is awfully sweet, but not the brightest bulb. One minute he is running alongside me and the next thing I know he's gone."

"Is he dead, Doc?" Benjamin asks.

"God, I hope not!" Mabel says. "I knew something like this would happen! I was only supposed to watch these dogs for a weekend, and then one of Maive's relatives goes and dies and now my good sense has expired."

Dr. Veck speaks in a calm voice. "I think he is going to be okay, but I need to get him back to my office and fix his leg. He's unconscious from the pain, but he'll make it."

Overjoyed at the news, Benjamin turns towards Mabel and hugs her. "I'm sorry, I don't even know you, but I'm so relieved." Benjamin says.

"Don't apologize, honey. I'll take a hug from you anytime!" Mabel grins.

"I'm Benjamin Koppel." He extends a hand.

"Mabel Hempstead." She grips his hand.

"I'm taking him now." Dr. Veck calls out.

"Wait a minute, Dr. Veck! I need to get your phone number. I'd like to take care of everything." Benjamin says.

"I couldn't possibly let you do that." Mabel interrupts him. "I shouldn't have let him off of the leash. Honestly, I don't know how Maive keeps up with the four of them."

"She's pretty spectacular!" Dr. Veck smiles, as he carefully places Buster on a blanket in the back of his wagon and puts an IV in his leg. He hands Benjamin one of his business cards. "You can call me in a few hours and I'll let you know how he's doing."

"Can I come with you?"

"You can if you want to, but it's not necessary. He'll be in surgery and then recovering for awhile." Dr. Veck gets into his car.

"Still, I'd like to make sure he's okay. I've never hit an animal before. I feel really awful."

"He's in the best of hands!" Mabel says. "I can use your help making sure I get the rest of these mutts home safely." She motions with her head to the other dogs.

"I only want to help."

"Then you better come with me. Dr. Veck will call with Buster's progress. Won't you, Dr. Veck?"

"Of course! Let me go now." He pulls away, leaving Mabel and Benjamin standing on the side of the road.

"I just live around the bend." Mabel points up the road.

"What about them?" Benjamin glances down at the dogs.

"They love riding in the car!" She opens the passenger door to Benjamin's car and puts Cricket on the floor in front of her. Dunkin jumps over on Benjamin's seat and Sammy sits on Mabel's lap.

"Is he driving?" Benjamin asks, as he looks down at the large German shepherd staring out the windshield.

"He probably can!" Mabel laughs. "He's a smart one."

Benjamin slowly opens the door and the dog snarls at him. He quickly backs up. "I don't know if this is such a good idea."

"He's protective, that's all!" Mabel assures him.

"Protective of what? It's my car!" He leans down to get into his car again and the dog snarls. Benjamin snarls back and Dunkin moves over so Benjamin can sit down. "Okay then, is everybody ready?" Benjamin calls out.

The three dogs bark and Mabel says, "Always!"

Rudy Filona

He waves his cigarette to and fro and then coughs before taking another drag. "It's five o'clock somewhere!" He declares, as he reads twelve noon on his watch and mixes himself a Bloody Mary.

Sundays! How he once loved the day, but especially the night, partying on Oak Lawn Street in Dallas, Texas. There wasn't a man he couldn't have! Names without faces bombard his brain until he gets bored and throws himself on his new overstuffed couch and flips through *Men's Fitness* magazine. "Jesus! Would you look at the body on him?"

He has subscriptions to every man's magazine ever published so he can stare at all of the models. Thank God it's a man's world, because if it was a woman's he'd be celibate! While it's true that the comings and goings of his apartment raise a brow or two among his neighbors, mostly retirees, he still prefers Sanibel to living in Miami, which he feels would be too passé for him.

He explains his occasional slip as his "sister's son" whenever his nosey neighbor, Mrs. Shading, sees one of his boy toys leaving. His sister's uterus would be down to her ankles by now if she actually gave birth to all the sons Rudy has claimed to be hers. He knows old lady Shading can't keep track because she's senile.

There isn't anything Rudy hasn't tried sexually; swapping, threesomes, foursomes, orgies, whips, blindfolds, Black, White, Asian, and Hispanic. He likes to think of himself as multi-cultural, but he is fondest of married men. He weaves his web of deceit anyway he can whenever he finds a straight man trolling the streets near the club scene.

"They can all be had!" He tells his wide-eyed assistant, who thinks her boyfriend is the butchest thing on earth. Little does she know Rudy's already blown him in the color room at the salon.

His latest conquest is a man named Henry. He's an older gentleman who tries to act half his age even though he has a hearing problem. He keeps calling Rudy for dates, but poor Henry doesn't understand that he was only sex to Rudy and nothing more. While Rudy is losing patience with him, he does find his words of sentiment kind of amusing. For a straight man he sure could suck cock!

Rudy is well aware that most gay men he knows refer to him as a vicious queen. He brushes these people off like a piece of lint. Besides, those bitter old queens are just jealous!

To the observing eye, he is a self-serving, egotistical, flame-throwing bitch, but to those who dare cross him he's far worse. While it may be true that he doesn't have a ton of friends, he does have a few who are very loyal to him. Maive is a gem and he and Desiree have a bond that can only be described as other-worldly. There's also his staff. He often wonders where they would be without him; probably working at some blue hair salon or worse, a beauty school.

Ugh! Just the thought of beauty school! Rudy remembers all those old bitties coming in for their weekly sets. The only joy he got out of doing their hair was dousing it with hand sanitizer and calling it a special hair elixir before he touched it. He did a lot of crazy shit when he went to hair school. And drugs, too!

What he wouldn't give for a line of coke right now. Billie probably has some. He should call her and see if she wants to go out. There's a new restaurant on the main strip that is supposed to be good. She's been acting weird lately, though. What if Desiree is right? What if Billie likes him? He dismisses the thought the minute it comes. Billie's smarter than that. They're just friends.

His phone rings and he picks it up despite the fact that it says "Private" on his Caller ID. "Hello!" He sings into the telephone.

"Hey, gorgeous!"

He recognizes the voice immediately. He rolls his eyes and sticks out his tongue. "Hey, Hank!"

"It's Henry." He sounds disheartened.

"I know it's you! Hank is short for Henry. How dense can a person be?"

"Dance? I love to dance! Where shall we go?"

Honest to God! Rudy doesn't have patience for this. "Are you a doctor, Hank?" Rudy is hopeful. A person can never have too many muscle relaxers.

"A doctor? Well yes, sort of. I'm a psychologist."

Nut bag! They're the worst! It doesn't matter

what kind of pills this guy can get, Rudy has got to kick this relationship to the curb.

"Psychologist, huh? I find that fascinating, Hank."

"Really, Rudy? Why is that?"

"You're preaching to people about their lives and what's wrong with them and you're pretending that you're straight."

"You're right! I do have strength. It takes a strong man to listen objectively and give advice."

"Straight, you queer! I said straight, not strength!"

"I do hear! It takes a lot of strength."

"Listen Hank, it's been fun and it's been real, but it ain't been real fun. You know what I'm saying?"

"Yes! I think it's been a lot of fun, too!"

"I'm bored with this! I'm going to Miami. I won't be able to see you for awhile. Like never." He mumbles the last sentence under his breath.

"Is she sick?"

"Is who sick?"

"You said you were going to your Auntie so I'm wondering if she is ill."

"Mother of God! I'm leaving the country and I don't know when I'll be back." Rudy yells into the receiver.

"Are you being deported, Rudy?"

"Deported? Oh, I get it! You think because my skin is darker that I'm here illegally." He pours more vodka in his drink. "This is great! Un-fucking believable!"

"Believe it, Rudy! I'm here to help you. Well,

actually my friend can help you. He's an attorney who deals with visa issues, green cards, and deportation."

Rudy raises his hands towards the ceiling. "What the fuck are you talking about, you old bastard?"

"Rudy, why are you yelling at me? What's gotten into you?"

"Not you, Hank! Not now! Not ever!" Rudy slams the phone down.

Katrina Emery

Sitting in Starbucks, she drinks a grande cup of coffee and looks through her library book. She overhears two women with heavy New York accents talk ing and tries tuning them out until they mention the name David.

"What was the name of that guy you were making out with?"

"Wasn't he cute? His name is David."

Katrina glances over at the girl who said David to try and get a better look at her. She appears to be in her early twenties and has shocking red hair with a sort of purple hue to it. She's wearing an earring in her nostril and a skull on a metal chain around her neck. It's obvious that it can't possibly be the same David she has recently met, so she turns back to her book.

"I didn't think he was so cute. When I saw you kiss him, I knew you were drunk!"

"Was not! He is so sweet. He said he is going to call me."

"They all say that! Does he live here in the city?"

"No, on the Island."

"Where?"

"I don't remember. I think it was something with a neck."

"Little Neck or Great Neck?"

"He could have said fat neck for all I know."

"I bet he's Jewish!"

"So what if he is?"

"What's his last name?"

"David Liebo something."

"Well there you have it! Do you honestly think a guy from Great Neck is going to call you back?"

Katrina looks up from her book and glances over at the girls again.

"He said he would!" The redhead looks out the window.

"Oh, okay!" Her friend rolls her eyes.

"What's wrong with you?"

"Well, he's Jewish and well, you're not."

"What does that matter?"

"It matters to someone in his family I can bet you that." She raises her finger in the air.

"You're being paranoid!" The redhead waves her off with a flip of her hand.

"Am I?"

Katrina realizes she may have dismissed the women prematurely. Perhaps the girls' words about religion are true. Can it be more common than she originally thought? She has heard of this scenario once before, but brushed it off as sour grapes and nothing more.

"He's only going to look at you as a good time."

"Well, if that's the case, then I'll make sure he has the best time ever!" She wiggles her breasts.

"I bet you will, you tramp!" She pushes her in the arm.

"You're just jealous."

"Maybe I am! Why did I have to pick a guy that got sick and left the party early?" She sticks out her bottom lip.

"Hey, maybe David has a friend for you!"

"Nah! I don't want to be somebody's good time anymore. I want a relationship."

"Yeah, me too!" The redhead puts her head on her hand.

"But you just said…"

"I was only joking. Screw that David guy! Tonight we should go to that new bar on Eighty-second and Amsterdam. I hear it's great!"

"Do you really think we'll meet somebody there?"

"If we don't, we can come back to my apartment and order Chinese."

"Deal!"

The two women shove their papers into their bags and walk out the door. Katrina thinks about the David she just met and wonders when or if she'll ever hear from him again. He was cute, dressed impeccably, and seemed interested in her.

But he's married.

Maybe he's unhappy in his marriage and planning on leaving his wife. After all, he didn't mention her right away. Still, she's had such bad luck with men lately, the last thing she needs to be is somebody else's good time. She shrugs her shoulders, takes a sip of coffee, and goes back to reading her book.

Rebecca (Billie) Lane

She stares at the phone, willing it to ring. It's Sunday and hardly one goes by where she and Rudy don't cruise the gay strip, get drunk, and make fun of people. Maybe she should call him. No, she should wait for him to call her. Before she knows it she's picking up the phone and dialing his number. It rings three times before she hears his voice.

"Yes?" Rudy answers.

"Hey, Rudy! It's Billie! What are you doing?" She nervously paces back and forth.

"Having a drink! What are you doing?"

"Nothin! Just kicked some guy out of my aunt's house." She lies.

"Give me all the dirt, Mary!"

Billie begins to embellish a fictitious story about how she brought a man back to her place last night. "I teased that fucker so bad he had blue balls when he left here."

She can hear Rudy gasping on the other end. It's not the reaction she wants.

"You whore! I can't believe you picked up some guy at that country fuck bar you go to. You could have gotten yourself raped. Or worse! And what kind of person brings a trick back to their aunt's house?"

Is this concern? She is hopeful. "What's the big

deal? You pick up guys all the time! Besides, my Aunt is on some spiritual retreat right now."

"Hello! My men are gay! You could have picked up one of those straight mother fuckers with macho issues. You know the kind I'm talking about! They drink too much tequila and then beat on women all in the name of fun. Maybe you need to go on a retreat, Billie! It might do you some good."

"Rudy, are you worried about me?" She looks in the mirror and smiles.

"Of course, girl! You're like a sister to me."

Sister! Damn it! It isn't the connection she is hoping for. Billie shuts down for the rest of the conversation.

"You want to head out tonight and catch the drag show?" He asks.

"I don't think so. I'm not feeling well."

"Are you sure?"

"I'm sure!" She exhales.

"Well, alright then. I'll talk to you in the morning. You ARE still planning on going in tomorrow, AREN'T you?"

"Yes, Rudy. I'll be there."

"See you then, girl!" He hangs up the phone.

Billie throws the phone across the room and begins to cry. "A sister!"

Mabel Hempstead

"So tell me, how long have you been on Sanibel?" Mabel yells to Benjamin over the wind whipping through her hair and the dogs' heavy panting.

"Not very long. I retired here."

"Nice!"

Dunkin looks up at Benjamin and licks his cheek. He can't help but laugh even though he is totally repulsed by the slimy residue it leaves behind. "I guess he's warmed up to me."

"If he hadn't, he would have bitten you by now. That one is a good judge of character."

Hearing this, Benjamin keeps one eye on the road and the other on Dunkin for the remainder of the ride.

"Just up here on the right." Mabel points.

Benjamin slows down abruptly, sending Dunkin's paws sliding across the dashboard of his car. He looks over at Benjamin and snarls.

"Sorry, big fella!" He turns into the cul-de-sac. "This is nice back here."

"We like it!" Mabel grins.

"You and your husband?"

"God no! I've already buried two of those!" She throws her hands in the air. "Maive and I live here."

"You must tell me more about Maive. First Dr.

Veck mentions her, and now you."

"She's my neighbor. A real nice kid, but lonely as hell. Hey, you should meet her!" Her eyes light up as she pokes him in the arm.

"You think so?" He coyly asks.

"She needs to meet a man, for God's sake! She spends every minute at the salon or with these dogs of hers. Except for last weekend when she went to a hair show. I agreed to watch her little treasures while she is away and then her mom calls and says her great-aunt died, so Maive has to be gone longer." She points to her house. "Over here on the right."

He pulls into the driveway of the one-story home and they both get out of the car.

"This is me! Maive lives over there." Mabel points to another one-story home across the street.

The neighborhood has only a few homes, each one neatly manicured. It's cozy, inviting, a place you would love to escape to at the end of a long day. Far different than the singles chateau he lives at.

"Well, I'm going to take these fellas over to her house and then I'll call Dr. Veck and see how Buster is doing. Maive will kill me if anything happens to one of her kids!" Mabel winks at Benjamin and fumbles for her keys inside an oversized bag.

He awkwardly stands in the driveway, wondering if he should leave or wait until Mabel gives him her next order.

"Well, ya coming or not? Time's a wastin' fella! I've got a canasta game to host this evening and a dog to get better within twenty-four hours." She motions with her hand for him to hurry up.

Benjamin follows behind Mabel and two of the dogs, while Dunkin, who has taken quite a liking to him, follows behind. The sight of this woman with black rimmed cat eye glasses, a red straw hat, and a bag the size of a suitcase being escorted by two dogs makes Benjamin chuckle. "What a spark plug this one is!" He mumbles under his breath.

"Damn straight I am! Can probably teach you a thing or two, young man!" She yells back to him without turning around.

Completely embarrassed, Benjamin stops walking. Dunkin nudges him in the tush and barks. "You're an impatient one, aren't you?" Benjamin turns towards the dog. Dunkin barks again and then runs ahead to catch up with Cricket and Sammy.

Mabel opens the door to Maive's home and Benjamin feels like he has discovered the Holy Grail. He reluctantly steps inside, and then wonders if this is such a good idea.

"Come on, already! Let's get these boys fed and watered and call the vet. The phone is in the kitchen." She calls out as she walks into a room and shuts the door.

"Which way is…"

"Straight ahead and to the right." She yells from behind a door.

He walks down a long hallway filled with pictures. His eyes wander from left to right, taking in all of Maive's history. "She's so beautiful!" He says aloud and then feels like an ass, knowing Mabel can probably hear him. He hears a toilet flush and is relieved that she is too busy doing something else to worry about what he is doing.

There are at least ten photos of her dogs hanging on one side of the hall. The other side has various photos of people who he assumes are friends and family. He moves in closer when he sees one of Maive standing on a beautiful beach, holding her hand to her mouth and laughing. He reaches for the photo and outlines her face with the tip of his finger. He quickly steps back, feeling as though he has invaded her privacy, and calls out for Mabel.

"Listen, Mabel, I'm as concerned about Buster as you are, but I also need to get going. You see, I'm supposed to be doing some work for a client." He walks into the kitchen.

"I thought you said you were retired."

"Well, I am, but occasionally I do have to keep my feet in the ring of fire. I'm quite addicted to what I once did for a living."

"Addicted, huh?" She gives him a disapproving look, her glasses sitting on the end of her nose.

"Perhaps addicted is the wrong word. I'm in stocks and bonds." He nervously glances around the room.

"Oh, yes! Stocks and bonds. My son is in the same business. He's married to this horrible tart of a woman! Never lets me spend time alone with my grandkids." She says with utter disgust, pouring dog food in three of the four bowls.

"She can't be that bad!"

"Bad? She is the absolute worst! He makes over

ten million a year, but is always asking me for money. Apparently he can't say no to little missy. I don't know where I went wrong with him! I just know I'm being punished for something by having that bitch as a daughter- in-law."

"I'd hate to get on your bad side." He shrugs his shoulders and grimaces.

A loud rumba sound comes from Mabel's pocket. She reaches in and pulls out a cell phone. "Mabel here! What? When? I'll be there as soon as I can!" She hangs up and smiles at Benjamin. "Well, I'll be! You're a good luck charm, Benny! That was my son. Apparently my daughter- in-law just had a fall and I have to go take care of my grandkids while they go to the doctor. "

"I'm so sorry! Is she going to be alright?"

"Sorry, hell! This is my chance to finally have those kids alone! I would have put a toy in her path years ago if I would have known it would give me an opportunity to prove myself."

"Well, I'm going to get going then and get out of your hair. I've been a nuisance long enough." He walks towards the door.

"Nuisance, hell! I need you to watch these mongrels until Maive gets back."

"Watch the dogs?" He swallows hard. "I don't know anything about dogs! They might die of starvation or something."

"Nonsense! You just have to remember they're like children."

"Children? You see, that's a problem for me. I don't like kids."

"Honey, nobody really likes kids unless they're your own or your grandkids."

"Really?"

"Please! There's nothing more annoying to me than some ugly, snotty nosed brat that comes up to me and starts yammering away." She moves her fingers back and forth.

"I thought all kids are supposed to be cute?" He rubs a hand through his hair.

"Cute? Have you seen some of the mugs on kids? When my sister gave birth I didn't know if it was a baby or that creature from *Star Wars!*" She laughs.

"Which one?" He smiles.

"The hairy one!"

"Chewbacca?" He laughs.

"Yeah, that's the one! I called him that behind my sister's back every time I referred to him. The laughs Herman and I used to have about that baby's plethora of body hair." She stares off and smiles.

Benjamin looks at her, wondering who Herman is.

Mabel catches his confused look and quickly fills in the blank. "Herman was my first husband. He was a very dear man who liked to eat too much cream cheese."

"Oh! Did he have a heart attack?" He holds his hand to his chest.

"God, no! He choked while he was in Boston. I wasn't there to give him the Heimlich. The chamber maid found him slumped over a room service tray with a half dozen bagels on it and a hunk of cream cheese in his mouth. I knew a schmear would be the end of him!"

Benjamin feels sick to his stomach, yet amused at the same time. Mabel appears to have the same casualness about death as she does life. "You know, Mabel, I feel as though I could listen to your stories for hours."

"Everybody says that! Maive spends almost every Friday night at my house flipping through my photo albums and asking question after question. You know, Benjamin, I go to temple every week without fail and the one thing I always say a prayer for is her. You hear that? Send her a man!" She yells to the ceiling.

"Now that I think about it, it's probably not a good idea if you stay here with the dogs. Maive doesn't know you and to make matters worse, you're Jewish. She will absolutely have a rhinoceros if she finds out you were in her sanctuary. It will be best if you take the dogs to your place." She starts packing a bag for them.

"What does being Jewish have to do with anything? And how did you know?"

"Honey, please! I'm not deaf and blind! You're good looking, have a generous nose, curly dark hair, and it's all wrapped in a fabulous sense of humor!"

"It's wavy!" He corrects her. "Why should I take care of her dogs if she is going to condemn me without even knowing me?"

"Listen, Benjamin, she's smart enough to know not every Jewish man is an ass, but I don't push the issue. I feel that if the right man comes along, it won't matter what he is!" She looks over her glasses again and winks at Benjamin.

"I see! Did I hear you correctly? Did you actually suggest I take the dogs to my place?"

"You have to take the dogs to your place because they can't stay at mine. I'm having the interior painted and I can't have those mongrels running under ladders." She extends the bag of food and treats to him.

He pushes the bag away. "Wait a second here, Mabel. I want to help, and I REALLY don't want to upset you, but I can't take these dogs to my place."

"Oh, Benjamin! Can't you see what we have here? This is fate, honey! You ran into Buster for a reason." She puts the handle of the bag in his hand.

"I ran into Buster because he was off of his leash."

"You're missing the big picture here! You know how I met Alfred?"

"Alfred?" He asks, confused.

"Alfred was my second husband. We were both on a bike tour of Tuscany."

"And you call that fate?" He gestures with his free hand.

"You didn't let me finish! We both lived within two miles of one another in Poughkeepsie, but never met. We went to the same stores, restaurants, even the same synagogue, but we never met until we went to Tuscany. It's fate, I tell ya! Just like you hitting Buster and just like you taking care of the dogs until Maive gets home." She opens the back door of Maive's house and grabs Benjamin by his free arm.

"But I'm not a dog person and I don't want them in my apartment."

"If you weren't a dog person, Dunkin would have

bitten your arm off when you sat next to him in the car. Now take the bag with all their stuff and be on your way. It will be like having a slumber party with hairy men." She pushes him out the door.

"Isn't she going to freak out when the dogs aren't here and a complete stranger is watching them? There must be someone more qualified to do this!" He holds up his hands.

"Nonsense! You must watch them! You can't mess with fate. Besides, the only other person she's close with is that flaming queen, Rudy. Believe me when I tell ya the dogs will be better off running the streets than staying with that pissy bastard."

Benjamin feels sheepish for not telling Mabel he has already met Maive. Call it Jewish guilt or just having a conscience, but he decides to tell her. "Listen, Mabel..."

"Enough already! Take the leashes and go!" She puts them over his shoulder.

"But I want to tell you something that's very important. It doesn't have to do with the dogs."

"What is it?" She taps her foot.

"I met Maive when I was getting my hair cut." He lowers his head towards his chest.

She punches him in the arm. "You did? Well, why didn't ya say something? You see, this is fantastic! It's fate! First you meet her and then you hit her dog, now you're going to take care of them. What a great story this will be to tell your grandchildren! Now write your number down on this piece of paper."

He scribbles it down and hands it back to her.

"Don't you think we should call her and tell her what has happened?"

"Are you kidding me? Let her be with her family now. I'll leave her a note explaining what has happened. You can handle this, Benjamin. This is your moment! Besides, Dr. Veck says Buster will be fine. Now go, Benjamin! Destiny awaits you!" Mabel motions with her hand, shooing him away. "Just remember!" She calls out to him as he gets into his car. "When you're taking care of the dogs, there's no such thing as too many walks, too many naps, or too many kisses!"

Benjamin sticks his head out of the car window. "Kisses?"

"They love them!" She slams the door.

Stacy Kornberg-Adelstein

She slips on her Lulu Guinness canvas shoes with the yellow and white lotus pattern, bright yellow Capri pants, and a hot pink Michael Stars t-shirt. She glances at herself in the mirror and begins to cry. "This is horrible!" She yells, and takes off the pants and top.

Rifling through the contents of her closet, she pulls shirt after shirt off of their hangers and tosses them on the floor. She grabs a blue skirt and holds it up to her body. "Damn it! This looks awful, too!" She throws the skirt to the floor and stands in her matching bra and panties, staring at herself in the mirror. "Look at ya, you're as big as a house!"

An inch-worm size roll appears at the fold in her tummy and she knows it was that weak moment yesterday when she delved into the M & Ms and ate three of them.

"It's these shoes! What am I thinking?" She kicks her feet one at a time and the shoes go flying in the air. She grabs her beige Tod's loafers, a white cotton skirt, a blue polo shirt, and stands back and admires her outfit in the mirror.

Her eyes begin to well up with tears, as she thinks about her younger years and the dream she had of becoming a fashion designer. She quickly wipes her eyes with her hand. She knows it's best to remain neutral when spending time with the Adelsteins. It's better to blend in with the crowd than cause a raised eyebrow, or at least see someone attempt to raise their eyebrow, if she were to dress differently.

All of nature's creatures camouflage themselves when facing dire situations. It's how they avoid their enemies until they can return to the safety of their natural habitat.

Going to Debbie's house is certainly no picnic, especially every Mother's Day. Debbie calls it brunch, but never puts out enough food, so everyone has taken to bringing something. This year Stacy is bringing donuts, really sugary ones!

The Adelsteins hate sugar! It may as well be crack cocaine, the way they avoid it. David's father is the worst! Since he started exercising and working out with a trainer, he has become so obsessed with his diet that he carries a calorie counter with him. It would make sense if he needed to lose weight, but the man looks like Ichabod Crane!

Although the brunch at Debbie's only lasts two hours, making the car drive there and back takes twice as long, which makes the event a complete waste of an afternoon. Stacy would rather clean her house than spend time with the Adelsteins.

"This time I'll be ready!" She tells the mirror, as David enters the room.

"Who are you talking to, Stacy?" David looks into his closet for a belt.

"No one! I was reminding myself to stop at the organic food stand and pick something up for the party. You know how Dan won't eat anything unless it's grown in overpriced compost and comes in an earth-friendly bag." Stacy goes through her jewelry box and carefully selects a few pieces.

"Debbie told us not to bring anything. She said she will have it all."

"Have it all? Is that what ya call three bagels and some cream cheese? Every time I have been to her house there's nothing to eat. She calls it brunch, throws us a bagel, and sends us on our way. Honestly, I don't know who she's trying to kid! She must weigh three hundred pounds. And don't even get me started on that husband of hers!" She tries on a pair of ruby earrings.

"What's wrong with Dan? He's a doctor!" David chooses a Hermes belt and slips it through the pant loops.

"You are so naïve, David! He may be a doctor, but I guess they didn't teach common courtesy or manners in medical school." She takes off the ruby earrings and tries the pearl ones on instead.

"What are you talking about?"

"The good grapes?" She stands with her hands on her hips.

"Good grapes?" David asks.

"Ya don't remember the last time they had us over for brunch? Your sister put out a platter of fruit that was more shriveled than my Bubbe. I've heard of re-gifting, but re-fruiting is another story! Anyway, she tried to put some champagne grapes on the tray and Dan admonished her for it." She looks at the pearl earrings and gives a disapproving look in the mirror.

"I still don't know what you're talking about."

"He said, 'Are those the good grapes?' and she said, 'Yes, Dan! They're the good grapes!' We were sitting right there when he said it. You don't remember me kicking you under the table?" She looks at David.

"I remember now." He had sported an enormous bruise for weeks. "You shouldn't let him bother you. You know he's like that with everybody."

"Hello! Does that make it okay then? Am I supposed to sit back while he corrects everyone and acts superior? And what's up with that English accent? Every time he talks down to someone he does it in an English accent."

"He spent some time abroad at Oxford. I told you that when we were first dating. "

"A semester, David! He spent a semester. And p.s., did he spend some time abroad or with one? A brute, I mean. What's the equivalent of broad, but means man?" She raises her eyebrows.

"What do you mean by that comment?" David looks at himself in the mirror, runs a hand down his shirt to smooth out the wrinkles, and closes his closet door.

"There's something creepy about him. He's lecherous! Pansy-ish! Just plain weird! You're not going to wear that old thing, are you?"

"I love this shirt! And you're wrong about Dan, there's nothing sexual about him."

"That shirt is ancient, just like all of your other casual clothes. And YOU'RE the one who is wrong about Dan! There's something not right about him. I think their marriage is a fraud! There's a term for a woman who is married to a gay man."

David ignores her and continues to get ready.

"I don't buy for one minute that he loves Debbie, because there is absolutely nothing to love! The term I am trying to think of is some kind of facial hair."

"I wasn't going to shave." He runs a hand over his chin.

"Not you! You're not even listening to me, David! I'm telling you that Debbie is a…a beard! That's it!"

"Debbie doesn't have a beard! I've seen her grow a bit of a moustache when she has been away on vacation, but never a beard."

"A woman who marries a man that is gay is called a beard!" She rolls her eyes at him. "I think it's a shame that you and your family have accepted his behavior. No one should ever be talked to in the manner in which he addresses people. Honestly! The way your family kowtows to him, you'd think he's royalty." She shoves the pearl earrings to the back of the box and grabs the diamond studs.

"He's not so bad!"

"You just keep telling yourself that, David, and maybe you and your family will feel better about how you pushed Debbie to marry him."

"What are you talking about?"

"Your mother has told me at least a half a dozen times that she hand-picked a husband for Debbie. Oh, excuse me, a suitable husband. P.S., suitable meaning a doctor! Doesn't it bother you when he corrects you like you're five?" She catches David pulling his shoes out from under the bed. "David! What are your shoes doing under the bed? Haven't I told you a hundred times to put them back in the closet?" She flails her arms.

"I was so tired last night that I must have forgotten. Don't give Dan a second thought. He's insecure, that's all."

"Well I don't appreciate his insecurity. He should go talk to somebody about it. Sometimes I think they invite us over to their house just so they can put us down and make themselves feel better. I actually feel sorry for your sister. It must be why she weighs so much."

"Come on, Stace! She's not so fat. Besides, Debbie and Dan just want to be close to us." He ties his shoes and walks towards his dresser.

"Close, schmose! She's a selfish, control-freak fatty and he's a know-it-all. Why would I want to associate with people like that?" She takes off the diamond studs and throws them back in the box, too.

"Because they're family! Besides, you don't have a choice; you have to associate with them. If it makes you feel any better, I think Dan is an ass and Debbie is bit selfish, but she has been that way her entire life." David spritzes himself with cologne.

"Thank you! You finally said something truthful. And did you say Debbie is a little selfish? I've never met a person more selfish in my life."

"You've met my mom haven't you?" He looks over at Stacy and smiles.

"Please! She can have all of the plastic surgeries she wants; she's still O-L-D! Why doesn't she own up to the fact and grow old gracefully?"

"Because she's a narcissist! We've been over this a thousand times, Stace. She's never going to change. You have to accept her and all of her faults."

"But there are just so many! It makes me wonder, though." She looks over her collection of perfumes.

"What's that, Stacy?"

"You know the old saying about the apple doesn't fall far from the tree?" She sprays herself with Marc Jacobs's perfume.

"Yes, what about it?"

"I'm wondering what side you fall from." Stacy goes into her closet and looks for a belt.

"Nothing to worry about there! I'm most like my father." David says, and then walks downstairs.

Stacy thinks about the day that lies ahead of her and becomes nauseous. Perfectly decorated rooms with wall-to-wall Ralph Lauren, fake smiles and phony sentiments wherever she turns, and a general feeling of being tolerated by people she loathes herself.

The worst part of the day will come when she sees Joshie and Lily's beautiful faces looking depressed and forlorn. Their watery eyes and stiff upper lips will give way to their disappointment and this will be Stacy's cue to find David and leave. Stacy will spend the car ride home explaining to her children that Ethel loves them the same as Zoe, despite the fact that she never spends more than an hour with them every other month, but manages to spend every weekend with Zoe.

Her stomach wells in pain. She runs to the bathroom and shoves a finger down her throat. Nothing comes up, so she tries again. This time she takes her toothbrush and shoves it to the farthest point possible. Within seconds the toilet is filled with bits of red that look like blood. Stacy shrieks, until she remembers the yogurt with strawberries she ate for breakfast.

She stands up, flushes the meal, and wipes her mouth with a damp cloth. She rinses with mouthwash and walks towards her bedroom door.

"Are you ready, Stacy?" David calls from the front hallway.

"Yes, David! I'm as ready as I'll ever be."

The Residence Of Dr. And Mrs. Daniel Weismann

"Hi, David! Hi, Stace!" Debbie opens the door to her refurbished McMansion, hugs them both, and then gives Stacy an exaggerated sweep, calculating how she is spending her brother's money.

Stacy hands her the bag with homemade donuts in it. "Here you go! We stopped at the organic farm stand and I couldn't resist!"

Debbie opens the bag and glances down at the six sugar donuts and her eyes widen. "Sugar donuts! I don't think these are organic, but I'll bet someone will eat them." She walks the bag into the kitchen like it's tainted with the Bubonic plague.

A few moments later Dan comes over and extends his hand. "David, my man! Glad to see you could make it." He turns towards Stacy, examining her face as though he is holding a Zeiss magnifier, squinting to get a better look at her skin. "Good to see you, Stacy."

"Is there something in your eye, Dan?"

"My eye? No, I was…it's so good of you to make the trip out here."

"Wouldn't miss it!" David answers, but Dan has already moved on to his next guest.

"Isn't that one of your parent's friends?" Stacy

whispers in David's ear.

He looks around the room. "They're all my parents' friends!"

"You mean they're all Dan's patients now!"

David and Stacy stand in the grand hallway watching Dan in action. He extends a hand to everyone and gives them a sweeping inventory with his eyes, inviting an inquisitive comment.

"You must see something, Dan! Do you think it's time for a face lift?" Stacy hears one of Ethel's friends ask him.

"We have so many new technologies. You should stop by my office one day next week." Dan smiles from ear to ear.

"Look at him, David! He's shameless! He may as well hand out business cards with his rates on them the way he works the room!"

"My sister probably has plans drawn up for another addition!" The two of them burst into laughter.

"I'm going to get a drink. Do ya want something?" Stacy asks David.

"No thanks! I'm going to head over to the food table and see what Debbie isn't serving." David makes his way to the buffet table and is surprised to see it covered with an array of food items.

Debbie comes up behind him. "It's so much easier to have a party when it's catered, but you can't call just anyone. I got these people from Mom."

"Is she footing the bill, too?" He laughs, but Debbie gives him a dirty look and turns away.

David helps himself to salad, roast beef, red

potatoes, and green beans with almonds. He walks over to his mom and dad. "Nice spread!"

"This salad is amazing! Do I detect jicama in here?" Adam asks Ethel.

Ethel takes a bite. "I think it is jicama. Ask Dan, he'll know. He's such a foodie!"

"How is your exercise regimen going, Dad?" David takes a bite of roast beef.

"I'm jogging now! Up to four miles a day!" He glances around the room. "I'm in better shape than any man here."

"I've been thinking about starting to run. Dan has a trainer who knows a guy that knows a running coach who has done over forty-five marathons. He said he can train me." Debbie says.

"It really takes off the weight, but it's the combination between your diet and exercise that works. You know what they say, calories in, calories out." Adam helps himself to a potato from David's plate.

"Are you saying I'm overweight, Daddy?" Debbie's eyes fill with tears.

"No, honey, you're perfect!" Ethel puts her arm around her. "Tell her, Adam!" She scolds him.

"Daddy loves you just the way your are, sugar plum." He squeezes Debbie's arm.

Stacy walks up behind David and whispers in his ear. "I see the donuts made it to the table, but she cut them into quarters and they look like a pile of dog turds."

"You should have a donut, Dad! Stacy picked them up at the farm stand."

His father looks at the plate. "Wow! Would you look at the sugar on those things! They do look yummy, but I can't. Well, maybe just a bite! Ethel, how about you and I split a quarter?"

"Not me! I'm going to save room for some peaches and frozen yogurt. Debbie tells me it's sugar-free." Ethel turns her nose up at the donuts.

"Not caloric-free, Ethel!" Dan comes up behind them, speaking in his English accent.

"Glad you're here, Dan! Ethel and I were just discussing the salad. We think there might be a trace of jicama. What do you think?" Adam and Ethel wait for Dan to take a bite, like he's Indiana Jones deciphering an ancient code.

"Good taste buds, you two! There is jicama in the salad."

"How's your mother, Stacy?" Adam asks.

"She was swimming in the ocean last week and was bitten by a shark."

"I love the ocean! Tell her I said hello." He walks towards the living room.

"I'm so busy that I had to cater the party this year." Debbie takes a plate of fruit. "Between school boards, charity work, and Zoe, I barely have time for myself."

"Did Debbie and Dan tell you that they had lunch with Kim Basinger last week?" Ethel beams from ear to ear.

"No, they didn't." David answers.

"She's gorgeous!" Debbie says.

"What did you talk to her about?" Stacy asks.

"I didn't get a chance to speak with her." Debbie

turns away from Stacy. "Hi, Mrs. Shannon! I'm so glad you could make it." She walks away.

Stacy turns towards David. "How could ya sit at a table with someone and not talk to them? What am I saying? Every time I eat with your family they manage to ignore me. The only thing your father ever asks me is, 'How is your mother?' Like he cares! I just told him she was bit by a shark and he didn't even hear me!" She laughs.

"You know how they are! If you're not a celebrity or Dan, they don't think you're worthy of a conversation. Besides, Debbie loves to let everyone know how important they are by being at the same function as a celebrity, but she neglects to give you the full details. Like how they bought their way in and that there were over four hundred people in attendance. She probably wasn't even sitting at the same table as Kim Basinger!"

"Is this luncheon the equivalent of me having my hair done at the same salon as Bette Midler, and then later bragging to everyone about how she and I spent the afternoon together?"

"You're quick!" David winks at her. "I'm getting another drink."

"Don't drink too much! You have to drive us home."

"We can always spend the night here!" David laughs.

"David, if I have a choice between sleeping here and hell, I'm sending ya to the store for marshmallows to roast!"

Desiree

The lights on the stage dim and the revving sound of motorcycle engines fill the room. This is the dancers cue to get in line and get ready to strut their stuff. Motley Crue's *Girls, Girls, Girls* blares out of the speakers and a procession of gorgeous women wearing stilettos step out from either side of the stage.

"Good evening, gentlemen! Here they come! New York's finest ladies on stage for your viewing pleasure!" The announcer yells into the microphone.

Tall, short, Asian, African American, Indian, Caucasian, tanned, black-haired, blonde, and red-haired girls circle the stage, wearing gloves pulled up to their elbows, boas wrapped around their shoulders, and various necklaces made of pearls and beads that hang from their tiny necks and fall comfortably into their whopping cleavage.

One by one the girls take a turn on the catwalk, each wearing a different colored evening gown with long slits up the leg. This part of the night is completely ridiculous because in no time at all the girls will be in nothing but a g-string. The men like it, though, as they roar like a pack of lions in the wild, their mouths gaping open, eyes bulging out of their sockets, looking like they are ready to pounce on the first thing that stops in front of them.

Desiree takes her turn on the catwalk in front of the howling men. A jerk in the front row screams at her, "Daddy's got something for you, gorgeous!" She doesn't even bother to look at him because his face is of no concern to her. George Clooney could be sitting in the front row and it still wouldn't matter. To her, every man in here is nothing more than a piece of paper.

She stares blankly into nowhere, arms to her sides, snapping her fingers to a beat known only to her, and then gives a slight wiggle with her hips from left to right before joining the other dancers on the procession line.

For the next two minutes most of the dancers do their best to tease and entice the men. Some rub their long fingers down their chests, while others run a hand up the leg and back down again. But not Desiree. She never waves her wares in front of men for free.

While she appears motionless, staring out over the crowd, she can feel the adrenaline rushing from her head all the way down to her toes, even though they are crammed into pointy five-inch heels.

The music beats louder and her heart beats faster. She's prey in the jungle being pursued by a bunch of horny hunters. The thrill of the hunt is all that matters to these men. It's all that matters to any man about anything, and for this they will have to pay.

The lights pan the hollering crowd so Desiree takes her gaze off of the DJ booth and carefully peruses the audience for one of her regulars. She is starving and dinner will be nice, especially if one of these losers pays for it. One man standing in the corner looks foreign and might possibly qualify for a prospective boyfriend if things with Gary don't work out.

The nerve of Gary! How dare he forego his usual weekly cash payments and suddenly switch to bi-weekly ones, subtracting four hundred dollars from them! His loss of money in the stock market is of no concern to her. A deal is a deal, and there is nothing Desiree abhors more than a cheap man.

The song switches to background music and the DJ begins his spiel about cocktail specials, so the girls move swiftly off the stage and back towards the locker room.

"Looks like a good crowd tonight." Tiffany, at least that's what she calls herself, slurs her words to Desiree.

Desiree ignores her and continues to line her lips in the mirror.

"What station are you working?" Tiffany sways back and forth on the wooden stool, rubbing oil on her breasts.

"I've got the front." Desiree rubs her lips together and blots them with a tissue.

"That's a drag! Never make any money there." She offers her the bottle of oil.

She abruptly raises her hand into a stop position. "Maybe you don't!"

"What's that supposed to mean?"

"Look at you! You're always doped up on something. How is anyone supposed to take you seriously?" She puts her lipstick back in her bag.

"Plenty of people take me seriously." She stumbles

to get off her chair.

"Like who?"

"Tommy!" Tiffany slurs his name.

"Listen up, little girl! Tommy takes whatever he can, whenever he wants, and don't forget it! The sooner you realize that, the sooner you'll get your head out of your ass, your mouth off his cock, and start making some real cash!" Desiree hears her name being called to the stage.

She turns away from Tiffany, takes one last look in the mirror, and then makes her way to the stage to make fools of men and take their money.

Maive Henry

First thing Monday morning she pulls into her driveway, happy to be home. She leaves her bags in the car and runs to the front door, listening for barks from her furry little friends. When she turns her key in the lock and still doesn't hear anything, she begins to worry.

Running from room to room she calls out their names. "Dunkin? Buster? Cricket? Sammy? Where are you guys?"

Maive goes out on the screened-in porch and then walks back inside the house searching again. In the kitchen she reaches for the phone, but sees Mabel's unmistakable handwriting scrawled on a piece of paper taped to the fridge.

Dearest Maive,

How do I tell you this rather than coming right out with it?

My daughter-in-law broke her ankle and I had to go stay with my son for awhile to take care of my grandkids. I'm so excited, but anyway, that's a whole other story entirely.

I met a very kind gentleman in the most unfortunate of circumstances, but thankfully everything turned out okay. He accidentally struck Buster while driving his car and he had to go to the vet.

Not the driver, the dog. Anyway, Dr. Veck fixed him and he is all better. He's such a nice man!

But an even nicer man is watching your dogs. His name is Benjamin. I don't know where I put his number, but Dr. Veck has it.

I have to go now, my son is waiting for me. I'll talk to you when I get back home. And don't worry! Everything is going to work out perfectly!
Love,
Mabel

Maive bursts into tears and immediately calls Dr. Veck.

"Dr. Veck!" He answers on the first ring.

"Dr. Veck, its Maive." She paces back and forth. "How's Buster? What happened? Is he going to be okay? I'm coming over right now to get him! Do you have my other dogs, too?"

"Maive, its' so good to hear from you! Hasn't anyone spoken to you yet?"

"No, but I did get a rather strange and disturbing note from Mabel. Perhaps you can tell me what happened."

"There's been a small accident, but everything is fine now."

"My Bussy! Mabel said something about him being hit. What happened to him?"

"He broke his leg, but he's fine. I'll let Mabel and Benjamin give you the details about what happened."

"Who is Benjamin? I'm very confused! Do you have Buster or don't you?"

"Benjamin has him."

"I don't understand. A complete stranger has Buster?"

"He's a friend of Mabel's. He is the one who accidentally hit Buster. But don't you worry, Maive! When Ben picked him up, Buster was acting as though nothing had ever happened to him."

"Who's Ben?" She shakes her head.

"Benjamin Koppel, Mabel's friend."

"I don't know any man named Benjamin Koppel! Dr. Veck, why would you entrust my dog's care with someone I don't even know?"

"Well he seemed to know Mabel and she promised me that he would take the best care of all your dogs."

"All four dogs? He has all of my babies?" She walks with the phone into the hallway and looks at all of their pictures.

"I didn't know what else to do. You know how they got the one time you had to board them here. I just spoke to Benjamin this morning and he told me the dogs can stay as long as they need to. Apparently he has become quite attached to them."

"Really? He actually said that?"

"Verbatim! I'll give you his address and phone number so you can make arrangements to go get them. I'm sure they will be as happy to see you as you are to reunite with them. Maive, I hope you know that I would never do anything to upset you. Will you call me if you need anything?"

"I know you were only doing what you thought was best for the dogs, Dr. Veck. When should I bring Buster back in to have the cast removed?" She rummages through her refrigerator for something quick to eat.

"I'll check on him in a couple of weeks and see how he is progressing, but the cast shouldn't come off for several weeks. It was a pretty bad fracture."

She loses her appetite with the news. "He'll be okay, won't he?"

"Of course he will! He's a real trooper!"

"He is a trooper. I love him so much! Thanks for taking such great care of him. You're a terrific vet, Dr. Veck, and a great friend." She hangs up the phone.

Benjamin Koppel? Who the hell is Benjamin Koppel? Maive has met every one of Mabel's friends and she is certain there is no Benjamin Koppel. She picks the phone back up and dials the number Dr. Veck gave her. No one answers after three rings so she hangs up and decides to drive over to his apartment.

Making her way around the curvy road to the other side of Sanibel, all thoughts of New York City and her running into Debbie are forgotten. She glances out at the ocean and admires the breathtaking sight of the sunshine casting its rays out upon the water.

From a distance she sees a man with dark hair being followed by three dogs. She slams on the breaks, pulls over to the shoulder of the road, and gets out of her car.

Dunkin and Cricket are walking on one side of him, Sammy is walking on the other, and Buster is being pulled in a red wagon behind them. The man looks familiar, but Maive can't recall why. It suddenly dawns on her that this man with her precious cargo is the same cad who asked about his few gray hairs at the salon.

But it can't be! How does Mabel know him? She never would have pegged this guy as a dog person. Perhaps she misread him. She dismisses the thought as quickly as it comes and calls out, "Hey, you there! I think you have something of mine."

David Adelstein

His Monday morning commute into the city is nothing out of the ordinary, a few old timers smelling like moth balls, a lot of young sharp shooters with too much hair grease, and a bunch of women talking full volume on their cell phones. When the conductor announces Penn Station as the next stop, David rises to his feet and walks towards the door.

The moment they open he rushes out and takes the steps two at a time, forcing his way past all of the commuters. He foregoes his usual stop at Starbucks on the corner and makes his way to the office, welcoming the fresh air into his lungs.

As he passes a bodega with colorful flowers adorning the entry, he pulls out his cell phone and calls the florist his company uses for special occasions. He can't think of anything more special than the occasion to which he is about to arise.

He smiles as he passes people, notices buildings, restaurants, and the hansom cabs. He even stops to pet a sinewy black and white horse before hailing a cab to his office.

He arrives at the building in record time and takes the elevator up to his floor. The doors to the elevator open and he sees Mary stretch her neck to see who has pressed the wrong button. No one is ever here at this hour except for her and that silly woman who works the desk in the lobby.

David steps off of the elevator and greets Mary with a pleasant smile. "Good morning, Mary! Can I get you some coffee?"

"Good morning to you, David! I'd love some coffee." She glances down at her watch and then taps it to make sure it's working.

"You drink it extra light and extra sweet, right?"

"Yes, David, thank you!"

He returns with his own coffee, hands Mary hers, and whistles all the way to his office before closing his door. The clock on his desk reads 8:00 a.m. He sits back and stares out the window in a dreamy gaze and mentally goes over what he'll do.

First he'll catch up on some accounts, giving Katrina ample time to receive the flowers. Once she calls to thank him, he'll tell her he has something that belongs to her and ask if he can bring it by. If she asks how he knows where she lives, he'll remind her that she told him it was above the French restaurant, explaining that he has dined there before so he knows exactly where it is. She doesn't need to know that he lied to Stacy about having to work on a new account, and that he came into the city over the weekend just to find her building.

He remembers Stacy being miffed. "Work on a weekend?"

And him answering, "I've got to pay for the caterers at Lily's party, don't I?"

Her preoccupation with a new interest like planning

a party will provide him with ample time to pursue his new interest, Katrina.

The day moves slowly and David glances up at the clock every fifteen minutes. When it finally reaches noon and he hasn't heard from Katrina, he starts to wonder if she received the flowers since he didn't have her apartment number. He picks up the phone and calls the florist, demanding to know if they were delivered and when.

"Those went out first thing this morning, Mr. Adelstein."

"You didn't have a problem finding her apartment?" He stares out his window.

"I knocked on a few doors, but I eventually found her."

"Are you sure it was the right apartment? Did the girl give you her name?"

"No, sir, but I'm certain she was the right woman."

"How can you be so sure?" He turns away from the window and looks out at Mary, who is shoving a donut into her mouth.

"She said how sweet it was of you to remember her. I'm sure that the flowers..."

David hangs up the phone in mid-sentence. He paces back and forth. Maybe he misread her. Maybe she thinks he's some stalker. Maybe he should throw her shopping bags into the garbage and forget all about her.

He closes the blinds to his office and unlocks his briefcase. First he tosses the bag from Bergdorfs into the trash can and then the Victoria's Secret one. The make-up makes a loud clatter as it reaches the bottom of the garbage, but the lingerie falls to a silent death.

He stares back out the window overlooking the busy streets down below and lets out a heavy sigh. Although he has two beautiful kids, a great job, tons of friends, and lives in one of the best neighborhoods on Long Island, he feels a tremendous sense of loss.

David looks back over his shoulder into the trash can. He sifts through papers, gum wrappers, and tissues, until he finds the two boxes of make-up and puts them back into their bag. The lingerie is another story. Those damn cleaning people! How many times has he asked them to make sure they empty the garbage every night?

His coffee from yesterday has gotten onto the bag. He frantically tries to brush off the brown liquid, but it only makes it worse. He pulls out the dainty bras, panties, and teddies, and lays them neatly on his desk to access the damage. The bras and teddies are fine, but a pair of baby blue lace panties is soaked. He lifts them up and tries wringing the delicate material out, but even if they dry they'll be stained. If he throws the two bags into a dumpster somewhere, he can be rid of them and any notion of doing something he might regret.

Rolling up the make-up into the lingerie, he places them inside his briefcase and slams it shut. He grabs his suit jacket off of the rack and walks towards his office door. Just as he reaches for the knob, his telephone rings.

It might be her!

He quickly runs back to his desk and pushes the

light blinking on his private line. "David Adelstein!"

"The David Adelstein who sent me the most beautiful flowers I have ever seen?" The sexy voice on the other end asks.

It's her! David scrambles for something to say; something witty, something charming, something poetic. "You got him!" Idiot!

"Isn't that a nice thought?" She says, in her deep, raspy voice.

David gulps hard and pulls his collar away from his neck. His tongue is tied, and he realizes the next thing he says will determine if he takes this any further than flirting, so he doesn't speak at all.

"Did I catch you at a bad time?"

"No, not at all. As a matter of fact, I just walked in."

"Just walked in, huh? My goodness! I guess you've already eaten lunch then?"

Knowing full well he is supposed to meet a client in a half hour at I Tre Merli, he lies instead. "Actually, I had a lunch meeting, but it got cancelled. I have just become available."

"Literally or figuratively?" She asks, and then laughs. "You don't have to answer that…yet!"

David avoids the question. "How about I meet you at I Tre Merli? Do you know where it is?"

"No, I don't get out much."

"It's in Soho. The address is 463 West Broadway, between Houston and Prince. Can you be there in a half an hour?"

"I'll make sure I am. By any chance, David, do you

have my shopping bags? I think I left them with you the day we bumped into each other."

David sweats under his arms and he can feel his neatly pressed blue shirt sticking to his skin. Should he lie or tell her the truth? "Yes, as a matter of fact I do have the bags. I found them in my briefcase. I hope I haven't inconvenienced you."

"No, not at all! I have plenty of what is in those bags already, but a girl can never have too many."

"Goodness! I must look in those bags!"

"You mean you haven't already?"

"Of course not! I put them in my briefcase when I realized you had left without them. I was going to have them sent over to you. I'll bring them with me. See you in a few minutes!"

"Look forward to it!" She hangs up the phone.

David grabs his briefcase and walks over to Mary's desk. "You need to call Dean Brasso and tell him I have to cancel lunch."

"Okay, David. Do you want me to give him a reason?"

"No, just ask him to reschedule, please. Something's come up." He gets inside the elevator, pushes the lobby button, and then remembers the stains under his armpits. Rushing back into his office, he takes another shirt from the supply he keeps hanging on the back of his door and changes into it.

As David passes Mary's desk for the second time, he smiles cordially and says, "Have to look the part!" He forces a laugh and gets into the elevator.

Mary grabs the phone, calls Dean Brassos' office,

and speaks to him directly. Thinking about David's peculiar behavior, she calls her friend Joanne, who works down the hall. "Have you noticed David Adelstein acting weird today?" She asks.

"I saw him in the lobby this morning at 7:30 a.m.!" Joanne answers.

"Wait till you hear this! He offered to get me a coffee and knew what I put in it. I wonder if there's trouble at home?" Mary asks wickedly.

"Well, it wouldn't surprise me! His wife is so nasty! If I was married to her, I'd rise with the roosters to get to work and make sure I didn't leave until the owls came out." Joanne chuckles.

"You're too much, Joanne!" Mary laughs and hangs up the phone.

Joanne is right. Stacy Adelstein is one mean bitch! Every time the phone rings in the office Mary holds her breath and hopes it isn't Stacy. The last time she called, she instructed Mary on how David should purchase a sweater for his father at Barneys. Like Stacy didn't have time to shop. It's all the woman does!

Since David has already left for lunch, Mary might as well go, too. She logs out of her computer and puts on her gray cable-knit sweater. The telephone rings and she picks it up before leaving. David is notorious for calling her about something he has forgotten to do. "Good morning, David Adelstein's office!" She says in a chipper tone.

"It's afternoon." Stacy corrects her.

Mary lets out a sigh. "Hello, Mrs. Adelstein."

"Let me speak to my husband!"

"He's not in right now."

"Where is he?"

Mary hesitates before answering.

"Hello! Can ya hear me? Where is he?"

"Uh, I don't know." Mary walks into David's office to look at his calendar.

"Ya don't know? How could ya not know? What if I was a client calling and wanted David? How do ya think that looks for the company?"

"I'm sorry, ma'am. I should have asked him." She looks at today's date, hoping to find something written down, but only sees doodles of hearts with arrows through them.

"Whatever! Tell him I called!" Stacy slams the phone in Mary's ear.

"One of these days, Stacy Adelstein, you're gonna get yours!" Mary yells into the receiver.

Mary Humphreys

Walking past Victoria's Secret, she stops to stare at the huge poster of the barely clad models and takes her anger for Stacy out on them. "Anorexics! Why don't you eat a pizza or something? You look sick! Sick like that awful Stacy Adelstein!" She puffs on her cigarette and stares into the large glass windows.

All of a sudden, someone in the store catches her eye. She drops her cigarette and rubs her eyes in disbelief. David is actually buying something for Stacy! She can hardly wait to tell Joanne! They have joked for a couple of years now that poor David must have a calloused right hand because they can't imagine him wanting to have sex with his wife. Mary can't even picture Stacy doing something nice for David, let alone wearing lingerie. She lights another cigarette and takes out her cell phone to call Joanne.

David pays for his purchases and walks towards the door to leave. He spots Mary staring through the window, talking on her phone. He immediately stops and looks back at the register. Should he stay in the store until she leaves, or walk out? He notices a cigarette in her right hand, which makes his choice an easy one.

"Mary! I can't believe you smoke! I'm so disappointed." David comes up behind her.

Startled, Mary quickly closes her phone. "I'm

trying to quit, but I'm going through a really tough time right now."

"Well, hopefully it will pass. Enjoy it now before they make it illegal to smoke anywhere in the city." He hails a cab.

Mary feels awful and wants to crawl in a hole. Not only is she thirty pounds overweight, her boss has seen her smoking and she knows how against it he is. Everyone seems to be against it these days. She knows it's a horrible habit. She knows she needs to be kinder to her body. She knows she needs to love herself more. It's in every single spiritual book she reads.

Maybe she'll go sign up for that yoga class she keeps thinking about. Deep breathing will do wonders for all of her stress. First she needs to get some lunch, though. Maybe she'll try that vegan place around the corner.

She walks around the block to the restaurant and peruses the menu, reading soy this, soy that, and looks directly at the desserts. Tofu cheesecake? The thought repulses her. How can a person ruin something like cheesecake by putting tofu in it? She rolls her eyes, and walks next door to Krispy Kreme and orders a half a dozen of glazed, fresh from the oven.

Katrina Emery

Sitting in a corner table at I Tre Merli, wearing a blue and white polka dot chiffon dress with a plunging ruffled neckline, she shoos away annoying staff members every few minutes who keep asking her breasts if they need anything.

"Can I buy you a drink, miss?" A tall man with an Italian accent asks her.

He's quite handsome as men go, but Katrina dismisses him, knowing David will be along at any moment. "I already have one, thank you."

Right on cue, David walks in the door. He looks around the restaurant like a child at the Museum of Natural History. He is cute in a boyish sort of way, but much shorter than she remembers so she is grateful she wore flats. She generally has a fondness for very tall men, but she hopes pursuing David will be well worth the effort.

She stands up and walks over to him. "Good afternoon, David! It's so nice to see you again."

He fumbles with his hands as he takes them out of his suit pockets and extends one towards Katrina. "I'm so glad you could meet me."

"It's my pleasure." She gives him a kiss on both cheeks.

David stands awkwardly, grinning from ear to ear,

looking like a boy with his first crush. Katrina takes his hand and directs him to the table.

The waiter approaches and gives David the once over. "You two are together? I mean, will you be joining the lady for lunch, sir?"

David stares at Katrina and doesn't answer him.

Katrina nods yes to the waiter and motions with her hand for a glass of wine. She puts her elbows on the table and leans in towards David, her two breasts brimming out over the ruffles of her dress. "Tell me about yourself, David."

David, oblivious to anyone else in the room, answers. "Oh, it's all so boring! You really don't want to know, do you?"

"Yes, I really do. I want to know everything about the man who was so kind-hearted to me in the train station." She reaches towards his hand and touches it lightly.

The waiter returns with the drink.

"I took the liberty of ordering you a glass of wine. I hope you don't mind." Katrina takes a sip of hers.

"Not at all! I always have a glass of wine with lunch."

"I rarely have time for lunch, with my acting and volunteer work. It's nice to sit down and have a meal with such a charming man."

David blushes. "Your life sounds far more glamorous than mine. I might have known you were an actress, you're so beautiful!"

Katrina turns her head coyly to the side. "Actually, I'm a work in progress. It has taken me much longer than I had originally planned to land the right part. I'm finding that there is always something to learn to better hone my craft. But enough about me, David. I want to hear all about you." She touches his hand again.

David begins to ramble on and on about his accounts and how he got his start in hedge funds. She sits back and listens intently to every word. Each time he glances up at her, their eyes meet and she smiles, looking more and more interested in what he has to say. He ends his story with, "and that's my life in a nutshell."

Katrina smiles kindly. "It sounds like you work so hard! Do you ever make time to play?"

"I don't know. I need to find more time to play. Perhaps you could help me with that."

"Why, David, are you flirting with me?" She twirls her long blonde hair around her pointer finger.

"Well, I guess I am." He smiles and takes another sip of wine.

"You're too cute!" She motions to the waiter for two more glasses.

David reaches for her shoulder and Katrina moves back a bit.

"I'm sorry. I was only trying to get a hair off your dress."

"Oh, I'll get it!" She finds the stray hair and tosses it on the floor.

Four glasses of wine later, and no food, David looks like he's ready for a nap.

Katrina leans in so no one else can hear her. "Don't

you have to get back to work?"

David laughs, "You're right, Katrina, but I don't think I am in any condition to go back there."

"Maybe you should sleep it off. I wouldn't want anything to happen to you."

"Could I crash at your place?" He cocks his head to the side.

"I barely know you, David." She looks around for the waiter.

"I think you know that I'm no serial killer."

"You may be no serial killer, but you might try and take advantage of me."

"Would you like that?" He asks, smiling from ear to ear.

"Let's get you in a cab first. I have a feeling you might pass out on me."

David takes several hundred dollar bills out of his wallet and throws them down on the table.

Katrina looks over the bill and hands David back six of them. "It's great to over tip, but there's no need to pay his rent for the month."

"Shall we go?" David asks, extending his hand towards Katrina.

The hostess holds open the door and the two of them walk outside and hail a cab.

"Uptown!" Katrina tells the driver.

"I feel hot." David tries to unbutton his jacket as the cab pulls away from the curb.

"Here, let me do that for you." Katrina leans in and undoes his buttons.

He looks into her eyes and she stares back at him.

Suddenly the two of them embrace in a passionate kiss.

"Wow!" He leans his head back on the seat.

"I don't think you should go back to work in this condition."

"You're probably right. I do have an image to uphold." He laughs. "How about we go to your place?"

"I have something better in mind." She leans towards the driver and directs him to the Four Seasons Hotel.

"Do you take all of your men there?" He sheepishly looks at her.

"You're offending me." She pouts.

David reaches for her hand and strokes it. "I'm sorry! I didn't mean to. I was only joking."

"Do I really seem like the kind of girl who does this sort of thing all the time?" She turns her face towards the window and ignores him.

"Not at all! It was just a joke. A really bad one." He puts his hands on her shoulders and turns her body towards him. "I'm sorry! You're so beautiful. I'm nervous, that's all. I keep wondering what the hell you're doing with me."

"Don't say that! You're wonderful, David." She leans in and kisses him again.

The cab driver keeps one eye on the road and the other on his rear view mirror as he heads towards the hotel.

Dr. Teresa Fine

"Alright, Maive, the last time you were here we were exploring possible options for extracurricular activities." She holds her pen, waiting to take notes.

"Oh, phooey! What does it matter? I'm destined to be single my entire life." Maive places her face in her hands.

"Well, that attitude certainly won't help you meet anyone."

"I don't care anymore! Life never works out for me. It only works out for people who are evil."

"What is it that is bothering you today, Maive?" She takes off her glasses and wipes them with a tissue.

"The usual!" She looks down at her hands and examines her nails.

"David?" Dr. Fine yawns.

"While I was in New York City, I ran into David's sister on the street."

"Debbie?" Dr. Fine gets up and pours herself some coffee and then motions to Maive to see if she wants any.

Maive shakes her head no. "Can you believe it? After all this time, there she was, "Little Debbie!" Well, big Debbie now, holding a little girl's hand."

"Was it her daughter?" She opens a pack of sugar

and stirs it into her coffee.

"I assumed it was. I noticed her a mile away, despite the fact that she had doubled in size. You know, with that stupid smile of hers!" Maive mimics the Colgate smile.

"I think I recall you saying something about it, yes." Dr. Fine sits back at her desk.

"I walked up to her and said hello and she looked at me as though she had never seen me before in her life."

"It has been four years, Maive! Actually, almost five. She has a child."

"Why are you taking her side? How can a person be so rude? Life has clearly moved on for Debbie!" She waves her hand in a gesture of dismissal.

Dr. Fine looks up at Maive and doesn't say a word.

"What? Why are you looking at me like that?"

"That's what people are supposed to do, Maive."

"What, be rude?" She gets up and walks over to the window.

"No, move on with their lives. I think we need to examine this further."

"What, Debbie?" She turns and looks at Dr. Fine.

"No, not Debbie! This approval you are always seeking." She reviews her notes.

"I don't understand."

"You expect a woman who barely knew you four years ago to remember you now."

"I remembered her." Maive raises her eyebrows.

"That's because she had such an impact on you."

"I know that! I just..."

"You just what?" Dr. Fine looks right at her and waits for an answer.

"I just wanted to choke her! She was so happy with her and her perfect family. I thought all this time that she and her husband were phonies, and I guess when I saw her I felt..." She paces back and forth, clutching a Kleenex until it's a shredded mess.

"Felt what?"

"Why does she have someone to love her and I don't?" She turns to look at Dr. Fine and waits for an answer.

"But you can! There must be someone who sparks your interest. You come into contact with a lot of people."

"There's no one, Dr. Fine." She looks right at her and rolls her eyes.

"Your neighbors don't know anyone? Someone you work with? A client?"

Maive stares off for a moment. "Well, there is this guy who watched my dogs."

"Wait a minute! We've been in session for fifteen minutes and you haven't said a word about any man except David." She looks at Maive in disbelief.

"It was a complete mishap! This playboy from the salon wound up watching my dogs for a weekend." Maive twirls her hair in her right hand and paces again.

"How do you know he's a playboy?" Dr. Fine gets her pen ready to write.

Maive stops pacing, looks right at Dr. Fine, and

puts her hands on her hips. "Because he looks like one!"

"You're judging people on their appearance, Maive. Do you like it when people do that to you?" She cocks an eyebrow and stares at her.

"Not at all, but this guy looks like he brings EVERYTHING home!"

"You're not being fair, Maive. Do you like it when people assume you're a flake just because you're a hairdresser?"

"No."

"Well, maybe you're wrong about this man. What's his name?"

"Benjamin. Benjamin Koppel." Maive looks right at Dr. Fine and raises an eyebrow.

"What's that look for?"

"Koppel? Need I say more?"

"Yes! Tell me all about him."

"He's a client at the salon. He accidentally hit my dog, Buster, and ended up taking him to the vet, paying the bill, and then watching all of the dogs until I got home from New York City."

"Hold the phone! Watched the dogs until you got home? He sounds like a playboy to me! Where do you suppose he kept four dogs while he was bringing women back to his love shack?" Dr. Fine laughs.

"Oh, I don't know! Maybe he's okay." She sits down and rummages through her purse, looking for her small mirror.

"Maybe he's okay?"

"Okay, he's fine!" She stares off for a moment.

"You know, now that I think about it, they actually liked him. When I saw him pulling Buster in the wagon, it made me well up with tears. Do you know, when I called out to Dunkin, Sammy and Cricket they all looked up to him before running to me?"

"Pulling Buster in a wagon? Come on, Maive! Aren't you the one who is always looking for signs? I'd say Benjamin is mural size!" Dr. Fine stands and then walks over to Maive.

"I think you're reading into this, Dr. Fine." Maive looks down at her watch. "I've got to get to work. See you next week?"

Dr. Fine throws her hands in the air. "Next week!"

Rudy Filona

On a Tuesday morning in June, Rudy wakes in a cold sweat. He reaches for another blanket at the foot of his bed and wraps it around his shivering body until he's a human cocoon. He must get out of bed and get ready for work. He's got to wrap a perm on one of his regular customers first thing today.

He rolls over, lights a cigarette, and brings it to his parched lips. The smoke makes direct contact with his nose and he covers his mouth to wretch. He moves as fast as his weakened body will let him, and only makes it to the edge of his bed before he vomits up Mexican food from the night prior all over the bedroom carpet.

"I'm getting too old for this." He moans, and crawls to the toilet to throw up again. When he throws up bile he crawls back into bed. Beads of sweat form on his tanned forehead so he reaches for a Kleenex, but the box falls on the floor. Completely void of energy and the will to get out of bed and pick it up, he uses his bed sheet instead. He rolls back over and falls into a deep sleep.

"Drew, I need you!" He mumbles in his sleep.

"Rudy! Mr. Rudy!"

Rudy opens his eyes to find Maria shaking him awake instead of his ex-lover Drew. "What the hell are you doing, you crazy bitch?" He rolls over on his side.

"Mr. Rudy, you late for work. I wake you up."

Rudy opens one eye and looks over at his alarm clock. "Ah, fuck! I've missed Mrs. Cook." He tries to stand on his feet, but lack of oxygen sends him falling backwards. Maria runs to catch him before he falls on the floor.

"Oh, Mamacita! I don't feel well."

"You party too much, Mr. Rudy. It gets to you after awhile."

"I don't need a lecture from you! Now get me my robe so I can take a shower. I've got to call the salon and make up some story."

He dials the phone and Jennifer yells at him. "I've called your place fourteen times, Rudy! Where the hell are you? Mrs. Cook threw a major fit when you never showed for her appointment. I don't get paid enough to put up with these demanding bitches!"

"Calm down, girl! Everything isn't about you! I was in a car accident last night and I've been in the hospital all morning."

"Rudy! Are you okay?"

"I'll be fine. Tell my clients I'm taking the day off and they'll have to reschedule."

"Of course, Rudy! Is there anything I can do?"

"Yeah! Don't call me at home today. I'll be in first thing tomorrow morning." He hangs up the phone.

"Mr. Rudy, I made you a bath and hair of dog." Maria puts a Bloody Mary on the bedside table.

"I can't drink that! Do you have any marijuana?"

"I out."

"Don't lie to me, Mary! Fork it over, sister!"

Maria goes into her purse and pulls out a joint and the two of them smoke it together.

Mabel Hempstead

As Mabel drones on about Benjamin Koppel, Maive sips on a cup of coffee and tries to change the subject, but somehow each topic reminds Mabel of Benjamin.

"How is your daughter-in-law doing? Was she pleased with the way you watched the kids?" Maive adds another sweetener to her coffee.

"She's worse! I didn't think it was possible. That girl really has it out for me! I did my damndest with those kids and everything I did was wrong." She reaches in the cabinet for some croissants.

"I'm sure you're exaggerating."

"I made peanut butter and jelly for the kids and she said I cut the bread wrong." She flails her hands as she speaks.

"That's too bad! Maybe one day she'll see your goodness. Do you want me to call her?" She reaches for the pad of paper and pencil sitting on the table.

"Will you, Maive?" She walks over and sits down next to her.

"In a second!"

"All we need is for you to have some kids and then I can be a grandmother to them."

Maive rolls her eyes and quickly changes the subject. "Your kitchen came out lovely! You have to give me the name of the painters you used. I've been thinking about doing my bedroom."

"That's an excellent idea, Maive! Get your place ready for a man, someone like Benjamin Koppel." She extends the plate of croissants to her.

"Mabel, please! He's just like all the others." She looks over the pastries and takes the smallest one.

"Is not!"

"Is too! And besides, what makes you his best friend all of a sudden?" She takes a bite of pastry.

"Because I know men! There is something very special about that fella. What kind of man would take in four dogs?" She looks at the croissants and takes the biggest one.

"That was nice of him, yes, but I think he did it out of guilt."

"Wrong! He didn't have to watch all four dogs. Hell! He could have kept driving after he hit Buster, but he didn't. He was crying like a baby when it happened." She takes an enormous bite and crumbs fall everywhere.

"Really? You never told me that." She looks over at her.

"Would it have mattered?" She picks at the crumbs with her finger and dabs them on her tongue.

"Well I..."

"Well you what? You haven't given anyone a chance since that damn idiot let you go." She gets up from the table and grabs two napkins.

"It's not that I don't want to. I don't have the time." She waves her right hand and takes a sip of coffee.

"Honey, you've got nothing but time! Let me tell you something right here and now, Maive. I love you like you're one of my own, but you have got to stop thinking every man is going to hurt you." She points a finger at her, her other hand on her hip.

"I don't think that!"

"You had one run-in with a creepy family and you think the rest of the world is like them. Personally, Maive, I resent the hell out of the fact that you think we're all like the Adelsteins!" She looks over at Maive, who looks wide-eyed. "I know David's family wasn't nice to you and I know they made you feel like you were less than human. I also know how much you loved him, and I'm quite certain he loved you just the same, if not more. What I'm trying to say, Maive, is that David was a coward and his family was shallow. You should never have to impress someone or prove yourself to them, they should love you just the way you are."

Maive bursts into tears so Mabel offers her a tissue from the counter. "Don't go and get all weepy on me. I understand your ambivalence towards Jewish men, but it's time to stop. Can't you see how you are acting the same way that David's family did towards you? They thought a hairdresser wasn't good enough for their precious boy and now you think every Jewish man is a jackass!"

She looks up at Mabel. "I know! It's true! In my heart I know it, but I'm so afraid of being hurt again, of feeling like I don't measure up. I don't understand why they didn't like me. I never thought things like education, money, and what I did for a living would matter. I was such a fool to think our love could be enough." She cries harder.

"Maive, you weren't a fool! Your love should have been enough, but David wasn't "the one" and you of all people shouldn't have to look for someone's approval, you should see it every single time someone looks at you." She rubs a hand on her shoulder.

"I wonder how many men I've snubbed because I thought they might have a family like the Adelsteins?"

"I have a friend named Suzy Horowitz who gave up sushi for years because a Japanese fellow dumped her. I kept telling her how great Philadelphia rolls were and she still wouldn't try them."

"Mabel, as much as I appreciate your stories, I don't see what this has to do with me."

"She, like you, wasted a lot of years being angry. You overlook every man who steps in your path and she overlooked the world's greatest food because it was Japanese. Until recently, that is.

"Okay, I get it! Please tell me there is a happy ending to Suzy."

"Eats sushi with me once a week! Sometimes twice when we splurge outside of the lunch special. She met the sushi chef one afternoon and has been dating him for six months now."

"How did you get her to eat sushi again?"

"Invited her over for lunch and proceeded to eat it in front of her. You know how I love my food, Maive!"

"Yes, I've seen you eat." She raises her brows.

"Well, my passion for food came in handy that day. And who are you to talk about eating habits? When I was watching your dogs, I found an empty bag of potato chips and a large amount of candy wrappers on your bedside table."

"I am choosing to ignore that comment." Maive turns her head away.

Mabel touches the top of Maive's hand. "Listen, Maive, my point is that you have to start fresh, give someone new a chance. It doesn't matter if they're Jewish or not. Let it play out. If he winds up having a creepy family, than know it has nothing to do with you. It doesn't matter if he's Jewish, Italian, African American or Chinese. Of course, if he happens to be a Jew, he certainly won't disappoint you in bed."

"Mabel, I'm getting a mental picture of you that I really don't want to have."

"Get over yourself, Maive! We all do it!"

Maive looks down for a moment and shakes her head.

"What is it, honey?"

"I want to move on, I really do, but right when I think I can forget about the Adelsteins, I think about the way I was treated by those awful girls. It had such an impact on me!"

"They were nothing more than a bunch of insecure bitches! They were jealous of you."

"You think so?"

"I know so!"

"Why didn't I stand up to them? Tell them off?"

"You were a different person than, Maive. Look

how much you've grown! How much you've learned from your experience with David."

"I guess you're right, but why do people have to be such creeps? Why do women put other women down so much? Why can't we look out for one another instead of seeing each other as competition?"

Mabel speaks with her mouth full. "Because people are insecure and have a desperate need to be accepted."

"But deep down inside I think we are all a bit insecure and want to be accepted. Don't you?" She twists her hair between her fingers.

"You're probably right, Maive, but there's a difference between people wanting acceptance and people acting entitled. You know the type I'm talking about! They have a Blackberry glued to their hand, talk down to people who wait on them, and never miss a chance to admonish somebody when they feel they have been wronged."

"You mean like those japs back in New York?"

"Now that's a term I can do without, thank you! How would you like it if someone called you a shiksa? It's just plain awful and racist!"

"How about yenta then?"

"A yenta is a gossip, a really meddlesome woman."

"Am I a yenta?" Maive asks.

"Of course not! You can't be a yenta because you're not Jewish. You could be a shenta, but you're not a gossip."

"A what?"

"A shenta! It's a term my friends and I came up

with years ago. It describes a gossipy woman who is really obnoxious, but isn't Jewish."

Maive looks confused.

"A shiksa that's a yenta. A shenta!" Mabel raises her hands.

"Is shenta the equivalent of jappy? I have heard women call other women jappy and they weren't even Jewish. I think people use it to describe someone obnoxious and materialistic without realizing that it is offensive to Jewish women. You should take out an ad, Mabel, and let people know about the term shenta."

"Mibby is another one we came up with."

"Mibby? What the heck does that mean?" Maive looks up at her.

"Materialistic, Insecure, Bitch!" Mabel says proudly.

"You mean a mib instead of a jap?" Maive thinks about it for a moment. "I like it!"

"Then it's settled! From now on, any woman you find offensive will be referred to as a mibby!"

"Sounds good!" Maive says, and the two of them burst into laughter.

Rebecca (Billie) Lane

She sits at her station inspecting her split ends and popping her chewing gum. When Rudy comes in this morning, she's going to confront him and tell him exactly how she feels about him. Sister, hell! Unless he's into incest, there's got to be more to their relationship than his concern for her as a friend.

Pop! Pop! Pop! She snaps her lips together with the large wad of pink bubblegum in between them. The client sitting in the chair next to her is one of Maive's and she keeps rolling her eyes at Billie. This only encourages Billie to make the popping sound louder. She decides to have some fun and really send the old bag into a panic, or at least running for the door.

Pulling her cell phone out of her purse, she fakes dialing a number. Maive's client pretends to bury herself in a *Good Housekeeping* magazine, but Billie knows she's listening to her.

"Hey, Baby! You up yet? Not like that, you nasty man! Thought you'd be sleeping in after the way I fucked you last night. Oh, yeah? Wait till I see you tonight! I'm going to lick you like an ice cream cone!"

She glances over at the older woman, now holding her shirt to her neck and staring nervously at the front door of the salon. "She's always late! If I were you I'd find a new colorist." Billie says, as she takes a cigarette from her purse and lights it.

"Billie!" Jennifer yells from the front of the salon.

Billie glances up at Jennifer who is waving a finger back and forth, signaling no smoking in the salon. "Alright! Alright!" She walks to the back of the salon and out the delivery door before taking a puff.

She thinks about what she'll say to Rudy and how he will react. At first he'll be surprised, but then he'll gaze at her with those deep brown eyes of his and he'll realize she's right. He's not actually gay, just promiscuous, and the two of them are meant to be together.

Holding the cigarette up to her lips, she takes a long drag and blows smoke circles into the air. From a distance she sees Maive's car turning the corner into the parking lot. "Fucking bitch!" She mumbles.

Convinced that Maive is standing in the way of her relationship with Rudy, Billie is determined to get her out of the picture. Marrying her off is next to impossible, and an accident will be too devious, even for Billie. There must be some way to get rid of Maive. Billie closes her eyes and thinks about it for a moment.

A set-up!

But will Rudy believe it? If it's done correctly, yes. After all, she has seen Maive take color home from the salon before. Everybody brings supplies home to do clients on the side. If a few extra boxes are missing, like, say thirty or so, Rudy will have to do something about it. He'll never suspect Billie since she doesn't even do hair color.

She throws the lit cigarette to the ground, ignoring the can designated for butts, and watches Maive fiddle with something in her car. Billie walks back into the salon towards her station, grabs her ginormous handbag, and heads into the color room. She opens the cupboards and starts grabbing handfuls of color boxes and throwing them into her purse. The small buckets of bleach that Rudy has shipped from Europe are quite pricey and will definitely raise an eyebrow if they go missing, so she shoves three of those in her bag as well. Billie hears Julianne's footsteps and quickly grabs a paper towel and soaks it with water.

Julianne walks in and sees Billie leaning against a counter. "Are you okay?"

"Actually no, I was feeling a bit warm so I thought I would try and cool myself down."

Julianne looks around and notices the cabinet doors open. "Can I help you with something?"

"The day you can help me will be the day I stop doing hair." Billie storms out of the room.

Julianne shakes her head in confusion. She is certain she closed the cabinet doors last night after doing inventory. She closes the cupboards and walks up front to look at Maive's schedule for the day.

Stacy Kornberg-Adelstein

After hiring her third maid in four weeks, she is pleasantly surprised to find one who is doing exactly what she asks her to do. If it wasn't for her old housekeeper Cecilia and her ridiculous notion of going back to school, she wouldn't be inconvenienced like this.

The house is quiet, which is the way she prefers it. It had been a stroke of luck getting Joshie into a full-day program at the local camp, since they rejected him at sleep-away camp. He is very mature for three and a half and would have been just fine going away for the summer, especially with Lily there to watch over him.

At least she has part of the day to herself, which gives her plenty of time to plan a vacation for her and David. She better book her parents now, since their social calendar seems to be far more important than spending time with their grandchildren these days.

She could never ask Ethel and Adam! Their social life is far busier than her own parents, not to mention the fact that Debbie has them booked three months in advance. Why Debbie had a child is beyond Stacy, since she never spends a moment alone with her. She's always shipping Zoe off somewhere.

When Lily comes home from camp, she and David will take the kids away for a family vacation. Which reminds her, she better call Beaches and make sure they have openings in their kids program. It fills up so quickly.

David works so hard these days. He is really feeling the pressure of everything that is going on in the economy. Stacy tries to be understanding about him spending four nights a week in the city, but going in on Saturdays is a bit much.

A smile covers her usual somber face, thinking about his willingness to meet her on most issues lately, the latest and most costly one being an extension on their bedroom. It makes no sense for David to sleep in the guestroom. If he is having trouble sleeping, he should be able to walk into a sitting area with a pull-out couch instead of going all the way downstairs.

In the past he would have put up a fuss about such a costly endeavor, but this time he only made one comment about her getting a job to help pay for it. Between school meetings, tennis lessons, cooking lessons, going to the club, and shopping, she's far too busy to think about going back to work.

The phone rings and Stacy rushes over to answer it. It might be David calling with plans for dinner. Maybe he'll want her to meet him in the city. "Hello?"

"Hi! This is Sandy Smith. I'm calling about a reference on your sitter, Sarah."

Stacy's mouth gapes open. "What?"

"I'm so excited to find a sitter! I haven't been able to leave the house since my baby was born. Does Sarah work for you?"

"Yeah! She babysits for us. Well, she used to

babysit for us. I don't use her anymore. She proved to be rather irresponsible." Stacy lies.

"Really? She seems like such a lovely girl."

"It's all an act! She had a party at my house and ruined the carpet."

"Oh, my! I'm so glad I called you. I guess we'll have to look for someone else. Do you know of anyone?"

"No, I only let my mom watch my children. Best of luck to ya!" Stacy hangs up with the woman and immediately calls her sitter. "Sarah, this is Mrs. Adelstein."

"Oh, hi!"

"I just got a very disturbing phone call. Why are ya giving your number out to people? You're my sitter!"

"Mrs. Adelstein, you know I would never desert you, but I only sit for you on Saturday nights. Mrs. Smith wants me to babysit during the day."

Babysitters are coveted and there is no way Stacy is going to share Sarah with anyone. "Well I'm glad ya feel that way. I gave her a terrific reference! I'm sure she'll call ya back. Ya didn't forget that I need ya earlier this Saturday, did ya?"

"No, Mrs. Adelstein."

"I'll have David pick ya up at four o'clock. We have a Bar Mitzvah to attend."

"See you then!" Sarah hangs up the phone.

Galled by the nerve of the woman who tried to take her sitter, she picks up the phone and calls her friend Sasha to hear the latest gossip, but only gets the answering machine. "Hey, Sasha! It's Stacy. You'll never believe what happened! Some woman called for a reference on my sitter. I'm so mad! Anyway, call me back. Maybe we can meet for lunch at the club." Stacy puts the phone back on the receiver and places it on the French antique bookshelves.

She glances at all of the photos sitting on the shelves. David getting his M.B.A. from N.Y.U., the two of them sailing on his parent's boat, family portraits of the Adelsteins and Kornberg's, Lily and Josh as babies, and her favorite, the one of herself on her wedding day.

How perfect she looked! Her skin so tanned against the custom-made, white Amsale wedding gown, her hair piled loosely on her head and secured with a diamond tiara. She's surrounded by four of her best friends, all clad in light blue gowns, each one beaming from ear to ear in the photo.

As she peruses the photos, she stops when she comes to the one of her and Debbie on Yom Kippur. "The two forks go on the left." Debbie directed Stacy, as they both set the table for the break-the-fast meal. Stacy is perfectly capable of having a meal catered and placing the food on her own china. Why does Debbie get to host it? She already hosts Mother's Day! She'd like to get rid of the photo, much like she'd like to get rid of Debbie, but appearances are all that matter to the Adelsteins, so Stacy keeps the photo on her shelf just in case one of them comes by for an unannounced visit.

It irks her to pack away the Vera Wang place settings she received as a wedding gift, since Thanksgiving is at her parent's home, Rosh Hashanah is at Bubbe's, and Passover is at Ethel's. While the Torah may have its rendition of Passover, spending an evening with Ethel is enough to make anyone want to "pass over" a holiday.

It's a shame Stacy doesn't like the Adelsteins more. At first meeting, their closeness to one another was rather charming, inviting even. It wasn't long after she took her vows, though, that she realized the Adelsteins used the word "close" as a disguise for their manipulative and controlling behavior.

How David's father puts up with Ethel really perplexes Stacy. He has to be cheating on her! Guilt does a lot to men, but far more for women. The way Stacy figures it, Adam Adelstein must be one horny bastard, because Ethel is dripping in jewels!

She hopes her David will never stray like poor Mitzi Silver's husband did. Stacy is convinced Mitzi lost Fred because she gained an awful lot of weight during their marriage. The thought of balding, skinny as a noodle, worst breath ever Fred being found attractive by another woman really bothers Stacy.

She wonders what kind of woman David would fall prey to. Probably some tart, like the one in the photo she had found while looking around David's old apartment. She never asked David about the photo. How could she? That would mean she was snooping, which in turn would mean she wasn't being honest.

Glancing back at her wedding photo, she walks over to the shelf and opens the back of the frame and takes out two smaller photos. She stares down at the gorgeous blonde with blue eyes, wearing jeans on her thin, long legs and a white t-shirt, which is probably one of David's. A long blue scarf holds back part of her hair and the rest is blowing in the wind. Stacy runs a hand through her own hair and bursts into tears. No matter how much money she spends getting her hair straightened or dyed, she will never look like the girl in the photo.

David looks besotted. His left arm squeezes the girl tightly, while the other is extended outward holding the camera. He looks different than he does now. Not just younger, it's something else. They have "it." Unmistakable, undeniably, "it."

Just as she once had.

She looks at the other small photo; one of a tanned young man with jet black hair. He's sitting on a large boulder with the Bay of Naples behind him. He's wearing a sleeveless white t-shirt and three of his seven tattoos can be seen on his perfectly toned biceps. His muscular thighs are bulging under his dark blue jeans and a pair of coffee brown loafers peeks out from under their hem. His lower lip is slightly pouting, but his green eyes are smiling like they always did whenever he looked at her.

She caresses the photo with her finger and whispers his name, "Gianni."

Katrina Emery

She walks into the living room suite at the Four Seasons Hotel, sits down on one of the comfortable couches, and looks over the room service menu. French toast with a wild blueberry compote and eggs Benedict both sound deliciously sinful, but she opts for the melon sampler and black coffee instead. David will prefer something hearty like an omelet with cheese. She calls room service and places the order.

David dozes soundly in the next room, sleeping off their morning romp. As far as lovers go, he's pretty average, but he's been so generous and kind in the two months they have been seeing one another that she overlooks the sex thing.

Life is quite glamorous when it's lived this way, but deep down inside every girl yearns for more. If David thinks she is going to be content remaining behind hotel walls and sneaking out to hideaways in the East Village where he knows his wife or her friends will never dine, then he had better wake up! If it's one thing Katrina knows, it's her worth.

She's not blind to the way men and women stare at her, she's too pretty to be hidden away. His wife is the one who should be hiding, hiding from the reality that her marriage is deteriorating. She has to notice the changes in David, and if she doesn't than his secretary, Mary, does.

She sits on the couch and flips through the television stations, wondering what David's wife is like. She must be a bore that bakes cookies all day, or one of those high maintenance bitches with a staff member for every finger that never gets lifted. His wife obviously has no tits, given the way David has taken possession of hers like a tiger protecting its' cubs. And the woman is as dumb as hell! Especially if she thinks David is working too hard to come home at night.

A knock at the hotel door startles her. She walks over and looks through the peep hole. Relieved to see an older gentleman with a room service tray, she opens the door.

"Good morning! Where would you like this, Mrs. Adelstein?" He smiles.

"You can put that over here." She motions with her hand towards the couch.

"If you will sign here, I'll be on my way." He presents her with a bill.

She forges David's signature and leaves an extra twenty percent gratuity. "Have a great day!"

"You too, Mrs. Adelstein!"

Mrs. Adelstein, indeed! That's exactly who she should be. Enough of this sneaking around! She's not about to become some trophy David puts on a shelf and takes down to fuck when he feels like it. She wants more! Patience may be a virtue, but so is being chaste.

She marches into the bedroom and watches David sleeping soundly on the king size bed. She crawls in next to him, wearing only her white bra and matching lace panties. "David! Oh, David! Wakeup, darling!" She whispers. "I thought you might be hungry."

"Yes, as a matter of fact, I'm starving! You really make me work up an appetite." He leans over and kisses her hard on the mouth.

"You're such a nasty boy! So nasty, I think I'm going to have to punish you." She takes her hand and smacks him on his ass.

"Ooh, I like being a bad boy!"

"I'm going to have to teach you a lesson." She straddles his legs and begins to gyrate on his crotch.

"I'm a slow learner."

"I'm a good teacher." She whispers in his right ear. "But not a patient one."

"Patience is a virtue." He boyishly smiles at her.

"So is being chaste! That's why I am no longer going to have sex with you until I know you are totally committed to me." She starts to climb off of him.

"Chaste? Why would you want to go and ruin such a great thing by being chaste?" He sits up, looking puzzled.

"I don't want you to think of me as a sex toy!" She sits on the side of the bed.

He reaches for her head to bring her closer to him.

"Don't touch my hair!" She snaps at him.

David quickly sits back.

She pouts. "I'm sorry, sweetie! I don't want to cuddle with you right now. It will only make me want you and I think it will be best if we stop the physical for awhile."

"You're joking, right? I thought we both liked it so much?"

She caresses his hair. "I do, darling, I do. It's just that...do you realize you've never asked anything about me? It really hurts my feelings, David."

He holds her by the arms. "Oh, baby, I want to know everything about you. I do! But when we're together I'm so attracted to you that I only want to hold you and never let you go. Will you forgive me for being so attracted to you?"

"I'm attracted to you too, David, but I need more than sex. I want to be married."

"Married? Where did that come from?" He shakes his head.

"I've always dreamt about being married, David, but I have never seen myself totally committed to someone until I met you. I don't want to carry on like this any longer. I need more." She gets up from the bed and starts to get dressed.

"I haven't thought about marriage. I mean, I'm already married. I thought we were..."

"Thought we were what? Having a good time? Is that all you think of me? If I were Jewish, would you think differently?" She buttons her blouse.

"Jewish? What does that have to do with anything?"

"I don't want you to see me as some sex object! I'm worried that down the road you won't want to be with me because we're not the same religion."

"Katrina, I'm a grown man! It doesn't matter to me if you're Jewish or not. Now stop worrying about all of this stuff and come back to bed." He pats the space next to him.

She ignores him and puts on her skirt.

"You're serious, aren't you?"

She turns and looks at him as she's slipping on her shoes. "Very!"

"What do you want me to do? Do you want more jewelry? Do you need some money? Do you want to see each other more?" He throws his hands in the air.

"I want you to leave your wife." She grabs her purse, puts on her sunglasses, and walks towards the door. It's a gamble for sure, but confident in how far they've come so quickly, it's a risk she's willing to take.

David jumps out of bed with a sheet wrapped around his body and runs towards the door of the hotel room to try and block her from leaving. "Baby, I'll do whatever you want! But I can't do that. I mean... Stacy and me! My family!"

"Does your wife listen to you the way that I do? Is she attracted to you the same way that I am? Does she make love to you the way that I do? If the answer is yes to any of these questions than you and I shouldn't be here together." She opens the hotel door.

He puts his arm in front of her. "No! The answer is no. Can't we give this some more time? There must be something else you want from me."

"No, David, I only want to be with you. That's all! I don't want to sneak around anymore. I want to be able to hold your hand on Madison Avenue and wake up next to you every morning. I want to be the one who gazes into your eyes as you relay your day, and the one to comfort you when something goes wrong. Am I being too selfish? I don't think so, David." She pushes his arm to the side and walks out the door.

"Katrina!" He calls out, standing half naked in the hallway.

She walks to the elevator and doesn't look back. The doors open and she steps inside, while a baffled David stands in the middle of the Four Seasons hallway in a hotel sheet.

Rudy Filona

Fearing he will be discovered at the waiting room in the county hospital, Rudy looks down at the scuffed floor, thinking up an excuse in case he is seen. People will still speculate regardless of what he tells them, especially a nosey queen. The first thing that will suffer is his career, and he can forget about ever getting laid again.

Why the hell did he have to visit his ex-lover Drew? What if the same thing happens to him? He rubs his head, trying to get rid of the image of Drew and how bad he looked, but he can't.

Drew had once been a Cary Grant look-alike, but now he looked more like Freddy Krueger. Lesions covered one side of his handsome face and Rudy found it difficult to look at him. He was frail as he gripped a metal pole with an IV attached to it, like it was a repelling line dangling from a cliff. The body that once worked out at the gym twice a day was now made exhausted every time he opened his mouth to simply take in a breath of air. His beautiful thick head of blonde hair was thin and dusty looking. "Make sure you see your doctor, Rudy." Drew had said before his nurse walked him back to his bed.

"Mr. Filona?" A heavy woman stuffed into a white nurse's uniform calls him.

He casually looks up and raises a pinky finger.

"Mr. Filona?" She bellows out his name again.

"You don't have to yell my name, Mary! Why don't you announce to the world that I'm here?" He snaps at her, and then follows her through two swinging doors. "Don't you have anything more private?" He glances around the tiny area.

"This ain't the Ritz, honey! If you prefer something more private, you'll have to see your own physician." She closes the curtain with one sweeping movement.

"I don't have one!" He crosses his arms to his chest.

"You don't have one? You know, you're about the tenth person to tell me that. Damn shame!" She takes a needle out of a drawer.

"I don't ever get sick."

"Mm hmm!" She puts a pair of gloves on her two large hands, places a tourniquet around his right arm, and then taps his forearm to produce a big, bulging vein.

"You find everything you need?" He asks sarcastically.

"You've got good veins! I like 'em when they're like this." She smiles from ear to ear.

"I think I'm going to faint." Rudy throws his free arm to his forehead.

"Lay back, Mr. Filona. This will only take a few minutes. Try to think about something pleasant."

The paper on the bed is cold and crinkles when he moves. He closes his eyes and takes a few deep breaths, counting to ten as he exhales.

Every winter, pine needles covered the ground

outside his family's cabin and the mountain tops were filled with glistening fresh snow. Pure, white snow! Everywhere he looked there were different shades of white, draping down hillsides like the elegant robes made for a queen. His parents' cabin was situated on a ravine where an icy blue river moved slowly towards a dam. The water was dark blue.

Blue, like the bike.

He was sitting in the corner looking through the *Sears* catalog for the bike he wanted. It was blue with red streamers that dangled from white plastic handles. It had a white banana seat and reflectors on both wheels. He had seen one just like it in the town store when he went with his mother to drop off the sewing she did for townspeople. His parents could barely afford to feed his two older brothers and three younger sisters, let alone buy him the bike, but his Uncle John could.

Every birthday, Easter, Thanksgiving, Valentine's Day, and Christmas, Uncle John showed up at their house with a large bag filled with presents for all of the kids. His mother hated Uncle John, but Rudy never knew why.

Not until that day.

All of Rudy's brothers and sisters had opened their presents from Uncle John while Rudy waited for his. Paper was strewn about the room, his sisters cuddling their new dolls, his brothers pushing their toy trucks back and forth. Rudy's mother was preparing the ham Uncle John had brought her.

"Where's my present, Uncle John?" Rudy had asked.

"It was too big to bring." He told him. "You'll have to take a drive into town with me so I can get it for you."

When his mother said no, his father came out of his drunken stupor long enough to curse at her, so she clutched her rosary beads in her hand and went back into the kitchen.

Uncle John took Rudy by the shoulder and walked him towards his car. Two hours later, Rudy returned with a brand new bike he would never ride, a disgust for his mother for allowing him to go, and a contempt for all mankind for what happened to him at the hands of his uncle.

"Okay, Mr. Filona!" The nurse holds four vials of blood. "Mr. Filona?" She sings his name.

He sits straight up.

"I'll have your results in about a week."

"A week? I can't wait that long!"

"I'm sorry, sir, but that's how long it takes. You're not the only person in here getting blood work done." She helps him to his feet.

"I've got a question for you." Rudy looks her in the eyes.

"Yes?"

He whispers, "Is it true that they actually give you a prescription for pot if you have cancer?"

"Yes, I believe they do."

He points with his finger in the hallway. "Where do I go to get tested for that?"

Benjamin Koppel

He returns to his apartment after meeting a client for coffee and throws his keys on the counter. He sure hates dressing up! He can hardly wait to get out of these clothes and into a pair of shorts and Tevas. First he needs something to eat. He would have eaten at the restaurant, but the guy he met was such a pretentious asshole he could hardly wait to leave.

He looks into his fridge and sees two packs of ketchup, a glass of orange juice, a container of coffee, and a half-eaten sandwich from Subway. He picks it up to take a bite and notices a bit of mold on the white cheese. There is no mistaking it for relish. He tosses it into the garbage and heads to the market to get a few things.

As he pulls into the parking lot, he sees Maive getting out of her car and heading into the store. Think fast Koppel! Should he go in or leave? What is it that Mabel says about fate? Oh, for God's sake! Now you're listening to that loon! Just get your groceries and go home. He grabs a cart and goes straight for the beer aisle.

"Hi, Benjamin!" He turns to see a woman he doesn't recognize, beaming from ear to ear.

"Hello there!"

"I'm Lisa Marshall. Your Aunt Kitzy may have

mentioned me." She smiles more.

Aunt Kitzy is always yammering about somebody, but he just tunes her out. "I don't recall her mentioning your name."

"Look, Julie! It's Benjamin Koppel!" She yells to her friend, who comes rushing over.

"Hi, Benjamin!" She speaks in a sing-song voice. "Didn't I see you at the nature preserve?"

Benjamin tries not to gasp at the sight of a human stick bug in high heels and gigantic Chanel sunglasses. "The nature preserve?" He suddenly remembers being with his aunt and mom. "Yes, I was with my family." He looks around the store.

"Your family? I didn't know you were married!"

"He's not! I told you about him." Lisa nudges her friend in the side.

"Well, that's a relief!"

"Julie, stop! You're embarrassing me!"

He sees Maive across the way. "Excuse me, ladies! I've got to get some fish before the market closes." He turns his cart so fast he almost runs down a ninety-five year old man grabbing a cereal box off of a shelf.

He reaches Maive just as she is putting her order in the cart. "It's so nice to see you again." He flashes his ultra white smile at her.

Maive turns and sees Benjamin. She forces a smile, nods appropriately, and tries pushing her cart past his.

He pulls up closer to her and traps her against the seafood counter. "Maive, how come you're clamming up on me?" He bursts into laughter.

She looks bewildered so he points her in the

direction of the fresh clams lying on chips of ice.

"Very funny! I guess I prefer to stay in my shell."

"Pretty good!" He chuckles again. "But seriously, I feel like I'm floundering here. Do you think we can have coffee together sometime?"

"Halibut I think about it and get back to you?" She smiles and turns her cart in the opposite direction.

"Are you worried that salmon might get the wrong impression if they see you talking to me?" He calls out to her.

She stops walking and turns back around. "I'm just a bit bassful." She smirks, and quickly turns her cart down an aisle before he can respond.

Quick witted and gorgeous! The combination is lethal. He chases after her, taking the quickest route to the check-out counter, throwing random items from the organic food aisle into his cart. He finally catches up to her. "So was that a yes or a no?"

She turns around to answer him, but is interrupted.

"Are we going to see you out on the town this Friday, Benjamin?"

He turns around and sees the two girls standing behind him. When opportunity knocks, Benjamin always answers. "No, I don't think so. I'm hoping Maive will go out with me instead." He motions with his hand towards her.

Both girls eye Maive up and down. "Aren't you that girl who does color at Rudolph's?"

"Actually, Lisa, you're wrong. Maive doesn't do color, she's a colorist and a fantastic one at that!" Benjamin replies.

"Oh, I see! Is that all you do?" Julie asks her.

"In her spare time she tries avoiding me and my advances." Benjamin laughs.

The two girls force a laugh and then leave their cart and the store.

Maive, whose face is bright red, looks at Benjamin. "Thank you."

"For what? They were so rude!" He shakes his head.

"They're mibbies!"

"They're what?"

"It's a term Mabel taught me." She glances down into Benjamin's cart and back up at him. "Thanks again for taking such good care of my dogs. I'm sure it wasn't easy for you."

"It was no problem at all! Once I understood they were in charge, we got along just fine."

She laughs and looks down at his cart again. "I've got to go, Benjamin. It was nice to see you." She pays the cashier and leaves the store.

Benjamin watches Maive walk away and wonders what the hell just happened.

"I'm going to have to get a price check for these soy hotdogs." The cashier looks up at him.

"Soy hotdogs?" He glances down at the package. "I wouldn't even know how to cook these. Hey, if it doesn't come from Yankee stadium or from a joint on the side of the road, I don't eat them. You know what I'm saying?"

The cashier looks at Benjamin, confused. "Does that mean you don't want the tofu eggs, either?"

"Tofu eggs? How do they do that? You know what? I don't even want to know! I'll pay for the beer and be on my way. I'm sorry for the confusion." He hands her a twenty dollar bill.

She rolls her eyes.

"Let me take these things back. I don't want to be a problem or anything. I like this store. It has the best selection."

"The best selection of WHAT?" The cashier gives him his change.

"You got me there! I'm a bachelor! What can I tell ya?" He grabs his beer and walks to his car. He sits in the seat and thinks about Maive. Where does he stand now? He doesn't have an answer about coffee and who knows when he will run into her again. Why is she so repulsed by him? He smells under his arm to see if he stinks. Nah! Still smells like Armani.

Was it the conversation? Who doesn't find fish humor funny? Who is he kidding? What a complete tool! "I'm floundering here?" "Clamming up?" And tofu eggs? She must think you're a real winner, Koppel! He puts his car into drive and heads to Dairy Queen to get something to eat.

Mary Humphreys

Mary started work at Advantage Edge Advisors the same day David did. He is okay as far as bosses go. A bit full of himself at times, but Mary figures a giant ego comes hand-in-hand with someone who has done so well at such a young age.

She flips through the television stations, trying to quiet her mind, and settles on the Food Network. Some overly perky woman talks about how to eat healthy and Mary loses interest. She turns on the DVD player and puts in *Casablanca* for the hundredth time. She reads the names of the actors and tries to focus on the dramatic music, but can only hear Stacy Adelstein's nagging voice instead.

"Where is my husband?" An agitated Stacy asked her.

"Uh, I'm not sure. He hasn't come in yet today." Mary admitted.

"What do ya mean, he hasn't come in yet?"

Mary had her suspicions that David had been seeing someone for about two months now, but had only confirmed it two days ago when he came back from a "lunch meeting" with Bill Howard, who she knew from his secretary, Trina, was on vacation.

The lingerie, the late lunches from which he returned smelling of perfume, early office exits, late morning arrivals with make-up smudges on his shirts, and calls from a sexy-voiced woman claiming to be a "new client" were only the beginning.

By far the most obvious give away was David himself. Humming as he walks around the office, smiling to clerks and mail delivery personnel, and carrying on conversations with people he has previously ignored. Even his wardrobe is different. Uptight David no longer exists. There is a sense of freedom about him that wasn't there before this "new client" came along.

Mary has her opinions as far as affairs go, but this girl certainly seems to be having a positive influence on David. And quite frankly, Stacy has it coming to her. Mary has often fantasized about the day she would tell Stacy off, but had no idea it would actually come to fruition.

"Honestly!" Stacy yelled at Mary. "Maybe if ya stopped stuffing your face with those donuts and paid more attention to details at the office, ya would know where my husband is."

All the years of Stacy Adelstein, Ms. Perfect Teeth, Ms. Perfect Life, Ms. Too Good to talk to anyone unless they have something to offer had taken their toll on Mary. It was one thing for Mary to take it from David's mother, the elderly were entitled to a little leeway, but she was not about to take it from some skinny little twit like Stacy any longer.

"Did you like the lingerie David bought you from Victoria's Secret?" Mary cocked one eyebrow as a devilish grin covered her face.

The instant the question intended to harm Stacy

flew out of Mary's mouth, she also knew she had just made David suspect, which is something she hadn't wanted to do. Unfortunately, one couldn't be done without the other.

It's for the best! David deserves better. Why the hell Stacy is so miserable when she appears to have it all is really bothersome to Mary. There isn't one woman alive who wouldn't trade places with Stacy and maybe David has finally found one.

As she chews on some cashews, the reality of what she has done finally dawns on her. What happens to her if David finds out she is the one who told Stacy about the affair? Will he fire her? What if something happens to David? What if Stacy is so angry she flies into a jealous rage and kills him?

Mary begins to panic. Should she call David on his cell phone and make sure he is okay? What if David doesn't know anything yet? Should she warn him of her conversation with Stacy? Or should she play innocent and act like she knows nothing at all?

She sits in silence with her thoughts, waiting for an answer that doesn't come. She needs to clear her head. She should meditate; people say that works. Or she could go outside and take a walk, a walk to the Haagen Dazs store.

Desiree

Every Wednesday morning for the past two years she has met Gary at the Plaza Hotel, and for the past two years he has always been late. Today is no exception.

As she walks from one end of the lobby to the other, she becomes more agitated by his tardiness. She pulls out a cigarette and then pauses to check out the scenery.

Sitting on one of the sofas is an older gentleman who appears to be in his sixties. His skin is a deep golden brown, his hair is black with silver streaks, and his glasses, made by David Eden, perch on his Romanesque nose.

A finely tailored suit, which appears to be Italian, probably a Caraceni, frames his build rather nicely. His shoes, much too pointed for New York men, are definitely European. His watch is a Rolex, a little mundane, but his taste in clothing and eyeglasses make up for his lack of character in jewelry. The only accessory that matters to her, however, is the one in his back pocket.

As if on cue, he retrieves his wallet. He pulls out a wad of Ben Franklins and gives one to the man who brought him an espresso. Desiree smiles in delight. She knew he wouldn't disappoint her.

She feels a tap on her shoulder and turns around

to annihilate the person who has touched her. "What the..."

"Hey, sweetheart! Have you been waiting long?" Gary leans in and kisses her.

She glances over at the prospect on his cell phone and he winks at her.

"Should we head upstairs?" Gary asks too eagerly.

Honestly! This used to work when she found him to be a challenge, but now he is beginning to bore her.

"What's your hurry? I thought we could have a drink first."

"But I have a meeting this afternoon. I can't be late for it."

"Fine! Go to your meeting! Forget about my feelings! If all you want is sex then you should get yourself a hooker!" She walks away and sits on the couch facing the European gentleman.

"Baby!" Gary rushes over to her. "You know that's not true! I don't know what else to do to show you how much I care for you."

"All I want is one little drink. I don't see the harm in that."

"You're right, honey! Let's order something." Gary motions the waiter over and orders a cup of coffee.

"I'd like a bottle of your finest champagne." Desiree smiles.

Gary's eyes widen. "I thought you only wanted one drink?"

"Are we going to fight again?" She lowers her head and pouts.

"Of course not! Whatever you want, princess!" He rubs her thigh.

Desiree smiles with her eyes at the man sitting across from her, while Gary kisses her on the cheek, telling her what he's going to do to her once they get upstairs.

"You promised me you'd leave that awful wife of yours." She says, extending her lower lip like a small child.

"Baby, I am! I'm waiting until I get some more money put away."

"Promise?"

"Of course!" He caresses her face.

She puts both of her hands on his thighs and faces him. "I need something from you, Gary. A small token that says you love me and that you mean what you say about leaving your wife."

"What do you want Poppa Bear to buy you, baby?"

"A little something I saw at Bvlgari." She runs a finger up his arm.

"Bvlgari?" He sighs heavily and stares off for a moment. "You know, honey, I've been wondering about something."

She pushes her chest into his and presses her lips against his ear. "What's that, sweetie?"

He puts his hands on her shoulders and looks into her eyes. "Would you be with me if I didn't have money?"

She cocks one eyebrow and stares back at him. "Gary, would you be with me if I didn't look like this?"

He smirks and drinks his coffee while she drinks a glass of the champagne in one gulp.

"Let's go visit Bvlgari." He gets up from the sofa, reaches for her hand, and the two of them head around the corner.

"This is the one I want!" She points to the Lucea blue topaz watch.

Gary looks at the price tag. "Are you sure you don't want to look around some more?"

She whispers in his ear. "Are you sure you want to have sex with me?"

Five minutes later they leave the store and head back to the hotel. She glances down at her latest accouterment and smirks like the Cheshire cat. "You've made me so happy, Gary! Are you ready to go upstairs now, Sugar Bear?" She leans into Gary, pushing her breasts up against him.

"Grrr!" Gary growls, as they get inside the elevator.

Rudy Filona

Late Wednesday morning, Rudy walks through the front door of his salon with a stagger in his footsteps that wasn't there before. Jennifer is on the phone, but manages to hold up a finger, signaling him to stop at the front desk. He leans against the podium for a moment and feels his chest pull tightly around his ribcage. He struggles to take a breath and uses all of his energy to walk to his station and sit down in the chair.

His eager-to-please assistant comes over with a smile from ear to ear. "Good morning, Rudy! Your first client is waiting. I'm stalling him at the sink with a conditioner on his head."

"Rinse him and bring him to me as fast as you can, please." He spins around in the chair and faces the mirror. He looks at himself and notices his skin has a rather gray and ashy appearance to it. The urge to throw up overwhelms him and he wants nothing more than to go home and crawl back into bed. He pulls open his drawer, grabs the over-the-counter speed pills he bought at the gas station, and pops two into his mouth.

He turns his chair back towards the sink and watches his staff working on all of their clients. It's like they are all moving in slow motion, dancing around one another with a terrific sense of timing. His head moves back and forth to the tempo of Maive's paint brush until he feels like he's going to fall onto the floor.

"Hey, sexy! How you doin'?" Billie smacks her gum.

Rudy looks up at her, moves his nostrils towards her, and then feels like he is going to be sick. "You need to put on some more of that French whore perfume you wear. You reek of cigarettes!" He turns away from her.

Billie slinks back to her station, but the cigarette smell stays behind. Nauseous, Rudy rushes to the back of the salon and throws up his morning breakfast of tomato juice, four egg whites, and three slices of turkey bacon into the color sink. He nervously grabs the paper towels and begins to wipe the sink before anyone sees what he is doing. Losing his breakfast is one thing, losing his composure in front of his staff is something he will not tolerate.

He shoves the vomit-ridden towels into the garbage and then throws an entire can of bleach on top of them to conceal the smell. He splashes his face with water, shoves four Altoids into his mouth, and prepares to greet his client.

Rudy's swish across the polished wood floors of his salon is minus a sway or two, but he still manages a smile for Mr. Todd. "Good morning, sir! How are you today?" Rudy picks up his comb and scissors.

"Enough with the chatter, I've got a meeting to get to this morning."

Their appointment appears to be nothing out of the ordinary. Mr. Todd reads his *Wall Street Journal* while Rudy searches for hair to trim. He knows Mr. Todd comes more out of routine than need, but will take his money regardless.

Without looking up from his paper, Mr. Todd leans to his right and whispers in Rudy's ear. "You're looking a little thin, Rudolph. Someone like me could stand to lose a few pounds, but if you lose any more weight people might begin to talk."

The stench of Mr. Todd's coffee breath lingers in the air, along with a statement so insightful, Rudy is astonished at his client's casual delivery of it. If this man, who only utters good morning and the occasional order has noticed Rudy's appearance, the whole world must. The statement leaves Rudy standing with scissors in hand, unable to answer. He cuts Mr. Todd's hair in record time.

"Make sure the girl up front puts me down for the same time in four weeks. You will be here, won't you?" Mr. Todd hands him a twenty.

"Certainly, sir! I never miss a day of work." Rudy answers him, and then rushes to the bathroom to throw up again.

He holds the porcelain sides of the toilet and notices the cleaning crew isn't doing a very good job. The vomit rushes from his stomach to the back of his throat and then finally gains momentum as it thrusts out of his mouth and into the bowl. He looks down into the toilet and watches the yellow bile mix with clear water. They swirl around one another, mixing a past with a future he doesn't want to see. He flushes the reminder out of sight and then stands and stares at himself in the mirror.

His handsome face is pale, despite the trip to the tanning booth yesterday. The gold and brown Dolce and Gabbana silk shirt that once fit his finely toned body now hangs on his frame like a young man wearing his daddy's shirt. He notices a trickle of bile running down the front of it, but feels helpless to do anything about it. He watches the bead of dribble fall onto his pants, unable to muster the strength to wipe it off.

The last two months have seen a steady decline in his health. Despite his attempts at telling himself its mind over matter, he can't help but think the matter he is trying to ignore is lying on white crumpled letterhead from the county hospital, inside his bedside dresser.

Past illnesses he could once cure with a large snifter of the finest brandy now linger like an unwanted houseguest. Trips to the gym find him exhausted and sweating profusely after only ten minutes, and now Mr. Todd, a man who doesn't notice anything outside of his precisely timed world, has noticed his weight loss.

"Fuck!" He falls over on the cold floor.

Someone knocks on the door of the bathroom, but he is unable to answer. He lies in a couture lump on the marble floor of the bathroom waiting for the dizzy spell to pass. The pain in his chest will not dissipate, along with the reality of what seems inevitable.

"Rudy?" He recognizes Maive's voice.

He whispers, “Yes,” but she doesn’t hear him.

“Rudy?” She pounds harder.

He hears feet gathering outside the door then a scrambling of heels running away.

“Don’t leave me!” He yells in a whisper.

He lies helpless on the floor for what seems like forever until a key turns the lock on the door and he sees Maive staring down at him. He tries to think of something witty or sarcastic to say, something that sounds vaguely like his usual dialogue, but all he can muster are the words, “Take me to the hospital.”

Maive Henry

She stands at her kitchen sink, washing dishes and thinking about what happened at the salon. It had been a blessing that she was the one who found Rudy. She quickly announced it was latte time and that she was buying, and the entire staff scrambled next door for a break. Everyone except for Billie, who insisted Maive tell her what was going on.

Billie has an unusual attachment to Rudy, but it's something Maive has seen before. The ideal of the perfect man is a myth unless you know a gay one, and Rudy fits the bill. He's charming, handsome, funny, loves to gossip, and loves to shop. But he is gay and no woman, no matter how appealing, is going to change that. Billie must know that! But her reaction to Rudy lying on the bathroom floor was so strange.

"Open the door of the salon and let's get him in your car." Maive held Rudy's head in her hands and turned towards Billie.

Billie said nothing, did nothing, she just stared in awe at Rudy.

"Damn it, Billie!" Maive yelled at her, and then dragged him to the back door herself.

"Don't put him in my car!"

Maive glared at her. "Then go get mine!"

Within a few minutes Billie returned with Maive's car.

"I'm leaving for the day." Billie covered her mouth as she looked down at Rudy and then ran towards her car, crying.

Tears fall down Maive's cheeks as she thinks about Rudy sitting in a hospital bed, not only fighting an illness, but the rumors that will inevitably spread once the word gets out that he's in there.

In the meantime, she'll do her best to keep things calm at the salon and try to think about happier times. Like vacations spent abroad, her four dogs and how much she loves them, and the time she saw Benjamin walking with them on the beach. "You get out of my head, you bastard!" She yells to the ceiling.

Despite her attempts at trying not to think about Benjamin, it seems that everywhere she goes she runs into him. Their meetings are always the same. He gives her a feisty schoolboy grin like he's seeing boobies for the first time and she gives a half smile, folds her arms, and sends off every unspoken signal she can think of to let him know to leave her alone.

But he's relentless. Like the time at the grocery store.

She had to admit that his charm was a tad contagious and his hazel eyes did twinkle rather nicely when he smiled at her. His teeth were perfectly straight and so white against the backdrop of his tanned skin. His arms were rather muscular and hairy, but not ape-like or too bulgy. A patch of chest hair had been visible at the opening in his shirt and the dark blue pants he was wearing certainly shaped him nicely, but he looked rather fancy for someone who was only grocery shopping. On the other hand, she looked like a frump, wearing cut off shorts, a t-shirt, and flip flops.

If she isn't mistaken, people like Rudy might refer to Benjamin as a metrosexual. And of course, everyone knows metrosexuals collect women like they collect clothing and they only eat fancy food. Like the items in his cart. Forget it! He's way too high maintenance for her. He would be repulsed if he saw what she ate.

But that boyish grin! And those hokey lines about the fish! She couldn't help but laugh or take in his scent, despite her best attempt at not trying to find him funny or attractive. Why did he have to be so damn handsome? And so healthy! It only makes her nervous.

She can appreciate the vegan thing, but organic? The only thing organic she has ever eaten were those carrots she planted last year and that was only because she bought the wrong package.

A man like Benjamin might think he wants to take someone like Maive out, but in the end he will find her too passé, too boring, not flashy enough. He is better off with someone like Frederica. They're both good-looking people and they both probably dress up to take the garbage out. Who is she kidding? They probably never take the garbage out.

"I can't! I can't do this again!" She scrubs furiously at a pan.

At a knock on the door she looks up into her reflection in the window and pushes her long hair behind her ears. She brushes her hands down her pants to remove any wrinkles and walks towards the door. Secretly, she hopes it will be Benjamin.

She imagines herself opening the door to find him standing there. They look up at one another and he pulls her towards him. He takes her in his arms as she inhales his cologne and his entire being in one breath. His lips touch hers first, kissing her softly then hard, until they are ravenous in their desire for one another. He pulls her across the kitchen floor and down the hallway into her bedroom, kissing her the entire time. He stops for only a moment to throw her on the bed, and then undresses himself in front of her while she lies in a trembling heap on her bed. Benjamin moves slowly towards her, like a cat ready to pounce, and then kisses her again. He removes her clothing, never looking down at her body or away from her face. "You're the most beautiful woman I have ever known." He whispers in her ear. She cries as she hears his words, and then says, "But you barely know me." He looks up at her and shakes his head in disbelief. "You're wrong, Maive. I do know you. I know that you have been hurt and are leery of every man who looks your way. I know you long to love someone and have that love returned. I know that you gave your heart to someone unworthy and in return you felt worthless. But mostly, Maive, I know I love you and I'll do whatever it takes to be with you."

"Anybody here?" Mabel's raspy voice calls out from the front hallway. She walks into the kitchen and sees Maive. "For the love of Abraham! I was beginning to think you were murdered or something."

Maive looks up at Mabel with a glaze in her eyes.

"What's gotten into you, Maive?"

"Nothing! I was just thinking. That's all."

"Thinking about what?"

"Nothing."

"I've been alive a long time and I have never seen "nothing" produce a look like that on someone's face."

The image of Rudy in the hospital returns and she begins to cry uncontrollably.

"What is it?" Mabel asks.

"Rudy's sick."

Katrina Emery

Pacing back and forth in front of the Park Avenue Café, she has an urge for a cigarette but asks a passerby for a stick of gum instead. Now is not the time to reveal a nasty habit, especially when she's so close to closing the deal.

It has been one week since she has seen David, a lot longer than she thought it would be, but she is certain this will be the meeting where he tells her he is going to leave his wife. If not, she will turn and walk away the moment he says otherwise.

She sees him in the distance. His hair is curly, not in the usual slicked-back manner, and he is smiling from ear to ear. He looks relaxed, so Katrina takes this as a good sign.

When David sees Katrina, he runs towards her and presents her with a pink rose. "You are more beautiful than this flower and I can hardly wait to spend the rest of my life with you."

She reaches her hands towards his. "Oh, David! I knew that you felt the same way about me as I do about you."

"I do, Katrina! I do! That's why I'm telling my wife about us tonight."

"Tonight? Honestly, David!" She takes her hands away and turns to leave.

"Wait! Don't go!"

"I can't take another minute of these false promises or false commitments."

"But I am committed! I have something that will show you how committed I am to you." David takes a small black box from his pocket. He gets down on the sidewalk on one knee and takes her hand. "This belonged to my grandmother. I want you to wear it until we can pick out something together." He opens the box.

Inside is the most beautiful ring Katrina has ever seen. The yellow diamond in the middle is at least four carats and the pear-shaped diamonds on either side of it must be a carat each. "David, it's gorgeous! I don't know what to say." She stares at the ring, her eyes becoming as large as the diamond itself as he places it on her left hand.

"Say you'll love me forever!"

"Oh, David! I will! I will!" She hugs him.

"You've made me so happy, Katrina!"

She stares down at the ring, admiring the way the sun shines on its many facets. "You make me so happy!" She waves her hand back and forth. "I love you!"

"I'm glad you like it! You have no idea what I went through to get it."

"I'm worth it!" She leans over and kisses him, pushing her breasts snugly up against his chest.

"Come have lunch with me." He holds her hands, motioning his head towards the restaurant.

She pouts. "Oh, darling, I wish I could, but I have my class this afternoon. Once you leave your wife, we can eat together whenever you want. Oh, Davie! I can hardly wait to show you how happy you've made me!"

"Are you sure you can't stay with me for awhile? We can go inside and have a drink to celebrate." He squeezes her hands.

"We will celebrate, David, as soon as you end things with your wife." She lets go of his hands.

This appeases David, who can only think of seeing her naked again. "I'll do it tonight. I promise!"

"Call me the moment you tell your wife. I want to know the second you've done it! No more running around, no more lies, no more quick love-making sessions. Just you and me, David! Together! Forever!" She blows him a kiss and hails a cab.

"Where to, miss?" The cabbie asks, as he blows smoke from his cigarette.

"Sixty-third and Third."

"Shall I take Park Avenue or Third?"

"Take whatever you want! You wouldn't happen to have another one of those, would you?" She points to his cigarette, and then turns back and waves goodbye to David.

David watches the cab until it is out of sight. He can hardly wait to end things with Stacy and fondle Katrina's beautiful breasts again. He hails a cab himself and tells the driver to take him to Penn Station. Tonight he'll tell Stacy the news, tomorrow he'll be on a plane to Chicago to close the biggest deal of his career, and Friday he'll be with Katrina.

Stacy Kornberg-Adelstein

Thursday morning Stacy rolls over to an empty side of the bed and bursts into tears. Perhaps the night before was only a nightmare. That's it! A nightmare! She calls out to David, awaiting his reply. "David? David?" She yells, but there is no answer.

Feeling weak, she makes her way to the kitchen to try and cook something to eat. She stares down at the package of bacon and the carton of eggs. It's a perfect combination, like peanut butter and jelly. Everybody has a perfect combination, even Debbie and Dan. But where's hers? It's certainly not David! She can't believe this is happening to her. Not again! She won't let it.

There is only one thing she can do to preserve her dignity and the perfect life she has worked so hard to maintain. She walks over to the telephone and dials her number.

Ethel's sandpaper voice answers after the fourth ring. "Hello?"

"Ethel, it's me, Stacy."

"What time is it? It must be before eleven! What is it, dear? Is David okay? Is something wrong with the kids?"

"It's David!" Stacy sobs.

"What's happened to him? Oy vay! My David!" Ethel begins to cry.

"Ethel, calm yourself! He's been cheating on me!"

"What?" She stops crying. "There must be some mistake."

"I'm so distraught! The girl who works in his office told me."

"Well you can't believe everything you hear and besides, that poor thing eats too much, her brain is probably clogged."

"No, it's true! She asked me about some lingerie I never received and there have been phone calls on his cell phone bill that I don't recognize. When I confronted him, he told me he isn't happy in our marriage. What am I going to do? I'll have to leave the area!"

"Nonsense, dear! You will do nothing of the sort! What exactly did David tell you?"

"He said he was leaving me! All this time I thought he was working in the city, Ethel. Now I've found out he was working, but it was on someone else! Oh, Ethel! What if he loves her?"

"Michegas! He can never love anyone like he loves you. You're the mother of his children and my daughter- in-law. I won't have any of this shanda! Tell me exactly what happened."

"I came home from lunch at the club and he was sitting in the living room having a drink. P.S., he's been doing a little too much of that lately. Anyway, he said he wanted to talk to me and I said, 'Is this about the lingerie you bought some whore?' He came at me, Ethel! I've never seen him like that before. He said, 'She's no whore! I love her, Stacy. This is so hard for me, but I want to leave you for her.'" Ethel doesn't speak, so Stacy continues. "I should have known something like this would happen. I found a photo!"

"There's a photo?" Ethel raises her voice an octave.

"Of a girl! I found it in David's apartment when we were dating. She's so beautiful! I bet she is the one he is seeing."

"Stacy, what are you talking about?"

"When David and I were dating, I found a picture of a girl on a beach. It looks like it was taken out at your summer house. He looks so happy in the photo."

"Stacy, this is very important. Did you show David the picture? Did he tell you the girl's name?"

"No, but I did call the number on his cell phone bill. A woman with a sexy voice answers but doesn't give her name. I'm so embarrassed! Everyone will find out! The kids! Bubbe! Oh, my Bubbe! She'll never be able to take the news. And you and Adam! This will ruin you in the community! What will everyone say?"

Stacy grins slightly. She can practically hear Ethel contemplating her choices. It's either death or a fast departure from the country. The first thing Ethel's friends will wonder is what she did wrong to raise a son who would do such a thing. She'll be the laughing stock. They'll all say how sorry they are to her face, but behind her back they'll all secretly revel in her failure as a mother. After all, everyone loves to see someone perfect fail.

"Don't you worry, Stacy. I'll make sure this mess

goes away. Since Lily is away at camp, I want you to take Joshie to Tuscany for awhile. You've been through a lot, dear, there's no need to worry yourself anymore about this little blip in your marriage."

"Blip? Ethel, I don't know if I can look past this indiscretion. I'm not sure I want David to have any influence over my new baby."

"New baby? You're pregnant?"

All she has to do is tell a small lie and she knows Ethel will be indebted to her forever. Stacy takes a deep breath. "Yes, a couple of weeks."

In the end, if David returns, a couple of weeks will mean nothing over the course of nine long months. All she has to do is get him to have sex with her, and with the help of her ovulation predictor, getting pregnant should be a snap. And if it doesn't happen right away or if David doesn't come home, Stacy will say she miscarried and blame it all on the stress of his leaving her.

"This is a hilf, Stacy!" Ethel sounds elated.

"A what?"

"A Godsend! A miracle! David is no fool. He will realize he needs to be with you and his family."

"But the shame of the affair! I don't think I can look past it, Ethel."

"Nonsense!" Ethel blurts out. "We've all learned to look past these indiscretions. If you take a look around your home and the life he has provided for you, it becomes relatively easy to do so. And if you have a hard time in the beginning, just spend a little more money. In a short time David will realize the only place he belongs is with you."

Stacy feels liberated as Ethel becomes human and divulges a side to her perfect marriage that is anything but. Apple, tree. David had said he was more like his father and apparently he was right.

At this moment Stacy realizes she has the upper hand. The affair, albeit painful and disgusting to her, has been the best thing that could have ever happened to her and her relationship with the Adelsteins. Only a short time ago she was a mere player in the game, but today she holds all the cards.

"Ethel? How can he do this to us? Aren't I a good wife and mother?" She awaits the response she longs to hear.

"Of course, dear! You're an amazing mom and a terrific wife. I hand-picked you myself! I attended synagogue every Friday night for months trying to find the right girl for David and just when I thought I was going to have to start looking in Hotzeplotz, I saw you. Do you remember, Stacy?"

"I do remember." Stacy says, rolling her eyes. Ethel hadn't been subtle when she knocked her purse on the floor in front of Stacy and asked for her help in picking up her items. Among a lipstick case, a pill case, and hand sanitizer, were pictures of David.

"I'm sure this is all a big misunderstanding. Tell me where David is right now."

"You can reach him on his cell phone. He went to Chicago. Oh, Ethel! What am I going to do?" Stacy begins to cry.

"You go upstairs and pack a suitcase for you and

Joshie. This will all be over soon."

Stacy knows she won't have to do anything to David because Ethel will do it all. Stacy doubts she will ever be compared to Janet Stein-Shapiro or Debbie and her snotty-nosed brat ever again.

"Thank you, Ethel! I knew ya would know what to do to avoid an embarrassment of such proportions. While we are being so close and sharing secrets, can I ask you a favor?" Stacy grins from ear to ear.

"You can ask me anything!"

"Do ya think the kids can call you grandma? It will mean so much to them! They already have a Bubbe and they call my mom Nanny. It will make them feel more secure, all of us more secure. With our roles, I mean."

Ethel is silent, but Stacy remains calm. She knows this trick too well. The longer the pause, the more Ethel intimidates, until finally you give in. But not this time!

"Of course, darling! It's such a novel idea."

"Thank you so much for understanding." Stacy hangs up the telephone, jumping up and down. Ethel agreeing to being called grandma is something to celebrate. Now all she has to do is put her marriage back together.

David's good points had waned early in their marriage once Stacy realized the line David walked veered closer towards Ethel than it did towards her. If she had known Ethel was going to be such a monster, she would have stayed in Italy and taken the chance that her family would disown her instead of marrying David.

But today is the beginning of something different, something grander than Stacy could have ever imagined. Only yesterday she feared the telephone when it rang, hoping it wasn't Ethel on the other line. From now on, Ethel will fear Stacy's calls, hoping it isn't more bad news about her precious David.

"A hilf, indeed!" Stacy smugly says.

Maive Henry

"Come on, guys! It's time for your walk."

All fours dogs come running from her bedroom and wait by the back door. She grabs their leashes and walks outside. They all run off in the same direction, lifting their legs to spray the tall grasses. Dunkin walks ahead of the others and begins to bark. Soon the other three join in and then take off towards the beach.

"Dunkin, come back here! Buster! Sammy! Cricket!" Maive yells to them, but they ignore her. Her heart races as she picks up speed and chases after them.

When she makes it over the top of the sand dune she sees Dunkin with his two front paws wrapped around a man's neck. The other three dogs are circling around him, wagging their tales and barking. He reaches down to pet them all until Dunkin knocks him off his feet. They all stand over him and lick his face.

Maive bursts into tears. This wonderful, handsome man has been trying for months to get her to notice that he is special and it has taken the dogs no time at all. How could she have cheated herself of such love?

"Benjamin?" She calls out to him.

"Hi, Maive! I sure do miss these guys!"

Maive smiles, and extends her hand to help him up.

"Sorry if my hand is a bit wet, Buster was licking it."

"That's okay! I'm used to his kisses." She looks down for a moment and then back at Benjamin. "I've been thinking, Benjamin!"

"Ah, don't do that!" He brushes off his pants.

"I hope you'll like what I was thinking."

"And what might that be?" He looks in her eyes.

She looks out at the ocean. "About coffee! You asked me if we could have coffee together."

"You mean it?"

"Yes, Benjamin! I'd love to have coffee with you, but only after we have dinner. I'll invite Mabel, too." She turns to look at him and waits for his response.

"Of course! I realize you're a person with a deep "sole" and you need time, so I'm willing to have dinner with her, too. We'll have a "whale" of a time!"

She bursts into laughter. "On one condition though."

"Any condition you request, Maive, except coloring my hair. I can't do the hair color thing. Not yet, anyway."

"No need to worry! Can you stop the fish talk? It's a little corny." She pinches her two fingers together.

He closes a pretend zipper across his mouth. "I'm "clamming" up as we speak."

They both look at each other and burst into laughter.

David Adelstein

Looking out the window of his hotel room, he gazes at the lights of the Chicago skyline and lets out a heavy sigh. He presses re-dial on his cell phone, but only gets Katrina's answering machine again. He'll watch some television and try her again later.

He flips through the channels, doing his best to forget about his conversation with Stacy and how hysterical she had become. Although he had originally not wanted to say too much, she had now heard it all. Even he had been surprised at himself and the overwhelming feeling he had to protect Maive when Stacy called her a whore.

Maive? Where did that come from? It's Katrina he's in love with. Maive is ancient history! Katrina is nothing like Maive.

He thinks about Maive for a moment and the last time he saw her. It had been the night she went out with Janet and a bunch of her friends. She looked so gorgeous! They had been together all afternoon eating lunch at E.J.'s, walking through Central Park, and making love at his apartment before she headed out for the night.

The night he realized that they could never be together.

Losing her had been the biggest loss of his life. He had hoped that she would get the letter and ignore it, come rushing after him, and tell him that they could get through anything together, but she hadn't. When several weeks went by and he still had not heard from her, he called the salon where she worked and learned she had moved out of Manhattan. She had obviously met someone else and moved on, just as he had expected she would. He knew then that she never truly cared for him the way he had cared for her, so he gave in to his family and their incessant meddling into his life and married Stacy.

His eyes begin to feel heavy as he watches an *I Dream of Genie* re-run, so he leans into his pillow and falls into a deep sleep.

He's at the helm of a sailboat again. The sun is bright and ocean surrounds him on all sides. He hears a woman call his name and he turns to smile at her. She waves to him and blows him a kiss and the warmth returns to his heart. He knows this is where he belongs, where he is finally home. With her. With Maive.

David sits straight up in bed. Sun light is peeking through the curtains of his hotel room. He turns to look at the clock on his bedside table and lets out a sigh of relief. Two minutes later the telephone rings with his wake up call.

Although he has a meeting in two hours and needs to mentally prepare, all he can think about is Maive. But why now? He's anxious, that's all. He's got Katrina. She's a wonderful girl and has so much to offer. He takes out a piece of paper and writes down the qualities he likes about Katrina.

Great in bed
Good listener
Dresses nice

Maive had all of those qualities, but so much more. There's something missing with Katrina. He thinks about it for a moment.

"Laughter!" He says, and throws his hands up in the air. Katrina never laughs at his jokes and he's a funny guy. He wants to laugh! And dessert, she never orders it! Maive always did. He can't freaking believe this! She IS a substitute for Maive. What he wants is Maive, not Katrina! It's always been Maive.

Where does he go from here?

First things first! He's got to take care of business. He'll go to his meeting and then he'll find a way to get Maive back. He'll deal with the messy business of breaking things off with Katrina later. She shouldn't take it so badly. They haven't been together that long! How committed can she possibly…

"Oh, shit!" He yells. "Grandma's ring!"

Maive Henry

"In our last session I talked to you about your need for the Adelsteins' approval. Have you given any thought to that?" She looks over her notes as she speaks.

"Yes, as a matter of fact I have, Dr. Fine, and I've realized two things." She sits in a chair and holds two fingers up.

"What's that, Maive?" Dr. Fine looks over her glasses at her.

"I think I've looked for approval my whole life; first with my parents, then with my friends, and finally with boyfriends. I don't know why, but I always look for someone to pat me on the head and tell me I'm terrific. I think I'm in the worst profession possible. It's people's hair, for Pete's sake! Nobody ever likes their own hair!"

"I suppose you're right about that." She rolls her pen back and forth in her hands and listens intently.

"And since I am always looking for approval, the worst people I could have ever met were the Adelsteins because they don't approve of anything. Not even each other! If my last name was Gucci they'd wish it was Prada!" She begins pacing back and forth, swaying her hands to and fro. "I had the worst self-esteem when I met them!"

"Why do you think that?" She folds her hands and waits for a response.

"Dr. Fine, that alone would keep me in therapy for the rest of my life. Who knows, maybe I wasn't told I was pretty enough or smart enough when I was a girl. Whatever the reason, it doesn't matter anymore. What matters now is that I have to stop trying to get everyone's approval." She walks over and pours herself a cup of coffee.

"My goodness! You've made such progress!"

"I've had to!" She stirs in a Sweet 'N Low and cream.

"What was the other thing you realized?"

She looks at Dr. Fine. "Without realizing it, I had become like the Adelsteins because I was judging people before I even got to know them. I understand now that it doesn't matter why David broke things off with me, he did and I'm better off for it."

"It makes me so happy to see that you have finally understood this."

"Well it's taken me long enough, hasn't it?"

Dr Fine moves her head back and forth.

"It's okay, Dr. Fine. I know I've been very stubborn. It takes some of us a bit longer to understand that there are creepy people wherever you go and race or religion has nothing to do with it." She sits back down in the chair. "I can't even think about how rotten I've been, not to mention ignorant, for completely disregarding people because of one bad experience. It was so wrong of me."

"Yes, it was wrong, but you were hurt. I knew you

would come around." Dr. Fine puts her hand on her shoulder.

"My neighbor called me a reverse snob."

"A reverse snob?"

"Yes! It makes perfect sense to me. The Adelsteins may have judged me for what I'm not, but I judged them for what they are."

"Which is?"

"Well everything I'm not! Rich, educated, Jewish. But those are just labels. Labels might be important to the Adelsteins, but they've never been important to me. Labels don't make a person better or worse, they don't define someone, don't guarantee acceptance. I could have gone to college, but I didn't want to. As far as money goes, I make a pretty decent living and don't want for anything, except maybe romance. As far as being Jewish goes, I had never had any experience with Jewish people before until I met David and his family. I made a very bad assumption that I would always have to put up with an Ethel if I dated another Jewish man."

"You are so right, Maive! About everything! I guess the real test will be if you are ready to let go and forgive."

"Oh, please, Dr. Fine! Are you going to tell me I have to forgive the Adelsteins for the way they treated me?" She looks up at Dr. Fine.

"No, I'm telling you to forgive yourself for having allowed them to."

Maive bursts into tears. "Look at me! I'm such a sap!"

Dr. Fine pushes the box of tissues towards her. "No you're not, you're finally opening up. You're allowing your heart to heal."

"I'm so afraid."

"Of course you are! Exposing yourself to people is never easy, but well worth it. Who knows, maybe if you really open up you might give this man named Benjamin a chance. What's going on with him anyway?" Dr. Fine crosses her legs and removes her glasses.

"I can't stop thinking about him! I feel giddy, like a little kid." She smiles from ear to ear. "He's the most marvelous man I've ever met! The other day he was on the beach and the dogs went running over to him. It was so great! I couldn't believe how he loved them, how they loved him."

"Have you made any plans to see him?" She wipes her glasses on a tissue.

"As a matter of fact, I'm having dinner with him. Well, him and my neighbor."

"Dinner? Wow! Good work, Maive! You sound like a person who has got it together."

"I think most of the credit belongs to you, Dr. Fine." She rummages through her purse and looks for her keys.

"So do you still think you need closure with David?"

Maive thinks about it for a moment. "I hope David found someone his family approves of and that she makes him happy."

"That's very generous of you." Dr. Fine looks at her and smiles.

"I really mean it! I've finally realized that I am better off without him. I don't have to question anything anymore. You know, like what to wear, if I'm saying the right thing, using the right fork, if I have something in my teeth. I just want to be myself and have someone love me for every faux pas." She looks down at her watch. "On that note, I've got to get home and start cooking." She gets up and walks towards Dr. Fine.

"Is your dinner tonight?"

"Yes! Can you believe it? I'm so nervous!" She wipes her hands down her jeans.

"You'll do great, Maive! Shall I schedule you for next week?" Dr. Fine looks down at her calendar.

Maive smiles at Dr. Fine. "Can I check in with you once in awhile?"

"Sure!"

Maive hugs Dr. Fine. "Goodbye, Dr. Fine. Thanks for everything!"

"Maive, it's been my pleasure. Perhaps you will see me on your appointment book one day."

"I'd like that, Dr. Fine. It will be a nice way for me to get back some of the money I've spent coming here."

"That's the attitude, Maive! Congratulations!"

She leaves Dr. Fine's office and takes a deep breath. For the first time in years she finally feels like she is seeing her life from a different perspective. As she drives along the shore, she glances out at the ocean and its endless array of blues. David used to tell her there were three things he never got tired of staring at; the ocean, a fire, and her.

"Sailor's delight." She smiles, as she looks up at the sky's brilliant shades of red and orange. That was another thing David taught her. He wasn't all bad, but he wasn't for Maive, she realizes that now. She needs someone stronger, more grounded, a real man. Someone not afraid to go after what he wants. Someone who will appreciate her the way she is and not try to change her.

As she pulls into the driveway, a song by Hot Tuna plays on the radio and she immediately thinks of Benjamin. She walks towards her door humming the tune. She hears the telephone ringing and runs to answer it. It might be Rudy's nurse calling from the hospital.

"Hello?" She answers, but the caller on the other end doesn't say a word. She hears breathing, but no one speaks. "Hello?" She asks again, but the only sound she hears is a hang up.

She steps back and stares at the phone. What if it were David? Suddenly everything she said to Dr. Fine goes away, along with her pleasant thoughts of Benjamin. Will she always be committed to David in her heart and be unable to move on?

Her phone rings again and she picks it up on the first ring. "Hello?"

"Maive, honey, it's Desiree."

"Oh, hi." She wonders how Desiree got her number. Rudy must have given it to her.

"Is there a death or something? Nice to hear your voice, too!" She blows smoke in the receiver.

"I'm sorry. I thought you might be someone else."

She rolls her eyes and looks on the shelves for something to eat.

"I have to talk to somebody and I can't get a hold of Rudy."

"He's been away." Maive hesitates, and then asks, "Is there something I can help you with?"

"No, I need to speak with Rudy. Hey, why didn't you call me when you were in the city?"

"I was real busy." She gets a mozzarella stick from the refrigerator and takes a bite.

"Busy, huh? I'm busy, too! I'm calling to ask Rudy to be in my wedding."

"Your wedding?" Maive drops the cheese.

"You sound shocked, Maive. Yes, my wedding! I've met this wonderful man and he's asked me to marry him."

"Really? Is this the married man you've been dating?" She pours herself some seltzer and gets another piece of cheese.

"Which one?" She laughs.

"The fashion guy." She looks through the cabinets for some crackers.

"No, not Gary! This is somebody new that I met who also happens to be married, but not for long."

"Well good for you, bad for her. Does he know what you do for a living?" She takes a bite of cracker.

"Yes! Well, sort of."

"How do you expect to have a decent marriage if it's not built on trust?" Buster runs in and Maive bends down to pet him.

"You and that God damn Catholic education! I

swear, that school ruined you." She blows smoke again.

"I was only there a year and it has nothing to do with the school. It's morally correct, that's all." She takes a sip of seltzer and looks over her list of things to do.

"Miss Morals! Do you want to hear about him or not?"

Maive rolls her eyes. She only wants to start making dinner for Benjamin and couldn't care less about Desiree's new man. "What's his name?" She takes a deep breath and exhales.

"David."

"Did you say David?" Maive puts down the crackers and looks out her kitchen window.

"Yes! You know, Maive, they say the hearing is the first thing to go."

Maive ignores the comment. "What does he look like? Where did you meet him? What does he do for a living?" She starts putting dishes in the sink and wiping them.

"What's the sudden interest?"

"Nothing! It's just that I dated someone named David once." She wipes the dishes and slams them in the drying rack.

"That's right! The one who broke your heart! Rudy has told me all about him. Honestly, Maive, do you really think you and I would attract the same man? Look at you! You don't even know your worth."

"What's that supposed to mean?" She puts down a plate she is washing.

"If you loved that guy so much and he loved you, why didn't you get something for it?"

"I did!"

"How many carats was it?"

"I didn't get jewelry, Desiree. I got companionship." She blows on a piece of hair that's in her face.

"Oh, please! You should hear yourself. Talk to me when you score a ring the size I did!"

"So your hard work finally paid off, huh? What's this guy do for a living?" She asks, while pulling out pots and pans.

"Finance!" She sings the word. "He works at a hedge fund. Razor's Edge, National Edge, something with an edge."

She drops a lid on the floor. "Advantage Edge?"

"Yeah, that's it! How'd you know? He makes a shit load of money! He didn't buy the ring he gave me, it's his grandmothers, but I'm not going to worry myself about that now. All that matters is that he's mine and so is all of his money!"

Maive picks up the lid. She takes a few deep breaths to calm herself. It can't possibly be the same David! "What exactly does your ring look like?"

"It's a round, yellow diamond with pear-shaped diamonds on either side of it."

It has to be a coincidence. There's no way Ethel would relinquish that ring. Maive had noticed it all the way across the dance floor at Debbie's wedding. She remembers commenting to Ethel about it later that evening and her telling Maive that it had been in her family for three generations.

"Are you taking his last name or are you going to keep yours? Whatever it is you are going by these days."

"No, I'm taking his! I'm ready to give up my past and taking his last name is just the accessory I need to do that."

"And what might that be?" Maive holds her breath.

"Adelstein! I am going to be Mrs. David Adelstein!"

Maive grabs her mouth as her stomach wretches. It can't be true! What could have happened to him? He must have changed. "I can't…I can't understand how…" She slides down the side of the stove and onto the floor.

"How what? How I'm so lucky and you're not? Maive, please! It all goes back to your worth. I keep telling you this."

"My worth, huh?" She shakes her head.

"Yes! You give yourself away. Always giving your time, your love, your kindness. Honestly, Maive! If you stopped giving so much of yourself away for free and started asking for things like I do, you might get engaged, too."

An anger surges through Maive that she has never felt before. She thinks about all of the time she has spent thinking about David, while he was off screwing someone like Desiree. How in the hell could he fall for someone like her? He's even worse than she ever could have imagined.

She screams into the phone, "I hope you and David will be happy! You two are clearly meant for one another! And you're wrong about me not knowing my worth, Desiree. At least I don't give myself away to the highest bidder night after night at a topless bar or fill my body with whatever drug I can find."

"You need to get laid, Maive!"

"You need to go to therapy, Desiree! And one more thing, don't ever call me again, you miserable, rotten, self-loathing bitch!" Maive hangs up and takes a deep breath.

The David Adelstein that Desiree is marrying cannot possibly be the same David Adelstein she was once in love with.

Or is he?

She throws a dishtowel across the kitchen and curses David at the top of her lungs. Not only is he married now, he's having an affair with Desiree. What a complete loser! She is so much better off without him. It could have been her he was screwing around on.

All of a sudden her anger is overcome by a loud, voracious laughter, thinking about Desiree sailing on David's boat. David better have a lot of money because he is going to need a staff of seven to appease Miss Maintenance.

Mabel is right! This time the ole gal is right. David was not the one.

She walks to her closet and takes down the box filled with a life that no longer exists. Lightness fills her body as she pitches it into the garbage. She lets herself think about the possibility of filling a new box with new memories and becomes excited at the idea. She had heard that you need to clear out the old before you can make way for the new, so she stares at the gaping hole on the top of her closet, wondering what the new will look like.

Her telephone rings and her heart flutters, hopeful that it is Benjamin.

David Adelstein

After spending the morning tracking her down, he stares down at the number and dials his phone.

"Hello?" She answers after the first ring.

"Maive? It's me, David."

There is no response.

"Maive, are you there? I've made a horrible mistake, Maive! I realize that now. I should have never let you go."

Still no response.

"Can you please say something so I know you hear me?"

"I'm here, David. How did you get my number?"

"I knew you moved to Sanibel Island because I kept tabs on you for awhile. I must have called every salon until I found the one you work at. Oh, Maive! Have you thought about me? Have you thought about what our lives would be like if we had gotten married?"

She doesn't answer.

"I've always loved you, Maive! I've never loved anyone else. I was weak. I never should have let you go. Do you think you could forgive me and give us another chance?"

She bursts into tears and David takes it as a yes.

"I've made some bad choices and I will have to pay for them. I never should have gotten married to my wife, Stacy. I never loved her, Maive. What you and I had was special. It was genuine."

Maive sighs heavily. "Aren't you forgetting someone?"

"What are you talking about?"

"The real reason you are leaving your wife."

"You're the reason! I've changed, Maive. You'll see!"

"David, if you're finished, I'd like to apologize."

"Apologize? You didn't do anything, Maive. It was all me."

"I'm sorry that your marriage has ended. I'm sorry you have just now discovered that what you and I had together was special, but mostly, David, I'm sorry that I let almost five years of my life go by thinking about someone as unworthy as you. I owe myself an apology, David, not you."

"Maive, what are you saying?" He runs a hand through his hair.

"You don't love me, David. I don't think you know what love is. How could you? It's not like you have a good example of being loved for who you are, but that's not my problem. You have always been more interested in what your parents want than what might be best for you."

"Maive, didn't you hear me? I'm leaving my wife for you!"

"Now why would you go and do a stupid thing like that? Your parents probably love her! I bet SHE has the proper resume, doesn't she?"

"Come on, Maive! You're being ridiculous! Do

you really think that matters to me?"

"In a word? Yes! It's all you've ever known! That, and how to rip people's hearts out!"

"I was young and foolish then. My mom was up to her old tricks and I fell for it. What was I supposed to do?" He sits on the bathroom counter.

She raises her voice. "Listen to your heart! You were supposed to listen to your heart! Just like I'm listening to mine now and it no longer speaks your name. Once a person can see that you have a price, David, they will always own you."

"Don't you think I know that? Maive, I've grown up! Can I come see you?" He starts putting clothes into his suitcase.

"Are you crazy?"

"Crazy for you!"

"You're not listening to a thing I'm saying! You and I have nothing in common, David. Nothing at all!"

"But Maive, I love you! I want you in my life!"

"I don't care what you want, David!"

He stares at himself in the mirror and shakes his head. He feels the pit return to his stomach so he takes a couple of antacids out of his dop kit.

"Did you hear what I said? You and I are through!"

"I heard you. I just… I'm sorry that I hurt you. I wish I could go back and change things, but I can't. I was different then, always concerned about what my parents thought. I actually thought that they wanted what was best for me. That's why I broke up with you. I realize now that all they ever cared about is what is best for them."

"David, if this is an Adelstein history lesson, I'm really not interested!"

"I can understand why you're not, but please know that it will be my greatest regret if you say you won't give me another chance."

She sighs heavily into the phone. "David, it's a little late for this confession, but I will accept the apology."

"Does this mean you will give us another try?" He smiles.

"Are you on drugs?"

"No! Well, actually I just took an antacid, but I'm sure that problem will go away once you say you'll have me back."

"You have one hell of an ego, David!"

"Me, ego? I happen to be one of the most humble people you will ever meet."

"Humble, huh? Is that what Desiree likes best about you?"

"Desiree?"

She exhales loudly. "You're unbelievable! I don't know what you're up to, but I know all about Desiree!"

"Who is Desiree?"

"Honestly, David! You make me sick!" She hangs up the receiver.

David stands with the phone in his hand, unable to hang up. As long as he holds the phone he is still connected to her. He dials her number again and again for the next ten minutes, but it only rings. He'll try her again later. In the meantime, he hangs up and dials Katrina.

Juanita Maria Mendez

She watches the tape from yesterday's show of the *Bold and the Beautiful* while running a brush through the long, blonde-haired wig sitting on the table in front of her. Her own black hair is piled on top of her head and covered with a deep conditioning mask. This is part of her daily ritual, just like working out and working it.

Known as Juanita Maria Mendez back in her homeland of Mexico, she felt that her birth name would never get her into the circles she aspired to be in, so once she moved to New York City her first priority became finding a new identity. After a stack of magazines and numerous television shows didn't inspire her, she turned to the streets of Manhattan.

One day while walking on Madison Avenue, she heard a young woman calling out to a tall, blonde woman getting into a limousine. "Katrina!" She yelled. "Katrina!"

The girl in the car turned around to see who was calling her and her beauty took Juanita's breath away. It was her double; her double if she had been born blonde and into the right family.

She was thin and graceful and moved her hands like a prima ballerina when she turned and waved. She was wearing a Chanel suit with matching shoes and handbag, her eyes hidden behind a large pair of black sunglasses.

Juanita wanted to be that girl, that Katrina, and so she became her.

Once she chose her new first name, she knew it was of the utmost importance to have a last name that gave no clue as to her past or heritage. While watching her favorite soap opera, she meticulously filed her nails, swearing she would get a manicure once a week the second she could afford it. As she glanced down at the file it suddenly dawned on her what a fabulous name it would make. Emery. Katrina Emery.

She uses the name Desiree when she dances. Desire, plus one extra "e." It's a name she adopted at a strip club in Texas. Dancing in clubs is where she first met Rudy. She had been so new to the business then and Rudy had been so kind to her. He used to fix all the girls' hair backstage before he moved away and decided to open up his own place. Even though he knows she has changed her name to Katrina, he still calls her Dez.

"You can't run from your past, girl! People don't change honey, no matter how many times they change their name!" He is quick to tell her.

She supposes he is right, but it would be nice if he would at least acknowledge her attempt at trying to do so, especially since she works so hard at it.

Every detail of her dress, mannerisms, speech, and affect has been perfected. When she's not "working it," she's working at it. Acting classes, keeping up on the latest financial news, hours spent at the library reading about poets, prophets, and even prostitutes. Reading about the latest bar and restaurant openings, who the wealthiest men in the world are, and what they are wearing are all part of her studies. She spends countless hours in clothing shops, jewelry stores, and on the internet to ensure that she doesn't waste any of her time on someone unworthy.

In addition to her studies, her body must remain in perfect condition. She does two-hour gym workouts, Botox and Restylane when needed, and has surgeries to take care of anything that can't be done in a gym. Two boob jobs, two nose jobs, liposuction on her thighs and ass, and a brow lift have all been necessities thus far. Add weekly facials, waxing, and body scrubs, and it's a wonder she has time to meet anyone.

Working men as a career chose her, she didn't choose it. She can't remember a time when she has been without one - a man, that is. They're such simple creatures. So easily lured by a beautiful face and fit body. Most of them are a complete waste of time, unless they are taking her shopping or paying her bills. In order for her to have the ultimate acceptance, she needs to marry one, but not just anyone, a VERY rich one. While she would prefer one that isn't divorced, since it only diminishes his value, she also knows that men can't stand to be alone, so her chances of meeting a wealthy man who hasn't already been married are slim.

She will, however, draw the line at children. They're nothing more than insurance. If she marries a man who wants children, she will only subject her perfect body to the indignity and pain of childbearing and birth if she feels her marriage is threatened in any way, or if there is money or jewelry to be gained by it.

She's quite fond of saying, "Everything you need to know about a man is in his accessories." Anyone can go into a store and have someone pick out a nice suit. Hell! Nowadays you can get a pretty decent one at a second-hand store. It's what they pair with it that counts.

Ties, watches, and shoes are child's play. She can spot a Hermes tie a mile away and when she's not certain of a brand, a simple, "My, what a lovely tie!" followed by a slight caress of the fabric and a very subtle turn to reveal the label always works. Watches were once hard to peg, with all the knock-offs, but she's an old pro now and anything under the value of a Constantin doesn't even get an acknowledgment from her, unless of course the suit is exquisite. Shoes are a no-brainer, and it's simple to distinguish between foreign and domestic.

But none of this means anything in the game of pursuit if the players don't know the rules, and she's far too valuable to play with amateurs.

Speaking of valuables, that reminds her.

She pulls the large canary diamond from its box and marvels at its brilliance. As soon as David gets back into town, she will insist they go to the justice of the peace and get married. An extravagant wedding will have to wait. Getting him to commit is first priority, and this time she isn't about to let anything stand in her way.

A quiver goes up her spine and she giggles like a little girl, imagining herself at the country club with bustling waiters rushing to her side, desperate to please the new Mrs. Adelstein. She is finally going to be the girl on Madison Avenue flitting in one shop and then another, with all of the envious salesgirls clamoring to wait on her.

If she has calculated David's worth correctly, she'll be more than well-off, even after his wife takes half for alimony and child support. His wife will get custody of the children. The power of the pussy will see to that! If Juanita finds out David is not as wealthy as she thinks, she'll divorce him and take what's left of him.

He's probably not as wealthy as Gary, but nobody is. She could have owned half of Madison Avenue if he would have married her. Damn him, anyway! It's all Gary's fault she is marrying David. It should be him she is marrying! He's perfect for her! His kids are older, he has no living relatives, and he never says no to her.

Maybe she should tell Gary she is getting married to someone else. Maybe it will change his mind about him leaving his wife. But what if it doesn't? She's waited so long already and she isn't getting any younger, according to the calendar. It's best to take the proposal she has. Gary had his chance! His meter has officially expired.

The steam from the bathroom pours out into the hallway, beckoning her to perform her daily ritual. She climbs into the tub, closes the curtain behind her, and begins to scrub her olive skin with gritty granules. She scrubs harder, certain that she can take the filth away for letting that Arab caress her breasts last night. At least she didn't take him up on his offer to go home with him and another woman for five thousand dollars. Until David gives her his last name, the playing field is open. Besides, he's still sleeping in the same bed with his wife.

She hears her telephone ring. She shuts off the water and rushes to the phone. It might be Gary begging her to come back to him! Just as she reaches the phone, she hears a hang up on her machine. It's the fifth time this morning.

"Probably that bore, David!" She says, as she climbs back into the shower to finish rinsing off her legs. "Or his wife!" She laughs.

Her phone rings again and she shuts off the water. This time she picks up the phone, ready to annihilate the caller who keeps hanging up on her machine. "What the hell do you want?" She yells into the receiver.

"Katrina? It's me, David. Can you hear me? I'm calling you from Chicago."

She changes her tone. "Hi, sweetheart!"

"I, um..."

"You what, sweetie?" She rolls her eyes.

"I need to get my ring back."

She hears the words, but they don't register at first. She doesn't let them. Although she has had more affairs with married men than she can count, she hasn't actually had one ask for her hand in marriage, only to have it retracted two days later.

She dries herself with a towel. "Is there something

wrong with it, darling?"

"No! Well, not exactly."

"David, you and I are engaged. I'm supposed to have a ring. Why don't you come over so we can talk? We've been away from each other for too long."

"No, that's not it! I can't do this! You see, you reminded me of someone else. Well, not the person, but the way you look, the way you made me feel."

She drops the towel and the sweet tone. "What are you talking about?"

"I never should have let her go. All this time I have been in love with her, unable to forget her, no matter how hard I try."

"I don't understand. Are you saying you don't love me anymore?" She reaches for a cigarette, but the pack is empty. She goes into her kitchen and grabs a bottle of wine and fumbles with the opener.

"That's just it! This is really hard for me to tell you, Katrina, but I never loved you, I just thought that I did."

She doesn't speak, so he continues.

"Katrina, you've meant a lot to me. You showed me how to love again and I am thankful for that, but you and I don't belong together. You must know that."

She stands naked in her kitchen, holding the bottle of wine. It slips through her hands and smashes onto the kitchen floor, along with all of her hopes of living a privileged life. No matter how many times she moves or changes her name, she'll always be Juanita Maria Mendez, the poor girl from Mexico who is only good enough to fuck.

"I'm sorry, Katrina. I really am. I didn't mean to hurt you."

"Well, fuck you!" She screams into the phone.

David pulls the phone from his ear for a moment and swallows hard. "I'm sure there is some way I can make this up to you. I only want the ring back. It belonged to my grandmother. I'm more than happy to help you out if I can, or buy you something. Barneys has really nice things. My wife loves it there!"

"Barneys? Are you fucking kidding me?" She laughs a maniacal laugh. "I don't give a fuck what your wife likes! She obviously has no taste, she likes you. The ring is mine, David! I earned it! I fucked you, remember? Believe me, that was no easy task!" She opens the cupboard and grabs a pint of rum.

"I don't understand. What's going on?"

"I'm going on! Going on with my new ring!"

"You mean you only went out with me to get a piece of jewelry?"

"Wake up, David! This is New York City. People do a lot more and get so much less!"

"What's gotten into you? You don't sound anything like Katrina. You sound like somebody else."

"I am somebody else, David. I'm your worst fucking nightmare! Now hang up the phone and don't ever, ever, call me or come by here again!" She pulls the phone from the wall and throws it across the room.

Ethel Adelstein

She gives her shopping bags to the coat-check girl and looks for Annabelle. She sees her across the salon and rushes over to her. "I love it!" She points to her head, filled with skunk-like striped highlights.

Annabelle stares at Ethel's hair. "You love it?"

"It's perfect!"

"You don't think it's too blonde?"

"There's no such thing! I've already made another appointment for six weeks from now and I want you to do the same thing." Ethel walks away.

She goes into the hallway and presses redial on her phone for the twenty-seventh time this morning. David answers on the first ring. "Are you ready to come home now? Or perhaps I should call back on Monday after you have had a weekend of debauchery."

"I can't have this conversation with you now. I have to get to the airport."

"Are you telling me that you don't have time for me?"

"That's not what I said."

Ethel grabs the robe she is wearing and takes a deep breath. "I can't believe how insensitive you are being! What has gotten into you?"

"Nothing! I just don't have time to talk now."

"You don't have time for your mother? David, you

are forcing me to do something I really don't want to do." She walks towards the pedicure room.

"What's that supposed to mean?"

"I am going to have to call my attorney and have you taken out of the will. I know you don't need the money, I will do it as a matter of principle. Do you really want to see Dan get your half? Believe me, David, I don't want to do something as drastic as this, but I am afraid you are leaving me with no alternative. God knows Stacy isn't the perfect wife, but that doesn't excuse your behavior, especially since she's expecting."

"What? She can't be!"

"I love you, David, surely you must know that. On some level, this mess is probably my fault since I never let the relationship you had with that hairdresser girl expire on its own, but I do know best, David! I know what works and what doesn't."

David doesn't speak.

"I will not have you ruin the good name of this family or shame your father and me after everything we've done for you over some shiksa. Do I make myself clear?" She picks up a bottle of bright red polish and dangles it in front of the manicurist's face.

"You're being way too dramatic, Mom."

"I don't know where this attitude is coming from, but I can tell you that I am very disappointed in you." She turns away from the manicurist and walks back down the hallway.

"You're always disappointed in me. I don't do anything right, but Dan always does!"

"Why are you bringing Dan up? He has nothing

to do with the mess you have made! He works too hard for you to put him down."

"We all work hard, Mom!"

"Well, maybe if you worked a little harder, you wouldn't have time for an affair!" She stops at the kitchen and taps on the counter with her fingernail.

"I am no longer having an affair. I called to break things off with her."

"You did?" She points to the tea sandwiches on the menu.

"I just hung up with her. Well, actually, she hung up on me."

"It doesn't matter who hung up on whom. What matters is that you've finally come to your senses. Goy cannot be trusted! I've told you that a hundred times. You have to stick with your own kind. Now get on the phone and call your wife before she gets on the next plane to Tuscany and winds up costing me a fortune." She snaps a finger at the waiter and points to her cup.

"It already has."

The manicurist comes to retrieve her and she holds up her hand to halt her. "What are you talking about, David?"

"I gave grandma's ring to Katrina."

She taps her phone. "Excuse me, David, there must be something wrong with my reception. I thought I heard you say that you gave some shiksa my great-grandmother's ring."

"There's no bad connection, Mom. I gave Katrina THE ring."

Ethel raises her brows, or at least tries to, and takes

a deep breath. "I can't believe what I am hearing! You gave that hairdresser my ring?"

"Katrina's not a hairdresser! What are you talking about?"

"That girl! The one you told us you wanted to marry the night I had a heart attack. Isn't she the one you are seeing?"

"No! You're thinking of Maive. I wish it was her. And you didn't have a heart attack!"

"Heart palpitations, heart attack, it's all the same thing! And you mean to tell me there is more than one shiksa? Oy vay! My son is a whore! Where did I go wrong?"

"I'm not a whore, Mom! I'm unhappy."

"You're unhappy? What do you have to be unhappy about? We have given you everything!"

"This isn't about material things!"

"I'm not talking about material things! Have you forgotten everything Daddy and I have done for you? Do you realize I was in labor for twenty-six hours with you? That's over a day, David! I went through hell to bring you into this world and this is how you repay me?"

"I wasn't seeing straight. I took the ring and gave it to Katrina as a promise that I would leave Stacy. I was going to take her and buy her a new one, but I didn't have time."

"I can't believe what I am hearing! Not only have I given birth to a cheating louse, he's a thief to boot." She runs a hand through her freshly coiffed hair.

"I wasn't stealing it, I was borrowing it. I'm sorry, Mom!"

"You're sorry, David? Why do you always make everything about you? What about me? What about what I am going through? How do you think this is going to affect our family? Once again I am going to have to step in and clean up another mess."

"Mom, I said I'm sorry. I never meant to hurt you. I made a mistake, that's all. Don't you ever make them?"

Ethel thinks about what David has said. Has she ever made a mistake? "Only one that I can think of! Two years ago I had a procedure done out of the country instead of New York and now I have to re-do my lips, but that's the only one I've ever made and that didn't hurt anyone but me." She sits down in the pedicure chair.

"I guess all I ever do is hurt people."

"Well you're a work in progress, David. I think you need to spend more time with me and Daddy. In no time at all you'll realize there is nothing more important than pleasing your family. It makes no sense to be..." She puts her feet in the water. "Too cold!" She points to the hot water faucet and the manicurist obliges.

"I know! I have been rather cold to you lately."

Ethel's mood lightens. "The first step in getting better is acknowledging your wrong doing to those who love you most, David."

"I don't know what I was thinking."

"You weren't thinking, David. It's never been your strong suit. Women, that is." She holds her right hand out in front of her and examines her nails.

"I guess you're right."

"Of course I am, dear. I knew when I saw Stacy she was the perfect girl for you. Mommy knows best!" She flutters her fingers in front of the manicurist, letting her know she needs a manicure, too.

Ethel hears David snivel. "Well, don't beat yourself up about it. Move on! Go back home and start over."

"What about the ring?"

"David, if there's one thing I know, it's how to get what I want. Give me the girl's number and address and I'll take care of everything."

Maive Henry

She watches Mabel drop the matzos into the boiling chicken broth and then open the oven to check on the brisket. "Are you sure you don't need help with anything?"

"God, no! What do you know about making matzo ball soup, brisket or kugel?"

"I might surprise you."

"You already have surprised me, Maive, by the way you handled David."

"I couldn't believe how easy it was!"

"That's because you're over him!"

"I guess I am, Mabel." She grins from ear to ear. "How long before we eat?"

"You should call Benjamin and tell him to come earlier. The food is going to be done sooner than I thought."

"I can handle that." She walks to the phone and picks up the receiver, but pauses.

"Well, go on!" Mabel nods her head.

"I don't know his number." She holds up a hand and shrugs her shoulders.

"It's on the pad next to the phone."

"Do you call him often?"

"Almost daily!" Mabel laughs.

"I don't know why I even bother to have a thought

since you seem to have this all figured out." Maive picks up the phone and takes a deep breath.

"You can do this, Maive!" Mabel pats her on the shoulder.

She presses the numbers on the phone and Benjamin answers after the second ring. His deep voice sends a quick shiver up her back. "Hi, Benjamin! It's Maive. Mabel told me to call you and ask if you can come earlier." She starts pacing with the phone.

"I'd love to! You'll save me from going to the gym."

Maive hangs up the phone and looks for Mabel. She walks from room to room and can't find her. She sees headlights out in front of Mabel's house and rushes to the front door to catch her.

Mabel backs out of the driveway and yells, "Don't play hard to get, it's a waste of time!"

"Mabel, don't you dare do this to me!" She pushes open the door and runs towards her car.

Mabel waves to Maive, honks the horn, and then drives away at lightning speed.

Maive's stomach turns and her palms begin to sweat. She can't imagine having dinner with Benjamin alone. What will she say to him? Oh, God! She doesn't know how to cut brisket! She goes back into the house and runs to Mabel's bathroom.

She pushes her long, blonde hair behind her ears and checks her lipstick again. As she leans in closer to the mirror she notices a woman has replaced the girl that once stared back at her. Her eyes are much older now, but they're filled with a wisdom that was never there before. Their blueness has returned and she smiles at the woman staring back at her.

How could she have put so much faith in David when he had none in himself? She shakes her head at how misguided she has been and realizes David was in her life to teach her about her own self-worth. She feels a tear starting to form for the young woman whose heart had become so bitter that she had been unkind and quick to judge others, and almost looked past a wonderful man like Benjamin.

"Not now!" She says, but it's too late. Her eyes overflow with tears and she begins to sob, crying until there is nothing left in her. When the sound of the doorbell catches her attention, Maive frantically wipes her eyes and searches for Visine in Mabel's cabinets. She grabs a tissue and heads for the door.

Smoke fills the entryway of the house. She opens the door and finds Benjamin standing there with a bottle of wine and flowers. "Come on in! I have to check the food." She rushes into the smoke-filled kitchen, grabs a potholder, and opens the oven door. Smoke escapes from the hot chamber and blinds her eyes for a moment. She reaches in and pulls out what was once a brisket.

"Mmm, brisket!" Benjamin says. "Just the way I like it, too!" He looks at Maive, whose face is filled with tears and he struggles not to laugh.

"I'm sorry! This is a disaster! Mabel left and I've never made brisket."

"It's okay, Maive. I can't stand the stuff!" He points a finger towards the back of his throat.

"Really? You don't like brisket? But Mabel made this Jewish meal. She said it would impress you." She throws her hands up in defeat.

He reaches for her arms and looks right into her eyes. "Maive, you impress me. I don't need a special meal."

Maive blushes. "What should we do about dinner?"

"Does she have any cereal? I'm a big fan of Special K." He smiles.

"I don't think so, but I do."

"Terrific! Let's go over to your place. You know, I can't believe how much I miss those kids of yours." He walks towards Mabel's front door.

Maive smiles and walks behind him. "Would you like to take a walk on the beach with me and the dogs after we have a bowl of cereal?"

He puts a finger up to his lips. "Shh! Did you hear that, Maive?"

"Hear what?" She looks puzzled.

"A wall! I think one just came crashing down." He looks at Maive and laughs, and she punches him in the arm.

"Steady now, fella! It took a very long time for ONE to fall. Can you imagine how long it will take the rest?"

"No I can't, Maive, but I make my money investing in things and I'm betting you're worth the wait." He smiles and winks at her, and then holds out his hand.

She looks down at his tanned hand and reluctantly

takes her own hand from her side and reaches towards his. He waits patiently with a smile until Maive finally places her hand, along with her heart, inside it. They walk towards her house and hear one of the dogs barking.

"That Sammy's got quite a bark, doesn't he?" Benjamin asks.

"I think that's Buster." Maive corrects him.

"I was wrong, that can only be Cricket." Benjamin sounds confident.

"We're both wrong!" She says, as they reach the porch and see Dunkin pawing at the door to get out.

Maive opens the front door and Dunkin runs towards Benjamin's car. He hops over the door, sits in the driver's seat, and stares straight ahead.

"I knew he only liked me for my car!" Benjamin looks over at Maive, and the two of them laugh hysterically.

Juanita Maria Mendez

She goes into her bedroom and opens the closet door. Throwing her collection of shoes to one side she carefully opens the loose wooden floor board. Reaching inside, she rifles through piles of cash and brings some to her nose. Nothing is more sexy than the smell of money, and there's plenty more where this came from, sitting in her safety deposit box at Chase Manhattan.

A pile of mail sits on the table next to her door, so she sifts through it, keeping the flyer for the French Institute and the bills for electric and phone that will need money orders. She comes across a white embossed envelope with the initials E.A. on it and flips it over. She has no idea who E.A. is, but the stationary is quite exquisite, and not the kind you can get anywhere.

She takes the note from the envelope, hoping it's an admirer who saw her dancing at the club. How he has found out where she lives is a concern, unless of course he turns out to be worth her while.

Upon opening the envelope, a business card falls onto the floor. It's from the St. Regis Hotel. The note simply reads:

Call me. We have business to discuss. The sooner you come the more lucrative it will be for you.
Ethel Adelstein

It sounds rather urgent to Juanita, but the thought of making anybody Adelstein wait until the next day sounds better, until curiosity gets the best of her and she dials the number. A crusty old woman answers the phone and proceeds to tell Juanita what the ring will be worth if she returns it this evening.

She dresses the part of a grieving girlfriend. One torn between loving a man and letting him go because his family needs him more. Puke! Puke! Puke! The Holly Hobby dress she chooses is one she bought eons ago. That old bastard from Hollywood used to like it when she dressed up like a baby doll. Too bad that one died! He was an easy lay, and worth a fortune!

Before leaving her apartment, she looks through her collection of foreign language books until she finds the Yiddish dictionary. She skips through the pages and gives herself a refresher course before she securely pins the blonde wig on her head and heads out her apartment door.

She takes a cab to the St. Regis Hotel, pays the driver, and checks out her reflection in a window pane. She pushes her long blonde hair over her breasts. Best not to show her assets too much; Ethel doesn't need to get a mental picture of her sweet David porking the hell out of Juanita.

When Juanita walks into the room, she recognizes Ethel immediately. It's JoJo, the cloth puppet she owned as a child. Only now, JoJo has been patched one too many times and she's drinking a martini with four olives. This is going to be fun!

She reaches Ethel's table and extends a hand, a

hand with Ethel's ring on it. "You must be Ethel!"

Ethel downs her drink. "Please, sit down." She foregoes shaking Juanita's hand and motions with hers instead to the seat across from her.

A waiter appears out of nowhere, asks Juanita if she would like a drink, and completely ignores Ethel.

"I'll have a bottle of Pellegrino." She answers in a girly voice.

"No alcohol, dear?" Ethel eats the olives.

"I never drink! It gives you premature wrinkles."

Juanita can see Ethel holding back a comment. She wonders how many more digs she can get in before the evening ends.

"You look familiar to me." Ethel says.

"You look familiar, too. But I'm sure it's because your look is very common in New York." She whispers, "All of you older gals must see the same surgeon."

Ethel tries to smile, but it's obvious that she's recently had Botox. "Katrina, dear, I wanted to talk to you about marriage, more specifically, doing what's right."

"Are you saying I'm not right?" She asks Ethel, enjoying the challenge.

"Not at all! I would never presume anything like that. What I'm saying is, it wasn't right of David to do such a thing. And you seem like such a lovely girl! I'm sure this has to be hard for you, but you must understand that David has to do what is best for the family."

This is going to be painful. Juanita reaffirms her belief that she should only pursue rich orphans. David's wife has her hands full for sure! Not that she feels sorry for her. After all, she did have a choice in saying no when he asked for her hand in marriage.

"But I love him! He needs some time, that's all." Juanita goes into overdrive.

"No one will ever love David the way that I do, Katrina. You wouldn't want to break up his family would you, dear? Did he tell you he has children? That his wife is expecting another one? Imagine their life without him! Family is everything to Jewish people. You mustn't let this go any further. I beg of you!" Ethel reaches for Juanita's hand and lightly taps the top of it.

Juanita backs away. Ethel's hand is cold, lifeless, and heavy like a corpse's.

"David doesn't understand what he does at times or why he does it. You see, on many levels, he still needs my guidance." She stares off for a second and then says, "We're like soul mates!"

"Soul mates?" Juanita looks at her in disbelief. This is all too much for her.

"Yes! He and I are so much alike. We both have the same sense of humor and the same weak stomach. This ordeal is really going to take a toll on his poor tummy."

Honestly! The way Ethel is going on about him, it's almost incestuous. It makes Juanita sick to see this over-tucked woman talk about her son like he's her lover. She wants to throw the ring at Ethel, grab her cashier's check, and run. The sooner she puts these people behind her the better. The last thing she needs is David hanging around messing up potential men who have far more to offer.

"What about me? I'm ready to spend my life with him, to mother his children!" Juanita grabs a tissue from her purse and brings it to her face, pretending to cry but actually hiding her grin. She decides that Ethel should never play poker. Her face gives too much away, even with all the work she's had done. Juanita's last comment about her mothering David's children looks like it might send Ethel to the psych ward. Juanita knew this would be fun!

"I'm sure that if you look at the amount on this check, you'll see that I have compensated you for your tremendous loss. You are so gorgeous and young, Katrina. You'll meet someone new in no time at all! As a matter of fact, I may know someone for you." She pushes the check towards Juanita.

"That's so kind of you, Edith, but I think I'm going to go away for awhile to try and get over David. I can't bear the thought of seeing anyone else right now. I need to heal my heart."

"It's Ethel, dear." She taps Juanita on the top of her hand.

Juanita backs away. "What did you say?"

"I understand."

"This whole ordeal has left me farshadat. I'll have to move!" She glances down at the cashier's check. "This will help me find a new place to live and allow me to put my ailing grandfather in a better home."

"It's the least I can do. I feel so awful about what has happened. It's all been such a big misunderstanding." Ethel holds out her hand and waits for Juanita to give her the ring.

"A misunderstanding?" Understanding perfectly well what Ethel means, Juanita sits back on the banquet and waits for an answer. Out of the corner of her eye she spots an older gentleman sitting up at the bar.

"What I meant was…"

"I know exactly what you meant!" Juanita smiles her wicked smile. "I'm beginning to feel rather ibbledick from this conversation."

Ethel feigns a smile. "How do you know Yiddish?"

"I know a lot of things, Edna. I make it my business to. Perhaps I should keep the ring. It will remind me of David and all that I have endured." She turns the ring on her finger.

"The ring means a lot to me. It was my grandmother's. David had no right to give it to you! There must be something else I can do for you."

"Where did you get those fantastic earrings?"

"These?" Ethel asks, nervously touching the sizeable emerald and diamond stones in her ears.

Juanita leans in and touches one of the diamonds. "Yes, those! I want to get a pair just like them."

"Well I'm sure that check will afford you a pair."

"I told you, the check is for my grandfather! You know, I don't think I like your tone, Emily."

"Take them!" She undoes the backs of her twenty-fifth wedding anniversary present from her Adam and hands them over to Juanita.

"You are so generous, Ethel! May your son prove to be as faithful to you as you are to him. Juanita hands her the ring. She gets up from the table, smiles at the older gentleman as she passes the bar, and then heads towards the front door of the St. Regis Hotel. There will always be another man at another bar, but right now she needs to get this check home.

She hails a cab and directs the driver to her building. She sits back and giggles to herself, thinking about all of the possibilities out there. And to think she almost wrote David off as another N.A.T.O.! Not Anything To Offer.

One hundred thousand dollars for the return of that stupid ring and a token gift from Ethel was too good of a deal to pass up. The ring was gorgeous, but money is money and if she pawned the thing, she would never make this kind of loot. The money will allow her a little breathing space and give her a much-needed break from dancing in the clubs. She has worked a lot of men over the years, but David was definitely the easiest and most lucrative if you consider how long she was at it.

She has to call Rudy and tell him about it! On second thought, maybe she'll go see him. He keeps asking her when she's coming for a visit, maybe she'll see what Sanibel has to offer. She pulls out her cell phone and dials his number. "Hey, Rudy! It's Dez. I've called the salon a hundred times, but nobody will tell me where you are. I can't call Maive! She's lost her mind and is completely envious of my life. I wonder where you are. You know what? I'm going to come see you! I'll call you when I get into town. Love ya!"

Her suitcase is still sitting in the corner from her

last getaway with Gary. She throws some clothes in it and looks around her apartment. If she left here today and never returned, she wonders if anyone would notice.

Gary won't miss her! And his wife definitely won't! She has to know he's fucking someone else, just as David's wife did. Juanita makes certain of it by meticulously placing long strands of her hair on the back of their clothing, spraying her perfume on their nicely pressed shirts, and shoving tubes of Chanel lipstick into their suit pockets.

It isn't so difficult to tell when a man is being unfaithful. Perhaps their wives know, but chose to do nothing about it. Maybe a person can learn to look the other way if someone is worth that much to them. Unfortunately, she's never met someone THAT wealthy. But she'd like to!

What is it about the wedding band that makes men cheat? Is it like a collar and a leash? Or is it more like a noose? Is it the thrill of being caught? The newness? The "I've never felt like this before in my life" feeling that diminishes once they get it whenever they want it? And because she believes the answer to every question is yes, she turns the backs on her shiny new earrings and says, "I almost pity the fucker who falls for me!"

Stacy And David

A cab pulls up into the driveway of their home. Stacy stands in front of the bay window and watches David walk towards their house. He takes out his key and puts it into the lock, expecting it not to work. When he opens the door, Stacy is waiting in the entryway.

"Hey! What are you doing here?"

"Sit down, David. I have something to tell ya."

"I know that you're pregnant, my mom told me." He throws his keys on the table.

She turns around and looks at him. "No, David. I'm not pregnant. It's something else."

"You're not pregnant? Then why did she tell me something like that? You know, she never knows when to quit!" He shakes his head and walks over to make himself a drink.

"I told your mother I was pregnant, but I don't want to lie anymore."

"What's going on? Where's Josh?"

"Joshie is with my mom. Will ya please sit down! I really need to tell ya something." She points to a chair.

"Fine!" He throws himself on the couch. To his surprise, a gesture that usually annoys her gets no response.

He looks down on the coffee table and sees a picture that looks familiar. He picks it up and his eyes widen. "Where did you get this?" He looks at the photo of Maive.

"I found it in your apartment in the city."

"You've had it that long?"

"Yes, but not as long as I've had this." She says, and hands him the photo of Gianni.

He looks confused. "Who is this?"

"His name is Gianni Maldano."

"Who the hell is Gianni? Why are you showing me this?" He throws the photo on the table.

"Because I want ya to know that I loved somebody once, too!"

David looks at her in disbelief.

Stacy walks over to the window and looks out at a tree blowing in the breeze. She closes her eyes and suddenly she's back in Italy and in the arms of Gianni Maldano.

"I met Gianni while spending a year abroad after college. I went to Italy with every intention of tickling my fancy in the language, customs, and fashion of Italy, and wound up having my fancy tickled by Gianni Maldano, son of a tailor in town.

He and I would slip away to his father's shop, lie among the many fabrics, and make love for hours. We talked about places we had gone, people we had met, and a future that would never come to fruition. For the first time in my life, I felt something for another human being I had never felt before. It helped that Gianni was gorgeous, but more than anything else he was attentive.

He would brush my hair while I talked about my dream of becoming a famous clothing designer. Most nights he would cook me meals made from recipes that had been passed down from his great-grandmother because he couldn't afford to take me out. When I told him he had to stop because I was gaining too much weight, he kissed me on the cheek and said he would love me no matter how much weight I gained.

I was convinced the Maldanos could have made a fortune if Gianni's father would only aspire to have his designs in the windows of Bergdorfs rather than those of the ramshackle shop he ran on the outskirts of town. Ya see, instead of accepting Visa, Master Card, or American Express, Mr. Maldano accepted chickens, goats, and wild geese as payment for his fine garments.

'We need nothing more than we already have,' Gianni was fond of saying. I admired his family's choices, envied them even, and could hardly wait to tell my parents about him. They had always told me that religion did not matter as long as I was happy, so I convinced myself that a life with Gianni was within my grasp. Unfortunately, when the year came to an end, so did my dream of living this idyllic life with Gianni."

David is mesmerized. This is a side of Stacy that he had never heard about. As she speaks about Gianni, her harshness melds into a softness he has never seen before. He can only muster, "What happened to him?"

"He just went away. He promised to write, but he never did. I would run to the mailbox everyday and wait for his letters. I knew that my parents weren't too keen on my having met a foreigner. I could tell the second I stepped off the plane that my mom did not approve of Gianni's influence on me."

"How could you tell that?" David shakes his head.

"My mom burst into tears the moment she saw me. I thought it was because she had missed me, but her words were so cruel. 'You're so fat! What happened to ya? We must get ya to Canyon Ranch!' I chose to ignore them and only said I was in love. 'With what, food?' She asked me. No, I told her, with Gianni Maldano. He's the son of a tailor and the most wonderful man I've ever known. 'Does he import?' I told her that he didn't and that the Maldanos had no phone or microwave and that their entire family slept in one house."

"I bet that went over real well!" David shakes his head.

"She told me that I was forbidden to converse with sheygets! And not just any sheygets, a shmegegge to boot! She also said that Gianni had only used me and that he had already forgotten about me. I was so young at the time, and I only wanted my parent's approval. There wasn't anything I could do about Gianni's background, nor did I want to. I loved him just the way he was. I was convinced that if my parents met him, they would see what a wonderful person he was and what his family did for a living wouldn't matter. All I needed was for Gianni to write me to prove to my mom that she was wrong about him. But he never did.

I sent so many letters to him and I never heard back from him."

"I don't understand why he didn't write you. It sounds like he loved you." David walks over to Stacy.

"One day my mom asked me to go get some stationery from my father's office and I found a piece of an envelope with a postage stamp from Italy on the floor by the shredder. Ya know my mom has never been sentimental, so I figured she had shredded my letters because she hates clutter until I looked closer at the stamp and postal marking.

The first day I arrived in Italy, I had gone to the Sorrento post office to purchase stamps and never used them all. The stamp I found in my father's office had been postmarked from Marina Puolo, the village where Gianni's family was from."

"There has to be a reason for that. Maybe you sent a letter from there and forgot."

"No, David! I didn't forget. My parents thought I was in Sorrento. I was very careful about keeping the fact that I wasn't from them."

"Do you realize what you are saying, Stacy?" David looks at Stacy, who is off in another world, probably one that includes Gianni.

"Did my mom do something to Gianni's letters? I still ask myself this question, even after marrying you and having two children. I've realized that the only thing worse than suspecting my mom of shredding letters from Gianni is finding out that she did such a thing.

After the postage stamp incident, I fell into a depression and began losing weight. The first ten pounds was lost, along with twenty more, and I began to look gaunt to everyone who saw me. Everyone but my mom, who did everything she could to make sure I didn't gain the weight back, and that I met someone she approved of."

Stacy looks over at David and says solemnly, "That's when I went to temple and met your mother. Who, quite frankly, is even more brazen than mine."

"I don't know what to say, Stacy. It's so sad. I had no idea." He looks right at her.

Tears run down her cheeks. "Ya see, David, I don't know if I ever loved you. I did what made my parents happy."

"Well, at least we have that in common!" David laughs. "That, and a controlling mother! They sure are a couple of yachnehs!"

"It's not fair! My entire life I have fulfilled every one of my mom's expectations."

"You're preaching to the choir, Stacy!" David shakes his head.

"Do ya know what it's like to think your own mother sabotaged your happiness? Think about it, David! My mom ruined my relationship with Gianni just so I would meet someone she felt was worthy enough."

"My mom did it to me with Maive." He points to the photo.

"Now that I think about it, my parents always found something wrong with the guys who didn't have money. I bet they would overlook my dating a psychopath as long as he went to Harvard or worked for Goldman Sachs!"

David bursts into laughter. "I guess you settled with me! I only went to Penn and certainly don't work for Goldman."

Stacy sits down next to him and lets out a loud sigh. "What are we supposed to do now, David?"

He reaches into his pocket and hands her his handkerchief. "I don't know, Stacy. Should we ask our mothers?" He laughs again and she tries to smile.

"I don't want to laugh, David! Stop saying things like that." She wipes her eyes.

"That's it!" He stands and walks around the room.

"What's it?" She looks at him, puzzled.

"Laugh! We have to laugh, Stacy! It's the only thing that is going to save us." He walks over to her.

"What are ya talking about? You've really lost your mind!" She shakes her head.

"No, I haven't! You and I never, ever laugh. I can't take it anymore!" He throws his hands up in the air.

"Obviously! Ya went and screwed the first thing that looked at ya! Ya could have at least picked somebody who wasn't so expensive. Ya could have had a hooker for every day of the year for what that beast cost!" She throws the handkerchief at him.

"You see, that's funny!" He picks it up and puts it back in his pocket.

"I'm serious!" She stands and walks towards the bookshelves.

"I know you are. Give me some more of that!" He motions with his hands towards himself.

"I don't want to! It makes my skin crawl and p.s.,

I could just throw up!" She turns and points a finger towards her throat.

"We both know you like to do that!" He rolls his eyes.

"David!" She stares right at him.

"Stacy!" He stares right back at her.

"That's only when I have to see that hideous family of yours!" She throws her right hand in the air.

"They are pretty hideous, aren't they? Did my mother have more work done?" He runs a hand under his chin.

"Oh, my God!" She puts her hands on her hips. "Is she doing her chin again? If that woman gets anymore surgery she's going to look like Charlie McCarthy!"

David laughs. "Hey, did the royal couple call while I was gone?"

"David, ya were gone for two nights! It's not Debbie's scheduled day to call, but I did hear they might be moving to Miami. Apparently Dan has been offered the position of Chief of Plastic Surgery there." She smiles.

"Moving, huh? Now we'll never get rid of my mother! She'll be over here all the time."

"No she won't! She only spends time with your sister's kid."

"That's true! Why would they move to Miami when they just built a new addition on their house?" David pours himself a drink.

"Because Dan probably has a boyfriend there! Besides, you know that their homes aren't personal to them. Everything about their lives is phony. Their homes are nothing more than movie sets and stage productions!"

David rolls his eyes. "All Debbie cares about is acquiring material things."

Stacy pours herself a seltzer. "Hello! I've been trying to tell ya that for as long as I've known ya! It's all your entire family cares about!"

"Hey, I have an idea!"

"Careful! The last time ya had one ya went and cost your mother a lot of money!"

"Hey, maybe you should have an affair and we can see how much money we can get from your mother." He walks towards her and extends his hands.

She pushes them away. "Very funny! What's your idea?"

"Maybe we should think about moving, too. Someplace far away, someplace like Italy. You could look up your lost love and see if he wants to rekindle things."

"It's a little late for that. I'm sure that Gianni has moved on. Besides, I don't want him anymore. I want what we had, what you had. I want to be loved."

He looks at Stacy and the way her face has softened. "Do you think it's too late for us?"

"I don't know, David. Ya cheated on me! But aside from that, ya love someone else. What about that?" She walks back to the couch and sits down.

"She doesn't want me anymore. She's moved on, just like your Gianni Fabulous." He follows her to the couch.

"Maldano!" She turns and looks at him.

"Whatever! Well, we do have two really great kids." He puts a hand on her leg.

"They are pretty great! I don't spend enough time with them. I know that I don't." She shoves his hand away.

"I'm probably guilty of that, too. Do you know what I just realized, Stace? You are the only person who understands what it's like to be me."

"What do ya mean?"

"Our families! We're both bullied by them! If you're not there to talk about Dan, who am I going to make fun of him with?"

"Oh, David! Is it enough?"

"It's a start!"

"So where do we stand, David?" She folds her legs and arms and turns towards David.

"In our living room! And p.s., we're not standing, we're sitting."

"Stop that!" She says, laughing, and hits him in the arm.

Rudy Filona

Early Saturday morning Rudy lies in his bed at Miami Hospital, waiting for a nurse to bring him his pain medication. When no one shows after twenty minutes he finally screams into the monitor. "Somebody bring me a God damn pill!"

"Just a minute, sir!" A nurse answers him.

"I don't have a God damn minute! I'm in pain!" He moves around in the bed, trying to get comfortable.

The nurse ignores him and continues doing her rounds while the other one turns down the volume at their station. At first they found his sarcasm humorous, but now they just find him a pain in the ass, especially since they know he is hoarding the medications. They found a stash in his shoe!

As he continues to press the call button, he stops for a moment and stares down at his hand and then looks at the other one. They're bony and pale and in desperate need of a manicure. He thinks about all the heads of hair he's coiffed through the years. The bimbos, brunettes, blondes, beauty queens, drag queens, the dregs of society, and the cream as well. Hands that once held onto a pair of scissors like they were an extension of his arm can barely hold a Dixie cup at the moment.

His fine Versace shirts and Gucci suits adorned

with fancy gold buttons have been replaced with hospital gowns that fasten in the back, if he could only summon the strength to tie them. His feet that once found home in Prada shoes are now confined to dingy hospital slippers when he makes his daily trips to the bathroom with the help of a nurse.

His constant banter about his latest conquests, shopping at the finest stores, and endless gossip about anyone and everyone has now been diminished to a few lines about his progress of getting up to look out the window for two minutes without passing out.

Maive has been so good to him! He is certain her new-found energy has something to do with the fact that she finally got that schmuck, David, out of her life. Not only is she covering for him at the salon, she waters his plants at home, sits with him for hours while he comes in and out of sleep, and brings him his mail every day.

He looks through the stack of bills, mostly from department stores, and sees a pink envelope with the return address of Oklahoma. He tears open the back and the unmistakable scent of Billie escapes. He reads the letter three times before he loses his grip and it falls to the floor. He passes out from exhaustion, saying the words, "Not worthy."

When he awakes, Maive is standing over him. She wipes his forehead with a cold cloth.

"Careful, Maive! I might get used to this and never leave here." He rolls over and looks at her with one eye.

"You absolutely cannot stay here! Who will tell me

when I'm wearing the wrong shirt? Warn me that the blueberry muffin I am going to eat will make my ass spread like a container of oleo? Who will I laugh at all those silly women with?" She dips the cloth in the bowl of water.

"Oh, honey! Anybody can do those things." He throws his hand in the air.

"But what about the things they can't?" She wipes his head again, looks right at him and begins to cry.

"Careful, doll! Too much salt is bad for the skin." He touches her hand.

"You're my best friend, Rudy! You let me work whenever I want, you always tell me how fabulous I am, and you never say you are too busy to talk to me even when I know I bore you beyond belief."

"Beyond the universe! Are you kidding me? I'm so glad I don't have to hear about that idiot anymore!" He throws his hand up again and closes his eyes.

"By the way, I know it was you who sent me those flowers a few months ago, pretending they were from a secret admirer." She looks down at him and smiles.

He smirks. "How did you know that?"

"Rudy, there isn't one straight man on Sanibel who would spend that much money on a bouquet and sign the card, "You're flawless!" She takes the cup of water with the straw in it and puts it to his lips.

"I always wondered why you never got worked up over those gorgeous flowers. Make sure that florist does my funeral, will you?" He takes a sip of water and some dribbles down the side of his mouth.

"Stop talking like that! You will be just fine!"

"Okay! Okay! How about they do your wedding then?" He tries lifting the pillow behind him.

Maive blushes and fluffs the pillow behind Rudy's head.

"Have you ah, you know…" He motions with his head.

"What?" She coyly asks.

"Are you Jewish by injection yet or what?"

Maive ignores the comment.

"Do I have to spell it out for you?"

"Rudy, we have not had sexual relations yet, if that's what you're trying to ask."

Rudy feigns throwing his arms in the air and winces in pain.

"Look at you, Rudy! You're so tired. You're not twenty-two anymore, you know!" She wipes his face.

"Shh! That cute boy nurse might hear you!"

"You're unbelievable! Are you actually trying to get lucky in a hospital?"

"You heard the doctor! He said I'm going to be fine. Besides, have you gotten a look at that guy?" He tries to whistle.

Maive dismisses him with a wave of her hand and gets up to look out in the hallway for the nurse.

"Maive, will you do me a favor?"

"Anything!" She rushes back to his side.

He grabs her hand. "I want you to write Billie and tell her I'm sorry."

"Sorry for what? The last time I saw her, she could hardly wait to leave the salon. I don't think you owe her an apology." She taps his hand.

"Yes, I do." He points to the letter on the floor.

"What's that?" She bends over and picks it up.

"Read it!"

Dear Rudy,

When I saw you lying on the floor of the salon I felt so helpless. I know now I should have helped Maive, but I was scared. All I wanted to do was run home and be with my momma. Imagine that! Me running home to my momma. I know you're probably laughing right now just thinking about it.

Anyway, it's like this Rudy. I love you. I've always loved you since I met you. Even though you're not nice to me, I still love you. I love your humor, your talent, and your vulnerability. I know why you push people away and act so hateful, Rudy, because I do the same thing.

I only want to protect my heart from hurting, but I've realized through the church that you only hurt more by doing this.

I wish you the best in everything you do and I will never forget our time together.

Fondly,
Billie

"Wow!" Maive says.

"Yeah!" He closes his eyes.

"Okay, so I'm going to pick up your dinner, download some new music, and write Billie for you. Did you want Thai tonight or Italian?"

He opens his eyes and looks up at her. "I'll take Italian, but only if he's under thirty."

Maive shakes her head and walks towards the door to leave.

"Maive!" Rudy calls to her.

"Yes, Rudy?"

"I don't want to hurt anymore."

"I know, Rudy. I'll ask your friend at the nurses' station if you can have more medication."

"Girl, I've got enough medication to float me for a year! I'm talking about my heart. I don't want my heart to hurt anymore. I'm so tired of hurting."

"Let go, Rudy! It doesn't do you any good to hold onto it anymore." She walks back over and hugs him.

"You think God will forgive me for all of the shitty things I've done?"

"Of course she will!"

"I knew you were going to say that!" He tries to laugh.

"You didn't think I would pass on that chance, did you?"

"You know, I've been thinking a lot about this heaven and hell thing." He looks up at her.

"Rudy, stop! " She straightens his covers.

"I can't! Those pills they give me are righteous! All I do is think about death. Last night I thought I saw an angel in here and then I realized it was that male nurse. Besides, I know where I'm going there aren't going to be any angels!"

"Don't even joke about something like that!"

"People in hell are going to need a lot of help with their hair, Maive! Much more than any of those angels would, floating around on clouds all day. The heat in hell alone has got to do a lot of damage!"

Maive bursts into laughter and so does Rudy.

"It's good to see you laugh, Maive."

"It's good to see you haven't lost your sense of humor!"

"Go on! Let me get some rest now." He closes his eyes.

"I love you, Rudy!" She blows him a kiss.

"I love you, Maive!"

Juanita Maria Mendez

As she opens the door to Rudy's hospital room, her hand cups her mouth and she gasps at the sight of him. An IV is taped to his pale, withered arm and he looks more like a man who is eighty years of age instead of forty. A machine that monitors his heart rate beeps every few seconds, letting her know that he's still breathing.

She pulls a chair over to his bedside and reaches for his frail hand. The reality of what has happened to him is an ugly reminder of what might happen to her if she doesn't find someone to marry.

"Life is so unkind." She whispers, thinking about the night she and Rudy went out for drinks in Dallas. She had listened intently as Rudy told her about the past that haunted him and the uncle responsible for it. It didn't matter how far Rudy moved away, or that his uncle had now moved to Hawaii, the damage that he had done to Rudy followed him wherever he went and it was never more present than now.

"Don't you worry, honey! Nobody is going to do this to a friend of mine and get away with it." She caresses his hand.

Tears form in the corners of her eyes and slowly roll down her face. She pounds the bed with her fist. "Bastards! Why are men such bastards? Why couldn't they have left us alone?" She puts her hands over her eyes and sobs. "I was just a little girl!"

After a few minutes, she wipes her eyes and watches the heart rate machine. "I bet if they hooked one of those things up to me, they wouldn't find a heart! At least that's what that fucker back in Texas would say. He should know, he's the one who took it from me."

She gets up from the chair and walks to the door of his room. She looks out the window, glances up and down the hallway, and then sits back down.

"I've always been different, Rudy, ever since I was a little girl. I was always stronger than my brother and sister and I never let anyone intimidate me. Not even him!

The moment he saw me, he knew I was different. He told me so every time he...

It was my mother's fault! So desperate to get ahead in this world, she would have sold her own soul, but instead she sold mine to that man she made me babysit for.

One afternoon he told me that he was very sad because he was lonely and needed a pretty girl to make him feel special. At the time I didn't understand what special meant, and when he said it was having sex with him, I flat out said no. When I threatened to tell my mother, he told me that she already knew and that if I told anyone else he would have us all deported."

She runs her hands over her arms, trying to warm herself. "You wouldn't believe the things he made me do to him. Three years, Rudy! That's how long I had to make him feel special, until I saw a movie that changed my life."

She stops talking and looks up at Rudy. "There's something about you and me, Rudy, something that makes us survivors." She caresses his cheek.

"The movie was called *Fatal Attraction*. The moment I saw it, the tables turned and that's when I knew that I was really different. I may have lost my virginity and every bit of dignity that I had, but in the end, I won.

I blackmailed that fucker for everything he had. He called me an evil whore and I laughed in his face as I bankrupted him and his wife's company. As a matter of fact, I still have the first hundred dollar bill I ever extorted from him in my wallet. It serves as a reminder for me that money is all any man has to offer."

She stares off for a moment and then looks at Rudy. "All men want me for is my looks. So you know what I'm going to do? I'm going to fuck over as many of them as I can and keep putting money away for the day my looks, like the men, will all be gone."

A nurse's voice over the intercom startles her. She picks up her purse and leans over and kisses Rudy on the cheek.

"Well, darling, I'd love to stay and chat with you some more, but I've got to call a travel agent and book my tickets to Hawaii. I found out Uncle John has a textile company there and I want to make sure I'm in the vicinity when he calls his next board meeting." She looks down at the brochure for Hawaii sticking out of her purse.

"I'll be back soon, along with a very large sum of money for you." She walks out of his room and heads towards the doors that exit the I.C.U. unit. She reaches into her purse to get her sunglasses and doesn't notice the brochure fall onto the floor.

As she pushes through one door, a man walks through the other and she bumps into his side. She turns and sees a handsome man in a white coat. He's wearing a name badge that reads: Dr. Daniel Weismann, M.D., F.A.C.S., and she smiles to the Gods.

"Won't you please forgive me?" She speaks in her finest Italian accent.

"It's quite alright." He says.

"You are too kind!" She pretends to read his nametag for the first time. "Dr. Weismann."

"Dan! Call me Dan. And you are?"

She glances around the corridor and sees an orderly removing a stack of copy paper from a dolly. The neatly stacked reams of paper all read the name Georgia Pacific. "Georgia. Georgia Pacificato." She extends her hand, and he shakes hers with a rather flimsy grip.

"I think you dropped something when we bumped into each other." He motions with his head towards the floor and then bends over to pick up the brochure. "Hawaii! One of my favorite places! I've been there so many times they should re-name one of the islands after me." He laughs. "This year I won't be able to go, though, since I might be moving here. They have made me a rather generous offer and I might just find myself leaving New York." He hands her the brochure.

She immediately does an evaluation of him. His hands are small, typical of a surgeon, but unadorned. He's neatly groomed and has on a Charvet tie. His shoes have an ostrich cap toe, his suit pants appear to be Ralph Lauren purple label, and his watch is a Patek Philippe. She only recently started doing research on this particular brand, so worst-case scenario, the style he is wearing is valued at seventy-nine thousand dollars, best-case scenario, it's worth two hundred and forty thousand dollars. She prefers best-case scenario, although with his impeccable taste, he might be gay. Where the hell is Rudy when you need him?

"Huh?" She manages a reply.

"This is your brochure, isn't it?" He smiles.

There's only one way to find out if he plays for the right team. "Yes, that is mine." As she reaches for the brochure she "accidentally" drops it back on the floor and bends down to pick it up. "I'm always dropping things!" She looks up at him coyly.

"Let me help you with that." He bends over and meets her at her chest. He stares down between the plunging crevice that separates her two bulging breasts and smiles.

Juanita feels an excitement race through her veins. She looks him right in his eyes and then reaches for his arm. "It's so sad! I was supposed to take my brother, but he's…" She puts a hand to her nose and sniffs, pretending to fight back tears.

He helps her up. "What is it?"

"He's too ill to travel. I don't know what I'm going to do." She quivers her bottom lip and Dr. Weismann puts his hand on her shoulder.

"I'm sorry to hear about your brother. Is he a patient here?"

"Yes! It's so hard to talk about." She pretends to cry as she leans into his shoulder.

Dr. Weismann looks at his watch. "You know, I have some time before I have to meet with the director of the hospital. Would you like to get a cup of coffee and talk?"

"Why, that's so kind of you!" She smiles and bats her eyelashes.

The two of them head into the cafeteria. Juanita stares into Dr. Weismann's eyes as he tells her about his job opportunity at the hospital. He doesn't even notice when she slips the brochure for Hawaii into the nearby trash can.

After all, there's no time like the present, Hawaii will always be there, and it's not every day you bump into a plastic surgeon.

Yiddish Vocabulary

Bubbe: Grandmother.

Farshadat: Pained, wounded.

Goy: Hebrew and Yiddish term for a non-Jewish person; synonymous with "gentile."

Hilf: A real help, a godsend.

Hotzeplotz: Timbuktu, the middle of nowhere.

Ibbledick: Nauseated, barfy.

JAP: (Jewish American Princess) A rich, snobby, Jewish girl. A female who collects designer fashion items and status symbols (including men).

Kugel: Baked Jewish pudding or casserole.

Mazel tov: Literally meaning "good luck."

Mishegas: Absurd or ridiculous idea or belief.

Oy Vay: Used when frustrated.

Schmatte: A rag.

Schmear: A spread of cream cheese on a bagel.

Shanda: Not only a pity or a shame, but a scandalous shame, an affront to decency.

Sheygets: A Gentile male.

Shiksa: Used as a disparaging term for a non-Jewish girl or woman.
Yiddish: "Shikse" literally means "female abom-ination."
Hebrew: "Sheketz" "detestable", "loathed," or "blemish."

Shmegegge: An un-admirable person, a nobody, an ordinary Joe who lacks the talent, intelligence, or moral stature to be considered a full-fledged person.

Yachneh: Annoying nag of a woman.

Yenta: A person, especially a woman, who is meddlesome or gossipy.

- ya
- rolling eyes